P9-DUJ-720

# THERE MUST BE SOME MISTAKE

## Also by Frederick Barthelme

*Rangoon*

*War and War*

*Moon Deluxe*

*Second Marriage*

*Tracer*

*Chroma: Stories*

*Two Against One*

*Natural Selection*

*The Brothers*

*Painted Desert*

*Bob the Gambler*

*Double Down: Reflections on Gambling and Loss*
(with Steven Barthelme)

*The Law of Averages: New and Selected Stories*

*Elroy Nights*

*Waveland*

# THERE MUST BE SOME MISTAKE

*A Novel*

FREDERICK BARTHELME

Little, Brown and Company
*New York Boston London*

The characters and events in this book are fictitious. Any similarity to real persons, living or dead, is coincidental and not intended by the author.



Little, Brown and Company
Hachette Book Group
1290 Avenue of the Americas, New York, NY 10104
littlebrown.com

First Edition: October 2014

Little, Brown and Company is a division of Hachette Book Group, Inc. The Little, Brown name and logo are trademarks of Hachette Book Group, Inc.

The publisher is not responsible for websites (or their content) that are not owned by the publisher.

The Hachette Speakers Bureau provides a wide range of authors for speaking events. To find out more, go to hachettespeakersbureau.com or call (866) 376-6591.

ISBN 978-0-316-23124-4
LCCN 2014940625

10 9 8 7 6 5 4 3 2 1

RRD-C

Printed in the United States of America

*For Joan*

# THERE MUST BE SOME MISTAKE

# 1

# JUNK TOWN

AT THREE in the afternoon I woke up and there was Jilly Rudolph out on the deck flipping through the local paper. She was a woman from my former office, midthirties, lanky, charming, a friend who had stuck with me when I was jettisoned from the design business. And she liked me, which made her a special favorite. She'd had a short and lousy marriage in her twenties and hadn't gone back to the altar. I was two decades older, widowed once, divorced once, and a partner at Point Blank Design, at least until the others decided I was past my use-by date and sent me into Neverland with a silver plate and some fine sentiments about my thirty years of service. To say I was shocked would understate it. You do something that long and you figure you've probably made the cut. But the new and the young are relentless, and will have their way. So it is written.

I was living in Kemah, halfway between Houston and Galveston, and working from home a lot, so I repaired to the condo to lick my wounds and figure out what might be the next move. I'd lived there since the last years of my second marriage, so it was comfortable enough, even if I wasn't. I didn't fish or hunt, I didn't collect stamps or books or baseball cards, I didn't cook, garden, or build model airplanes, so when they let me go I was, to say the least, at a loss. I suppose I could have looked for work at another shop, but I felt a little long in the tooth for that, and I had a decent safety net, so I did nothing, and doing nothing I was very pleased that Jilly made a habit, after my embarrassing fall from grace, of visiting more often than I'd imagined she might. She was a quiet woman, kind of stoical, wry, what people call *older than her years.* We had been close at the office and were closer now. I was grateful. That, too, understates the thing.

I went out onto the deck and gave Jilly a hug, settled into the chair next to hers. Even with the sun surrounded by clouds it was way too bright.

"Visiting the halt and the lame?" I said.

"Per usual," she said, closing the paper and sliding it my way. "An act of mercy for which I reap great wealth and beauty in the next life. You, on the other hand, reap disreputableness."

"I'm fine," I said, sticking a hand through my hair. "It's only my hair. It's waking up. We went to bed at seven."

"How glamorous," she said. "You must be refreshed by this hour."

"I missed you," I said. "I do every time you go home. Didn't you just go home a couple days ago? Not to be forward."

"I did," she said. "To carry out my responsibilities. To spy on your former employers—my current employers—while living it up with them and our other friends in the big town. All the while clinging to a paycheck."

"And I missed you while you were gone. Did I say that already?" I said.

"You did. Thanks," she said. "I found a kid who writes code. He's sweet and ridiculously young. In the teen area."

"Attractive?"

"In the little-brother way, yes," she said. "What's news?"

"My neighbor, Forest Ng, died in a car crash," I said. "His name is spelled 'Ng' but pronounced 'Eng'—I looked it up."

"Everybody knows that," she said.

"I liked him. He crashed his car over by one of the marinas. In the early morning hours. A 'shots rang out' thing."

She tapped the paper. "If there's a picture in here, I didn't see it."

"It was, apparently, a completely accidental car accident."

This was March, still bearable out. Jilly was in jeans and a white button-down shirt and wore a scent that made the world around her seem wonderful and mysterious. I couldn't help feeling lucky. In the waning days of my tenure at the design shop she was what made it worthwhile.

The dead neighbor was a guy I talked to from time to time. He'd recently bought the condo next to mine, moved in with a herd of people, so many I couldn't figure out who went with whom. There were seven adults in the house—three men, four women—all between twenty-five and forty-five. One time Ng said they were relatives; another time he said they were coworkers in his nail salons. He said he had salons in Kemah, Seabrook, Texas City, Beaumont, Sugar Land, and Waikiki.

Waikiki? I said.

Kid you not, he said.

Together they had seven Mercedes-Benzes, all black, and not the cheap ones, either, for which there was insufficient parking, so the cars ended up in the yard, in my driveway, in the carefully tended green space.

"He struck a curb," I said. "Then he hit a building, flipped the car, busted a hydrant, landed upside down in the culvert. And the whole thing burst into flames," I said. "It was on TV at five A.M. this morning."

She picked up her water bottle and shooed a gnat away from her hair. "Get away," she said. "I remember you whined about the cars. You were intimidated by the cars."

"Well, maybe. But I did not whine. Not once. I asked him to keep them on his property. He was friendly about it. I liked him. He was a Mac person. We were pals."

"You don't have so many pals, usually."

"I'm trying to change my ways," I said. "It's your influence. Interacting with other human beings is therapeutic."

"Duh," she said.

"He made a fortune in mani-pedi," I said. "If the cars mean anything."

She shook her head. "They don't. Probably leased. Besides, you think everybody made a fortune."

"True," I said, swatting my hair again, both hands this time. "You look very very pretty today." Kathy Najimy's old routine.

She just nodded at that. "Good one," she said.

I liked Ng because he was straightforward about lying to me. He exaggerated everything. He had houses in three cities, he did Bill Clinton's toes one time, he bought an eighty-inch flat-screen television to watch American football, his yard guy was nine hundred a month and was the brother of a Green Bay Packers running back. Ng was small and wiry, and he gestured like a maniac when he complained about the neighborhood. One night he brought me a pork chop he had cooked "Oulipo style." One of the women was probably his wife, but I was afraid to ask which one.

My neighbor on the other side talked too much and wasn't so interesting. He was like a cook on a ship in a fifties Navy movie, except unnecessarily cheerful. He'd moved down from Clifton, New Jersey, and he was working on a miniature perpetual-motion engine in his garage. It was "scalable," he assured me. His name was Bruce Spores. Told me he was a Yale grad and he was rated as the fifth-smartest male in the country back in the eighties. He took an exam, won an award. The thing was, his brother was even smarter, ranked fourth smartest.

"You are a couple of smart cookies," I said when he told me about it.

He shook his head and grinned. He was always grinning. I wanted to ask him how he scored on modesty.

Roberta Spores was a short, thick woman with lots of ideas about what was needed to make Forgetful Bay Condominiums a more prestigious address. She had eyes on the leadership of our homeowners' association.

"Ng was OK," I said. "He always talked about money. How much he paid for the new triple-zone heat pump he had installed in his condo. He had a thing."

"Who doesn't?" Jilly said. She picked up the paper and opened it. "I'm going to look."

"I don't advise it," I said.

My first wife, and the mother of my daughter, Morgan, was Lucy Meringue, a lovely woman, a singer who died of throat cancer seven years after we married. The last months were a horror.

Years later I met Diane and we got married and bought a house in Houston, but after a time Houston got too ugly and crowded and we started looking for something quieter.

We rented a place in Kemah and I worked from there, going up to Houston maybe twice a week. Diane suggested we make it permanent, so we bought the condo. We were fine for a couple years. Morgan was four when her mother died, eight when Diane and I married. All the parenting after her mother's death was done with a light touch because Morgan was the best kid in the world. We were so lucky. She was a quick learner, self-motivated, interested in everything, so smart she almost raised herself. Real magic.

After ten years with Diane the marriage was belly up and we divorced. Amicably. I got the condo; she got the house in

Houston. Morgan stayed with me in Kemah. She was finishing high school, going through college brochures and websites, sending letters of inquiry, making applications, planning what she might study. We talked about it often. She was thinking architecture, which was my father's profession and something she'd always liked. Watching her mature was staggering just as it's said to be and changed everything for me. One world ended. Another began. Toward the end of high school she was as much friend as daughter. For college she chose Rice University, and I was relieved she wasn't going farther.

Diane's father died a couple years after the divorce, and she moved to Rhode Island and took on his estate. He was a hugely successful doctor, so she was well taken care of. We kept in touch, and from what I could gather she spent most of her time volunteering for good causes—small museums and animals, mostly dogs. The dogs she did in person, the museums by checkbook. And there were elephants. She had a thing about them. We got along better at the new distance.

Jilly would visit, we'd go to dinner or the beach or shopping at Walmart, sometimes a movie during the day when the theaters were empty. Once she couldn't get a motel because of the boat show, so she stayed at the condo—all perfectly proper. It wasn't strained or uncomfortable, so it became routine. At the office she'd always been pleasant, delivering a wry, playful commentary about our work that I liked, and she was a help during the divorce. She was fun, and having her visit was flattering, and if sometimes in my head there was a thought of what might have been, or what might be, more often I was realistic and simply happy to have the company. Her presence brightened everything.

I was a night person, so usually up until first light, sleeping into the afternoon. I liked the silence, the quiet of night, but also the idea that after two or three A.M. nobody else had anything to do, either.

The condo was up on concrete pilings sunk a good distance into the ground and chock-full of rebar. It had been hurricane-proofed and then some. On the east was Galveston Bay, Trinity Bay, and the Houston Ship Channel—all one huge body of water opening, farther south, into the Gulf. Along the bay there was a rundown coast lined with all the seedy charm an old body of water like that will breed at its edges. To the south were the refineries of Texas City, and eventually Galveston Island, and to the west was Clear Lake and the enormous NASA empire that had kudzued the entire area.

When I was a kid Kemah was dinky and charming, but it had been developed with an elaborate boardwalk, shopping mall, multiscreen cinema, amusement park, "resort-style" hotel, and, of course, a roller coaster, without which a vacation destination cannot apparently be imagined. The whole town was spectacularly kitschy. We still had that high bridge over the inlet to Clear Lake, so elegant and lovely in the late afternoons, but almost everything else belonged to a world where people didn't know how to leave well enough alone. It got better as you got out of town and down by the condo, which was a bit south; we were lucky. The development was done by a Galveston architect, a woman who had some sense of place, so the design was restrained. Each condo had a tiny bit of ground around it and was situated in a way that made the most of the views of Galveston Bay, which didn't look bad from a distance. A few older houses were scattered around us, but they were low and we looked over their tops. There were two dozen condos, all similar, and another couple dozen semidetached cottages built around a little lake on a few acres between Highway 146 and the bay. My place was three bedrooms, four if you counted the den, with wraparound decks so I got sunrises over the bay, sunsets to the west. The cottages were at the south end by the lake, which was called Smoky Lake because it was. Maybe four acres of water, maybe five when swollen in its banks.

A thin blacktop road wiggled through the place. We had a homeowners' association, so there was some upkeep for the trees and grass, and there was a path that went down by the seawall. Sometimes we envied the fancy high-rises over in Clear Lake, and sometimes we envied the more authentic world of hurt down in Texas City, a refinery town, but the envy was largely rhetorical in both cases.

"It's a tub," she said. "A brown-water bathtub."

It was a bay, after all, not the Gulf. But we sat there and listened to the sloshing and slight lapping, the seagulls, the wind shifting through the trees that leaned around the buildings at Forgetful Bay. It wasn't that bad.

"We are lucky," I said. "We got it easy out here. Just right for an old guy."

"Oh, quit that," she said. "You're barely sixty."

"Not funny," I said.

"Sorry. What are you, fifty-something? Women love men your age. You're just right for those among us who tend to the woeful and the downtrod. We serve at your pleasure."

I nodded. "For which I am grateful."

"I am the beautiful stranger," Jilly said.

The name of a wonderful book I'd given her years before, and exactly how I thought of her. "So fetch me another beer, will you?" I said, squinting at her long enough for her to imagine I wasn't joking.

"You need a nap," she said, getting out of her chair. "Me, I am going out. I am a young person on the go. When I return we will visit one of our finer eateries. Say, Wendy's."

"Way to plan things," I said.

"I'm all about the Frosty," she said.

## 2

# EX

Jilly's ex-husband Cal was a tough piece of business in his midforties, a guy she had married right out of college. She was twenty-two, he was thirty, and she regretted the marriage instantly. It took her a few years to cut herself free. I never got the details, but she gave the impression the marriage was on the nasty side. Like TV-show nasty, true-crime nasty. And the worst part was Cal was hard to shake. At Point Blank we saw him at office parties, Christmas parties, and whatnot, and he kept coming after their divorce. He got friendly with other people at the office, and with Diane, and stayed friendly. After my divorce he started coming to see me, too, like we had this in common, both of us living alone after marriage. He was always dropping by to commiserate or calling to suggest we grab dinner. A couple years later, when I left and Jilly started visiting, he tracked her to Kemah and stopped by the condo to visit her.

And he liked Morgan too much. I suggested he give her a wide berth, but when she started college in Houston he'd meet up with her and her friends at their hangouts. I tried to discourage this, but Morgan refused to "dignify" my complaints. Cal called it "a little harmless fun" and chuckled in a way that made me want to smack him silly when I talked to him about it. Then he showed up on her Facebook page, which I checked more often than a father is supposed to. There were snapshots of him and the girls at a college bar playing pool. Morgan seemed to be having a good time in the pictures. The girls were always grinning in silly group snapshots and looking as wacky as possible, sometimes hanging around the necks of men, sometimes sticking their tongues out between their first and second fingers, a gesture I tried to not think about.

She said it was just fun. I said Cal was too old to be having fun with college girls. Morgan loved that, of course.

After a while she seemed more inclined to hang out with kids who looked like gas-station employees but had, at least, the virtue of being near her age. It struck me odd that Rice students would look like gas-station attendants, but then I realized everyone under thirty looked like a gas-station attendant to me. Then I realized there weren't any gas-station attendants anymore. On her FB page Morgan was often seen smiling one-beer-too-many big between a scruffy-looking cowboy and three other guys who looked younger than and less reputable than Cal. That or she was with a guy who looked like a teen lawyer, always decked out in suit pants and a really thin tie, like he'd come from the office. I preferred the cowboy.

"Oh please" is all Morgan would say whenever I brought up the guys on her page. "Really."

# 3

# PAINTED

A FEW weeks after Ng crashed his car, a woman at the other end of our development was found in her kitchen, her hands bound with the picture-hanging wire from the back of her prize art print and blue paint smeared all over her. The print and the paint were Yves Klein blue, which everyone recognizes, at least everyone who ever took a modern art class. It was this guy's special blue, sort of French blue, but more so. He was an amusing heretic in the ancient art world of the forties and fifties, and the print was from his Anthropométrie series (so said the note on the back of the frame), in which he used nude women as paintbrushes. A powerful concept. He showed these paintings with performances of his *Monotone-Silence Symphony,* which was a solitary note played for twenty minutes, followed by twenty minutes of silence, thus locating himself among the very first minimalist composers. And there's a famous photograph of him flying over a wall that every art student sees sooner or later. He's known for that, too.

The cops came to interview the victim of the Klein attack. Apparently she was fine but curiously could not remember a thing about the skirmish. She was questioned extensively, but nothing came of it. She recalled answering the door to find a person standing there in a large rabbit mask holding a paintbrush and a gallon paint can. She thought it was a friend of hers. Turned out she was wrong.

The paint, which was water based, washed off.

The woman was Chantal White. I called Diane about the attack, and she said she'd met the woman once or twice and that the woman was snooty.

When I ran into my neighbor Bruce, he said, "This woman is like that nurse Jackie on that TV show is what I hear. You know, the slut drug-addict nurse with a really nice husband? We're supposed to feel for her because she works so hard and is a druggie? That cunt sets every guy's teeth on edge week after week," he said.

"Never saw it," I said. I was lying, naturally. I'd seen it. It was hard to figure out what the point of it was, but it was harder to figure Bruce getting upset.

"There's nothing a guy hates more than being cuckolded by his own damn wife," Bruce said.

"Who better?" I said, then quickly corrected myself, saying, "Amen to that."

"This guy on the show is so nice and modern with his cunt wife that he never even imagines she'd cheat on him, never gives it a thought. So we gotta deal with that. I mean, I keep pointing at the screen every time the actress screws the pharmacist in the pharmacy, in the car, in a fucking tree." Here he stopped and sort of got his bearings. He whistled for his dog, an ugly little pug-like something. "Anyway," he said. "Maybe I shouldn't let the show get to me, huh?"

"Think you're watching reruns," I said. "This year she's trying to be a better person."

"Well," he said.

"So what about the Chantal woman?" I said.

"She's a hydrologist," he said. "Divorced. One child grown and gone. Was a nurse, gave it up, and studied water somewhere. Got a degree and then I think she was EPA for a while. Bought that restaurant and bar down the coast. Velodrome, it's called. Used to be a bike racetrack or something. Under fifty, dates around pretty good. Nice-looking woman."

"Man, you got the inside track on this thing," I said. "Did anybody see anything? What about the paint?"

"The paint was blue," he said. "Splashed all over her supposedly. Cops were over there taking pictures when I went by. Newspaper guy was there. He's like sixteen or something. It's shit who they got writing the news these days. The *Sentinel* is not one of our great papers."

"They're all small these days," I said.

"They ought to rename it the *Wynden Weekly*," Bruce said. Wynden Drive, where Ng had his accident, was the prominent boulevard that ran over toward Clear Lake.

"She wasn't, you know, like, messed with or anything?"

"Apparently not," Bruce said. "She's good as gold is what I heard. Tough cookie."

For a few weeks the police were all over the neighborhood like mice. They were asking questions, coming in twos to everyone's door, inviting themselves in, sitting on the edges of sofas and wing chairs with their little tablets, little flip books where they took notes whether the interviewees knew a thing or not. I said I didn't know the woman and wouldn't recognize her if I saw her on the street, but still the questions. How often did you... Do you remember seeing anyone who... Did the victim have any habits that you... All this was oddly reassuring. Like your life imitating television—murders and drive-bys and robberies and whatever happening to people all around you. Chantal White put me in mind of the creepy guy attacking the hoodie kid in the Florida gated community. He kills the kid and the fucking guy walks. Go figure.

This woman Chantal wasn't around much after the incident, but she was widely discussed. There was speculation that she had something to do with Duncan Parker, the president of our homeowners' association. He was a loudmouth many Forgetful Bay folks didn't like all that much, but he wanted to be president of the HOA and almost nobody else, other than Roberta Spores, did.

Jilly was staying over when the cops came for their second visit and she made coffee and they wanted to talk to her. She told them she was a friend of mine and didn't know the neighbors, but that didn't faze them. I stayed out of it. Didn't even listen from the next room. I was out on the deck with the iPad, playing Monkey Pong Duets.

* * *

At the homeowners' meeting the following Monday, a monthly meeting I hadn't attended since Diane left, I joined an overflow crowd of residents eager for news about the rash of events at Forgetful Bay.

Parker ran the meeting. He was a short ex-marine with too many years in the service of his country to ever forget his service to his country, or at least that's what he told anyone who would listen or who happened to walk by his house when he was out working on the grass, which was anytime weather permitted. His grass got an awful lot of attention, and water, not to mention bags and bags of food and close scrutiny from the neighbors. All this was not lost on the grass, which always presented itself in dress greens, with military precision. The neighbors would routinely endure Duncan Parker's political and economic views, which were something short of enlightened, and his vision for the future of this great country of ours, which was plain terrifying, in order to get a little advice on how to get the brown socks off their grass, how to deal with birds pooping in the yards, how to get that glistening green that he managed to muster almost year-round, even in dead of winter.

"As most of you know, we've had some problems lately," Duncan Parker said, wiggling a finger at some slackers still busy chatting at the back of the small room in the community clubhouse, a miniature house that had once been the sales office. "And I thought we'd better gather to talk about things, try to defuse some rumors, and generally clear the air." Here he paused, waiting again for the full attention of all who were present. Finally he lost patience. "Hilton," he said, waving at a short fellow with a beard at the back of the room. "Could you save it for later?"

"Sure thing, boss man," Hilton said, grinning and sitting up straight in his folding chair. Hilton Bagbee never behaved, at meetings or elsewhere. He was a happy man, said to be wealthy, family money, but also said to be something of a gambler—casinos, horses, football. He had one of the fanciest condos in the group and felt this warranted special privilege. "I'm ready," Hilton said. "Fire away."

Parker waved a thanks, shuffled some papers in front of him, and started again. "We've had this problem. Chantal White, whom many of you know personally, was cruelly assaulted in her home a few days ago, by an unknown intruder." He lavished a lot of praise on that word, "intruder." It was as if he couldn't keep it in his mouth long enough, didn't want to let it go, and, when he did, wanted to pause a good while after to let the word dash around the room.

Eventually we heard about Ng, Chantal, a couple other inexplicable things, and got no new information. Nobody knew anything. Ms. White's wounds were bruise and paint oriented. The police were investigating. There were no leads. Parker said he preferred that we channel all neighborhood information through him.

* * *

The following week, on Sunday morning, a woman—not a resident of Forgetful Bay this time—was found at first light, dancing dreamily in Duncan Parker's driveway to some music on her iPhone. She was decked out in a black slip and heels, and Duncan Parker, when summoned from his bed, said, "I don't recognize her. Maybe she's from the rental-management office?"

His wife, Ella Maria Parker, was not heard on the matter.

This event joined the Chantal White attack and the Ng crash as topic one at Forgetful Bay. People chattered about it in groups of two or three, standing in driveways, by mailboxes, in yards.

I started catching up on the Scandinavian noir movies and TV shows everyone had been talking about and had to order an all-region DVD player from Amazon to play the import DVDs. I was also making small drawings, a thing I'd started again after being run out of the workplace. I was doing these pieces on the Mac and printing them on Frottage's Photo Rag Duo 276gsm paper on a fancy Epson I'd swiped from the company. I was having a good time.

Jilly often called from Houston to say good night, which was fun. Once we got to talking about Morgan and Cal, and the dangers of being young and good looking, and she said I should stop worrying. "Morgan is going to do what she wants. There's no messing with that. Besides, I thought she was off Cal and on to younger things."

"She is," I said. "But she won't listen to me anyway." I was combing through my mashed potatoes with the tines of my fork. I had been eating mashed potatoes when she called.

"Call her mother."

"In the great beyond," I said. "I told you."

"Duh. I was thinking of her other mother."

"Oh. I guess I could do that."

"You want me to talk to Morgan for you?"

"No. I'll call her."

"That would be good practice for you," she said.

I thanked her for that. We talked a little more and I told her what I knew about recent events, bits and pieces I'd picked up from neighbors, and pretty soon it was time to quit the conversation.

"I'll make you some gravy one day," she said.

"Got plenty gravy," I said.

"Right. OK. Well, I gotta hop. Call you tomorrow?"

"Sure. You coming down sometime?"

"Probably Friday," she said. "Can you wait that long? Are you OK?"

"Why do you always ask me if I'm OK?"

"Just checking," she said.

And she hung up, leaving me sitting there on a stool at the kitchen counter staring at my reflection in the dark sliding glass doors that led out to the deck. I got up and went to the pantry to see if there was any gravy there.

The next week Cal was picked up by the police for having sex with a minor, one of the Facebook girls whose picture Morgan pointed out to me on the computer. An acquaintance, not a friend, she reported. Morgan was staying with me for a few days.

"We always knew she was creepy," she said. "She was always after something from Cal."

"She got it," I said.

Morgan did a big eye roll. "Uncool, Dad."

I changed the subject. "I've been thinking that I want to go to church," I said. "I'm thinking this is a good time to bring it up. Are you interested? I think Jilly's interested. I've talked to her about it."

"What church?"

"Catholic church. I was raised Catholic, and my brother Raleigh tells me there are now twenty-two recognized and approved versions of Catholicism around the world."

"Your brother Raleigh tells you," Morgan said. "Huh. Well, it is the one true church."

"Yep. In twenty-two divisions, apparently. Papally sanctioned. It's a new world out there, and I'm thinking about joining."

"So, what are they? The versions?"

"No idea," I said. "I'm reporting what Raleigh said. He's a Marmonite or something. Mallomar. I don't remember."

"Did he come to you in a dream? I think you gotta get serious about this if you're gonna do it," she said. "How long since you been to church?"

"Thirty years plus," I said. "I'm that guy in the Clint Eastwood movie who says it's been thirty years since my last confession."

"Seen that a hundred times. Say seven Our Fathers and seven Hail Marys."

"They don't do that anymore," I said. "You stand at the back of the church where nobody can see you and you apologize under your breath for all your sins. Silently. Presto-change-o you're good as gold."

"At least that saves us the confessional scenes in movies," Morgan said. "Dangerous priests behind ornate grillwork. You're not really going, are you? You even know where a church is?"

"Mmm, not really. Probably look it up. I used to love going to churches. They smelled good."

Morgan got up and twisted her hair into a thing, pinned it up. "I don't think they're like that these days. Not the churches I've been to."

"Which?" I said.

"Can't remember. Maybe Episcopal. They're sort of semi-Catholics anyway, aren't they? Without the hard parts?"

"We don't have hard parts anymore. Too discouraging."

"You can go to mass on TV," she said.

"Done it. Grotesque. Like Howdy Doody mass, you know? Howdy Doody? Buffalo Bob? It's like they're in a dry cleaners."

"I know who Howdy Doody is," Morgan said. "He's cute."

"He's great," I said. "You want him praying for you."

* * *

When Jilly came to visit on the weekend Morgan had already returned to Houston. Cal got out on bail and flew to Rhode Island to see Diane. She called long distance to tell me all about it. The lawyer said Cal should remain calm and quiet and wait for the court date and then they would postpone, postpone, postpone, thus draining the girl's resolve and her parents' resolve, and eventually Cal would prevail. "It will take two years at a minimum," Diane said.

"Cal is up there with you? Are you nuts?"

"I'm expanding my experience," Diane said.

"I mean, is this . . . I don't want to pry, but is this a new thing?" I said.

"You mean did I sleep with him before?"

"Sure. If that applies."

"Well," she said.

"Never mind," I said. "I suddenly don't want to know."

"Well, there's you and Jilly," she said. "And she's practically a daughter."

"I never did anything with Jilly."

"That's not what Cal says."

"Yeah, well, you listen to Cal you're gonna hear a lot of things that aren't necessarily so."

"I never thought about Cal this way before," she said. "You get to know him and he seems more like a flightless bird than a criminal."

"You're about half in the park there."

"He's a wounded soldier, is what he is."

"You were a great wife, Diane."

"There are worse," she said.

At my end I nodded agreement and said, "I believe you. But sleeping with Cal hurts my feelings. It makes me feel bad. I feel weakened."

"So how is Jilly doing? You still with her?"

"I am not 'with her' in the sense you mean," I said.

"Not for want of wanting," Diane said. "You better get started, Wallace. You can't live by yourself forever."

"Maybe I could try, in my advanced years, something new," I said. "Like Cal."

She punched a button on her phone to send a nasty beep down the line. "You are a pig, Wallace."

"Gee, thanks," I said.

"I think I gotta run anyway."

"Let's talk soon," I said.

"Right," Diane said.

I was in the kitchen during all this. Jilly was carefully prepping vegetables, carrots, cutting on the cutting board, and the fine edge of the knife clapping on the wood reminded me, as silly as it sounds, of the guillotine dropping at the end of *Dialogues of the Carmelites,* the opera. One of three I was acquainted with. In the end these nuns are singing the "Salve Regina" as they process to their deaths by beheading, one by one. My first wife, Lucy, introduced me to this opera years before, but then I'd heard it again recently on NPR one day when I was out in the car driving around in the rain. Now Jilly's knife brought the opera, and Lucy, back in an instant—the lovely voices of the diminishing choir, the thwack of the guillotine, the thinning chorale, finally a single voice, a falling blade, silence. I watched Jilly work the vegetables. I lifted my hand off the telephone. I listened to the water running intricately in the sink, a lovely sound, a blissful unbroken sound.

# 4

# DESTIN

I RENTED a condo on the Florida Gulf Coast for a few days in April. Jilly drove over with me; Morgan joined us on the weekend. The town of Destin was pristine and plenty touristy, like Galveston but prettier, a coastal island known for powder-white sand and bright green water. The rental was in a beachfront high-rise with a view of the Gulf. "I ought to buy one of these and rent it when I'm not here," I said, when we got inside the place. "Like an investment. My dentist has two units in this building and he says they pay for themselves."

"Don't they have a lot of tarantulas in Florida?" Jilly said, looking out at the frothy water. "Per capita?"

"No," I said.

The rental was a three-bedroom on the sixth floor overlooking a pool, some parking lots, a few two-story cottages, a lake, the beach drive, bright white sand, and then the flickering water. It was a big change from Kemah. High ceilings, clean grounds, quiet except at night when the wind was up and howling through the ductwork. Don't ask me why that happened. It was a little creepy. There were six TVs in the place, all forty-two-inch flat screens.

Morgan arrived on Friday. She liked the place from the minute she saw it. "You definitely need to get one of these, Dad," she said.

"Yeah, Dad," Jilly said. She did that sometimes when Morgan was around, called me that.

"I'm thinking about it," I said. "Prices aren't bad." I had gotten some information from the on-site rental-management woman, who said rentals were up and that owners had a good chance of making enough renting to offset the mortgage. The three of us were in the living room, strewn about on the beachy furniture, which was floral and bright, and would have been grotesque anywhere else.

"Count me in," Morgan said. "Maybe Diane would take a piece of the action."

"Maybe not," I said. "I think she's busy sleeping with Cal."

She looked at me like I was a nutcase. "I may have heard something about that," she said. "The trifecta."

I looked to Jilly for an explanation.

"He's a lucky guy," Jilly said, getting up. "I'm going to rest a bit."

No help there.

"Let's reconvene in an hour or so," Morgan said. "Let me get moved in." She asked which was her room, and I showed her and then went to mine for a nap.

I got trifecta after a while. Some things are so cold in this world.

* * *

We spent the weekend looking at beach places—houses for a million bucks, condos at the Dunes—the place we were in—and in buildings called the Pelican, the Sandpiper, the Tern, the Flower Drum Song Super Towers, and a couple others. They all had the names going for them, beach names, the beachier the better. We met up with a real estate guy at an open house on Sunday. He had a flattop and talked a good game, so we began looking at properties with him. He was pleasant company, an ex-pilot, laughed a good deal, knew the area. He was writing a book about the Russian Mafia, nonfiction.

The financial crisis had hit Florida real estate hard, like 50 percent hard, so you could get places for two hundred thousand that had been five hundred a few years before. There wasn't much chance of the boom coming back, but there was, according to our guy, a good chance for growth. He owned a couple of condos himself, rented them out on VRBO, swore by the whole deal. He was always running late or rescheduling because he had to go and clean up his condos for incoming guests. We looked in Sandestin, a ritzy development with six golf courses and every kind of dwelling, from detached homes to condos, bungalows, high-rises, town houses, you name it. It was all a little too rich for my blood, and too Stepford. On its own the Stepford part wouldn't have kept me out—I like a good dose of restrictive and compulsory decorum—but the money was a nonstarter.

Morgan went to the beach more than we did. She looked great all decked out. She was tall and stringy with nicely acne-scarred skin and auburn hair, and she had that walk some girls have, a cowboy walk, real loose and relaxed, powerful. She had gained a lot of self-confidence, and it showed. She had a wisecracking way about her without actually cracking wise all the time. She did it with subtle things, cocks of the head, eye stuff, quick goofy facial expressions. She reminded me of her mother and made me happy all over again that we'd had a child.

Saturday morning Jilly and I went for a walk on the beach at dawn. I hadn't been to bed yet and she'd been asleep for ten hours. That happened sometimes. It was early and there were not many people on the beach, a few joggers, a couple old people. I said, "What do you think about this Cal thing with Diane?"

She made a face, not disgust or disinterest, but something oddly blank. "I don't envy her," she said. "Cal was scum in my twenties and he's scum now. Maybe she can make something of him, I don't know. Anyway, it's not your business. Leave it alone."

I nodded for a minute, then waved at the beach, the water, the sky. "You like it here? Florida?"

"Sure," she said. "It's pretty. Right now I'd like some Eggos."

"Eggos are so over," I said.

"Yet within our grasp, grocerywise," she said.

"True," I said. "We could leave this lovely beach right now, get a couple boxes of Eggos at Winn-Dixie, douse 'em with Log Cabin, wolf 'em down."

"I don't think I want 'em anymore," she said.

"That was quick."

"Maybe I'm a bad person," she said.

"Absolutely," I said. "Everybody tells me that."

She said things like that sometimes, as if the only thing she was worried about was being a bad person. It was touching, but also rhetorical, a request for reassurance. That's what was touching.

"Never mind," she said.

"I was asking what you think about a condo here. Think it's a good idea? Would you come all this way? Like, to visit?"

Seagulls swirled around us. "Might," Jilly said.

"I'm getting older and older," I said. "I like Kemah, but this is cleaner."

"It could be short on character," she said. "But character might be overrated."

The sand was dusty white and the water Kool-Aid Kiwi Lime, jittery in the morning light. I didn't have much idea what Jilly was about, apart from being friendly. She did not telegraph her intentions. We were hanging out together but keeping our distance. I didn't mind it, but I was aware of it. I thought I should let it alone, play it out. It was fun just being with her. Still, I had to remind myself of the baselines.

"Cal's kind of scummy," Jilly said.

"You said that," I said. "But I don't worry about Diane so

much, not anymore. Or maybe it's that she doesn't come to mind. There ought to be a point when your ex is your ex, know what I mean? A statute of limitations on their emotional bite."

"Cal's got bad teeth," Jilly said.

"Way to contribute to the conversation," I said.

"He could use some whitener," she said. She plopped down in the sand and I sat alongside her, both of us facing the water, which was wavy, waves rushing at us, rushing away.

"So you think I should get a condo? I could get a two-bedroom pretty cheap."

"Rent it when you're not here?" she said. "Let it pay for itself?"

"Exactly."

"Hmm," she said.

We sat on the beach for another fifteen minutes and then went back to the Dunes. Morgan was buttering toast when we arrived.

That night we went to dinner at Olive Garden. My choice. We squeezed into a booth, all three of us, and each of us studied the menu carefully. The seats were sticky plastic and squealed whenever anyone moved. Finally, Jilly said, "I don't think Diane should be sleeping with Cal."

Morgan said, "Me neither."

I said, "Delay of game!"

"Diane probably thinks it makes things more interesting if

she sleeps with him," Jilly said. "She hasn't thought about it carefully."

"Duh," said Morgan.

I reached for their hands across the table. "I'm glad that you two have spoken up. I was worried it was just me for a while there."

"I know you were," Jilly said.

"Diane's a slut anyway," Morgan said.

"I'll be right back," I said, starting out of the booth. "Get me some pasta, will you?"

"Stay put, Dad," Morgan said. She pointed me back into my seat.

"I don't know," Jilly said. "She's lonely maybe."

"We're all lonely," Morgan said. "And we're all sluts."

"What are you talking about?" I said to Morgan.

"I've done my share of slutty stuff," she said.

"I've got to get out of this booth," I said.

"Dad," Morgan said.

"I'm going to be sick," I said.

The waitress was wearing a stained white shirt. She was suddenly alongside the table, pen poised. Jilly took over and ordered for herself and for me. I was getting spaghetti and meatballs. She and Morgan were having salads, wonderful, complicated salads. The waitress vanished.

"Let's move on to other topics," Jilly said.

"Good," I said. "I don't want to hear any more about Cal. What's done is done. I mean, we're here at Olive Garden. *Fantastico!* Christ."

"Wallace," Jilly said. "You want your children to talk to you, yes?"

"Sure," I said. "There's one child, and I want her to be an attractive young woman with no boyfriends. No sex, love, anger, worry. No pets."

"He doesn't mean that," Jilly said.

"Pets are OK," I said.

"It was just once," Morgan said.

"You're making it worse, sweetheart," Jilly said.

Our food arrived in due course. Mine was execrable, in the best possible way, as usual. Thick, gloppy, greasy, misshapen, lukewarm, and inedible. We dined in silence, unless slurps and other sucking noises are to be counted.

# 5

# THE VIRGIN MARY

When we got back to Kemah I had neighbors coming out of my ears with rumors about the things that had happened at Forgetful Bay. The assaultee, Chantal White, was now said to be, variously, a druggie, a woman recently in business with unsavory types, an LGBT pioneer, transgendered division, a woman with sexual appetites described as "voracious," a word I seldom used myself. The dancing woman remained a mystery, but it was acknowledged she was connected to Duncan Parker, who had apparently been asked by the members of the board to vacate his presidency of our HOA and had been replaced by an interim president, a woman who was relatively new to the development and about whom I knew nothing but her name: Bernadette Loo. This was a crushing blow to Roberta Spores, who was, I was told, embittered. There was, also, a new peculiar event in the neighborhood, which was that someone had stolen—under cover of darkness, presumably—a dozen mailboxes, these being removed whole, post and all, like teeth pulled right out of their sockets, and installed in the shallows of Smoky Lake. By this time the neighbors were sure that one of our own was the culprit, the engineer of all carnage.

One afternoon coming home from Target where I had two prescriptions filled and bought some Orange Milanos, the Pepperidge Farm cookies my mother used to like so much before she died, I thought about my mother on the drive, remembering her at different points in her life, and in mine—when I was a kid at Saint Michael's, when I went off to college for the first time, when I went the second and third times, and then much later, in her last years, when she was approaching eighty and something of a recluse. My father had long since passed away, and Mother was living alone in a small town house among a group of town houses set aside for seniors where the fees, which were ridiculous, covered a good deal of care and attention from a staff that included RNs and PAs and assorted additional semi-medical people, not to mention staff that cooked and cleaned. The place was an old-folks home, though it was at pains to represent itself as something more modern and inoffensive.

I visited her often in those days, staying for an afternoon, for dinner and occasionally overnight, alone, often with Diane, who liked Mother tremendously and didn't object. Those were not bad times for us, for all of us, even Mother, who, in spite of her age, was still healthy and cheerful, funny, pretty much all there. It was only in the last few months that things hit the skids.

So I was coming home and I drove into our little community, which was dotted with some trees I suspected we paid a fortune to get to grow in the soil there, and with more recent low bushes designed to look natural, which of course they weren't, and I admired once again the plot plan of the place, the units set back with balconies or decks over tiny but impeccable yards, the better to be easily cared for, all providing pleasant outdoor space and detached housing units that, through careful design, did not impinge too much, one on the next. Our two-lane road circled the community so that the two entrances—they were only several hundred yards apart—could live up to their distinct signage, one saying NORTH ENTRANCE and the other saying SOUTH ENTRANCE.

I rolled past the condos of a half-dozen neighbors, none of whom I knew other than to wave at or wish a good day. A gay couple—two guys who looked maybe a little more working class than most of the regulars, and who were, by and large, younger than the average residents—had recently bought the condo four units down from mine. We hadn't talked much. They were very nice and sociable and had brought me some rather unattractive barbecued shrimp one weekend a few days after they moved in, probably because Jilly had chatted one of them up when she was out for a run the day they arrived.

I hadn't met these guys, but I had said hello and waved on several occasions when entering or leaving, and this particular afternoon, as I entered Forgetful Bay, I noticed their garage door was up, and inside, standing on a white Styrofoam ice chest with a blue top, was a statue of the Blessed Virgin Mary. It wasn't news that they owned such a statue. I had seen it before a couple of times, displayed at various positions in their front yard, in every case staying in one place only a day or two before being moved to a new location, and another, until it had disappeared entirely a week or so before.

Jilly had remarked that the statue was in poor condition. It was about twenty-four inches tall, and a hand was missing, and the paint was badly flaked, but it was perfectly recognizable as the Blessed Virgin Mary, with her flowing white floor-length gown and her pale blue cape and cowl, her right hand held out with what appeared to be a rosary—an actual rosary, not part of the statue—draped over it, and her other arm similarly posed, but missing the hand.

We were both, Jilly and me, taken with this statue, a little surprised to see it at the new neighbors' house because it was not the sort of thing people routinely put in their yards. Mostly they put in their yards seasonal decorations—Christmas wreaths and candy canes, Halloween orange and black crepe paper, goblins and ghouls on a stick, rabbits at Easter, and, of course, American flags of all sizes, some with glitter.

And here was Mary in the neighbors' garage. Mary the Mother of God. Since there did not seem to be anyone around, I pulled out my phone to record the event—*Mary on an Ice Chest*—and, as luck would have it, at that minute the smaller of the two gay men emerged from the other side of the garage, a door there to a storeroom, and saw me holding the iPhone in that unmistakable pose necessary for taking a picture, which in no way resembled the way one holds the phone when using it, so there was no getting around what was going on. "Taking a picture of Mary," I said, thinking the best way to handle the situation was directly. "You don't see enough of her these days."

The guy came to the car window and looked back to see what the shot was, then stuck out his hand and said, "I've been wanting to introduce myself. I'm Gil. We moved down from Houston recently."

"Wallace Webster," I said, sticking my hand out the window. "I used to live there, Houston, out Memorial. Moved here some years ago with my ex-wife."

"Was that her, the Jilly person I met?" he said.

"No. Jilly's a friend I used to work with. She keeps me company down here sometimes. And I have a daughter, Morgan, you may have seen. We live down the way here." I pointed out the windshield. "Thanks for the shrimp, by the way. Delicious."

"We have Mary to keep us company," Gil said, turning to give her another look. "I'm getting ready to clean her up some, maybe repaint—that blue's a little faded. We like to have her around. I always say there's no reason not to have things around you that make you feel better, whatever your beliefs. You don't think anyone will be upset, do you?"

"Can't imagine," I said.

"We talked to a couple of folks. People walk by, so we talk to them and they all say the same thing. They like it—they said, anyway. We're not pressuring anyone, but it's a good feeling you get when you come home and she's standing there, watching over things. We like her."

"She's nice," I said. "I was raised Catholic, so she's an old friend. I'm glad she's in the neighborhood."

"Great," he said. "We should have dinner sometime. I cook, we could eat out on the deck there. We've got some other statuary coming."

"I don't get out much," I said. "Please don't take offense, but I don't socialize much, not at all, really. And my schedule's all screwed up, so—but it's a kind invitation and I thank you for the thought."

"Well, all right," he said, now backing a step away from the car. "I'm pleased to have met you and look forward to seeing you, uh, when I see you. How's that?"

"Perfect," I said.

"And you can fill me in on the gossip down here. I mean, there are a lot of rumors, and we're not in the loop, if you know what I mean."

"Probably more than I am," I said. "Pleasure meeting you, too. I'm going on to the house." I pointed out the windshield again and lifted my foot off the brake and let the car roll slowly forward.

"Maybe you could send me a copy of that picture," he said.

"Sure," I said, toeing the brake to receive the business card he was handing me. It had nothing but his name and an e-mail address on it.

"I'd appreciate that," Gil said. "Let's chat again."

"Will do," I said, giving him a little salute and pulling away.

# 6

# VELODROME

ONE AFTERNOON later in the month driving south, toward Texas City, I got caught in a merciless thunderstorm and took refuge at Chantal White's bar and restaurant, Velodrome. She was once a beauty, apparently, as evidenced by beauty-contest photos hung lopsidedly around the room, but in person she was comfortably weathered. I introduced myself, told her I had a place at Forgetful Bay, and said that she knew my ex-wife, Diane.

"I do?" she said. "So, we're neighbors. Wait—Diane Webster?"

"Yes," I said. "My name is Wallace."

"Well, I'm pleased to meet you," she said. "I liked Diane. I used to talk to her when she was out walking. I think I even walked with her once or twice. She's been gone awhile now, hasn't she?"

"She has," I said. "You appear recovered from the Yves Klein malefactor."

"That was strange," she said. "I was terrified."

"I'll bet. Sounded crazy."

She was attractive, judicious with the makeup, attractive in that way middle-aged folks aim for. She could wear tights without embarrassment, and did—leggings and a shirt. I liked her right away. We sat at what I took to be her table, in a corner of the restaurant, chatting about Forgetful Bay, watching the rain out the window. We had coffee, then coffee and pie, and pretty soon the storm was gone and the night-shift people were coming in. I was nervous sticking around but curious about her, and after a bit we took the stairs to the apartment she had above the bar and had drinks. "For those dangerous nights," she said, waving her drink at the apartment.

We chatted more and in time decided to have an early dinner, which she had brought up from the restaurant. When that was done she went down for fifteen minutes to look in on the business, and when she got back we decided to take a drive down the coast to catch the wind and the smell of the bay after the storm. It was prettier out there at night. So was she.

We got back late and the bar was lit up with floods high on the telephone poles in the lot and I got the midnight view—the building was like a giant rock, made out of that blow-it-on concrete that people make odd-shaped buildings with, except here the shape wasn't geometric, it was like a boulder the size of a small hay barn, all chiseled planes, small cliffs, irregular flat spots, poorly framed square holes for the windows, and with what looked to be a small Airstream trailer stuck up on top. Homemade architecture, what we once called ad hoc design.

“How about that?” she said. “I bought it because it’s so strange. You’ve got to admire it. It speaks a language all its own.”

“It’s terrific,” I said. “Peculiar.”

“And the trailer’s not decoration,” she said. “You can go right through the apartment ceiling into the trailer. Sleep up there, whatever.”

“I look forward to it,” I said.

“Really?” she said.

The rock building sat low off the highway, sunk into an oystershell parking lot at the edge of a thirty-foot-wide strip of water she called a creek, but was really a cut in the marshland that surrounded the bay there. Next door there was one of those fenced high-voltage setups with the weird-looking curly electrical posts sticking out at odd angles from the tops of two-dozen red weatherproof cabinets. “Cancer farm,” she said. “I’m going to open it up one day and turn everything off.”

On the other side of the building there was a steep hill maybe twenty-five feet high and we climbed up to the top, where you could see what had once been the bike racetrack—a good-sized crater with a banked track that was half sunk in the ground and half built out of it. We went back down and then entered through a short tunnel to the track itself, where there was standing water, the banked sides leaning up and away from us like a sideshow trick. A wedge at one end had completely collapsed. We climbed back up on the inside, to a point near the trailer, and had a look over the layout, there in the moonlight.

"I like it here," she said. "Sometimes I even have enough business to pay for the place. There are days in summer my lot is full of trucks and boat trailers. The boats launch, guys are gone all day, they come back in the dark, want a steak and some drinks. Nothing much."

"Sounds great," I said.

She led me back up to her apartment over the bar and then up the ladder to the Airstream. It was tiny inside. We were kidding around about the place being like a tiny dungeon, all that giant rock stuff below and the cramped quarters inside. I laughed about it and stretched out on the bed. It was OK, pretty paint on the walls, small windows with what must have been postcard views of the bay, though at night all you could see was the lit-up parking lot. There were fresh linens on the bed, a little TV, all the comforts of home, and I thought I might be comfortable there for a while. "I could get used to this," I said.

"You were a commercial artist?" she said.

"I was a regular artist first," I said.

"Who isn't?" she said. "I want to hear your story, whatever it is."

"It's not fancy," I said.

"That's fine," she said. "Unfancy is good."

"Maybe I'll hang out here for a while," I said. "How'd that be?"

"Is it a *long* story?" she said.

"Ain't short. We can start tomorrow."

"Thought you said you were an all-night guy."

"Not tonight," I said. "Tonight I could sleep for a week."

She shrugged. I always like people who shrug instead of speaking. There are lots of different kinds of shrugs, but hers were the best kind. Tiny, offhand, a lot of it the eyes, the brows.

I fell asleep in the trailer, and when Chantal came to check on me later I said I probably ought to go home, but I knew I wasn't going home. "I've got to close up downstairs," she said, and I waved as she went back out. She closed the trapdoor and then, oddly, locked it. I listened to the deadbolt slide into place, and I was surprised, then amused.

So I stayed put for a few days. She ran the restaurant. Sometimes I was locked in the trailer, sometimes I was free to move around. It was a curious game.

At night, after she locked up, we rode around or watched television in her apartment. Eventually we had sex, which wasn't too bad. It wasn't Hollywood, but it wasn't awkward and messy, either. It was OK. There was some oral copulation and some non-oral. Nights, while Chantal tended the business, I read or was online or sat at the Airstream door and watched the clouds go by like chilly streamers. I smelled the food cooking. I listened to the sounds from downstairs, the laughter, the jukebox music, the arguments. There were always arguments. A few loud remarks would be exchanged and then people would spill out into the parking lot and a car would screech away, and then more laughter, the screen door slapping against the jamb as people settled down, got back to their real business. And at the end of every night she'd come up to the trailer and sit for a while, and then go down to her apartment. I stayed up in the trailer or went out and walked the parking lot or the shoreline across from the place; sometimes I took the laptop down to the bar and sat there until daylight.

Days passed. The sun was nice in the morning. Some afternoons we drove around, ran errands, took in the Kemah Boardwalk, a noisy tourist thing that still managed to have that mark of decay about it, even though it was new. The town wasn't pretty, and the huge bay didn't help that much. It was an acquired taste, we decided. Kemah was twenty miles up from Galveston but had been a fiefdom of the Galveston Mafia, sort of a suburban extension and playground. My grandparents told me about the Galveston Mafia. I remembered mostly the names of the gambling and nightclub spots in Galveston—the Balinese Room, the Hollywood Dinner Club, Murdoch's, and a couple others supposedly notorious. By the time I got there, all that was gone, much whispered of.

I was satisfied hidden up in that trailer. Chantal gave up on the lock, but I didn't budge. Every once in a while we took a drive. My divorce was years gone, and it hadn't been particularly bad, but I still felt only half connected, so it was a relief to hang out with her. I called Morgan to let her know where I was, tell her I was OK.

"The attacked woman?" she said. "Is she still blue?"

"Funny," I said.

"Well, she's age appropriate," Morgan said.

"Use the condo if you want," I said. "Call Jilly. Tell her I'll be missing awhile."

"Gee, thanks," she said.

I thought I was starting something new this way, in that trailer, alone at night and aimless by day. Chantal and I spent a lot of time in the car. We ate in the car, drank in the car, smoked in the car. Everything was a day trip, because at night she had to open the place. I started making postcards to send to old friends from my New York days, people I hadn't been in touch with for years. It was a small thing, the postcards, but it was something. And there was a precedent, there were several precedents. I was making things again, and making something, almost anything, seemed like a giant step.

"You look businesslike," Chantal said to me one afternoon when she caught me at work on one of the cards. "You're impressive that way. I like it." She put her arm around me, pulled me to her, pressed her head into my neck.

"Always thinking," I said. The card read WALLACE WEBSTER'S ONE-MAN SHOW CLOSED TODAY. "Thought I'd mail this out to some people," I said.

She had that fresh smell in her hair, on her skin, that scent I'd become attached to quickly. It wasn't ornamental, it was plain scrubbed, soaped, always the same Dial soap. I liked the ads for Dial that I saw on television, mostly because she used it, because we both used it now, but also because Dial was so ordinary. I liked that we were the same as other people.

I guess I thought I'd be with Chantal for a while. I started telling her stuff all the time, stuff about my family, my background, all that. It wasn't extraordinary, but it was stuff I didn't tell everybody.

7

# DILETTANTE'S GUIDE

JILLY CALLED and left a message on my phone, but I didn't call back. I was still with Chantal, talking too much, pleased to have a fresh audience. I told her one of my favorite early memories was of car trips from Houston to Galveston to visit my grandparents, my father's parents. They had moved to Galveston from Long Island in some long-since-lost fog of history. By boat, they had moved *by boat* from Long Island to Galveston. My grandfather was a Triple-A ballplayer who owned a bar in New York, and my grandmother was a short, stout woman from Poughkeepsie, which, being Texans through and through, my brother Raleigh and I thought was the strangest thing we'd ever heard. What kind of name was that? So we mispronounced it in every possible way we could think of on those long drives and laughed hysterically, made up facts about it, and generally misbehaved in the car the way kids did.

I recalled my father at the wheel of his precious yellow 1957 Chevrolet convertible, already by that time a classic, with the top down, my mother's pinned gray hair blowing in the wind as we sailed down the two-lane Gulf Freeway to the old, slightly disreputable beach town where the houses were carpenter gothic, the palms seriously grizzled, the awnings orange striped and wind whipped, and the sandy streets had names like Avenue I½, which, when spoken, was "Avenue I and a half." Half an *I*—confounding wonder. Over the course of my childhood we visited often enough for me to see this little city, hear about its past, and to remember the long weekend drives to and from my grandparents' house on Cedar Lawn North. We went fishing out by the causeway or in the surf at Stewart Beach and, later, West Beach. We ate Sunday dinners at John's Oyster Resort, which was barely there by that time, and occasionally the Galvez, and we drove the seawall for late-afternoon entertainment.

"Everybody's been to John's," Chantal said. "Even me. I saw a mouse running around in that place the last time I was there. We were eating and we were the only ones there and this mouse had the run of the place. Is John's still there?"

"Doubt it," I said.

"Food was great," she said.

"I always liked Galveston," I said.

More than any other broke-down Gulf Coast town, Galveston was all about the air, that army-brown water that wouldn't give an inch when asked to be beautiful, and the sand thrown around in breezes all the time. I loved the way the beach seemed the abrupt and not-a-moment-too-soon end of everything. The Dead End of the World.

The Galveston Mafia stories were the icing on the cake, the benevolent Maceos and the less benevolent Fertittas, the hushed talk of gangland empires, smuggling, gambling, bootlegging, and other dark pursuits. One of the Maceo brothers had lived right across the street from my grandparents behind an eight-foot brick wall. Of course, by the time I came along all the intrigue was largely a thing of the past, veneered by then with the upright facades of ordinary businesses.

I never lost that feeling of being at the edge of the world when I went down to Galveston, and that feeling was always more poignant on the Gulf Coast than anywhere else. Towns on the Atlantic coast, in New York, Virginia, Georgia, were still connected to the rest of the country, while the Gulf Coast was something else, some shank of the land where things flat ran out. The Pacific coast was showtime, *Arizona Highways,* and all that. Picturesque to the point of parody. But Galveston—and Kemah, Texas City, Matagorda—all the little bay and coastal towns were places nobody stayed unless they had to, unless they were aiming to steer clear of the line of fire. Everywhere along the coast, from south Texas to Louisiana, there was this worn-out feel, some godforsakenness that drifted through the air like sad Latin music. Things were slowed down and nothing seemed to matter all that much. You did your business at a stately pace, meaning if you got around to it, and if you didn't there was always tomorrow, or the day after.

"That's what made Kemah my target when I was looking to get out of Houston," I said. "Maybe the coast is no different from the suburbs, as superficial and empty, but it's still a little bit haunting. Probably the endless water, and memory, before memory was forgotten."

She looked a little puzzled, reared an eyebrow.

"Never mind," I said.

We went to dinner at a shack on the bay called Leitter's Oysters, big pine decking up on phone-pole pilings, two piers running out and bridged with these oddly irregular cuts of wood, the main part wood siding with zipped-down plastic sheeting for windows, and the kitchen another trailer stuck on the back end of the place, right on the edge of a shell lot.

"You been here?" she asked me.

"Sure," I said, like I was an old hand, though I'd only been there once.

We put in our orders and went back through the main shack, sat out by the edge of the place, water lapping up under us maybe five feet below the decking. We could see it right through the gaps in the so-called floor.

I told Chantal I'd driven the whole Texas coast in my early twenties, one end to the other, starting at Brownsville, where the town was trying hard not to be Mexico, and where it was impossible to imagine why it wasn't. I had gone down there with a friend who was headed into Mexico permanently, for reasons unknown, and I rented a car, a Cadillac, some years old and black with gray leather, and I began the long drive up the coast, staying as close to it as I could, stopping at every dinky town on the route. Some I knew, like Port Isabel, Tonsil City, Corpus Christi, and Aransas Pass, and some I didn't know at all, like Seadrift, Teacup, and Boiler, which was one stinky little town.

A woman came out with a couple of red plastic baskets piled with oysters and fries and called out Chantal's name. "White?" she said, and we waved her over.

"So what happened on the trip?" Chantal said, squeezing a lot of lemon on her oysters.

"I kept going," I said. "Went up to Beaumont, and then, for a laugh, threaded my way across the Louisiana swamps from Houma up to New Orleans, down to Grand Isle, up to Slidell, and then across the coast of dreadful Mississippi, where gambling had not yet become the salvation so desperately needed."

"They got it eventually," she said.

"I know," I said. The oysters were a knockout, and the fries weren't bad, either. I kept eating and talking, and explained that I went through Biloxi and on to the industrial burnout of Pascagoula, which looked about the way it sounded, and then across Alabama via the Dauphin Island Ferry to Gulf Shores and Orange Beach and into the garish far-western Panhandle of Florida at Perdido Key, and drove right on to Gulf Breeze, home of the Gulf Breeze Sightings, and Santa Rosa Island and then steadily along the long Florida run to Mary Esther and Fort Walton and 30A, to Pine Log and Panacea, Seaside, Apalachicola, and eventually turning south toward Crystal Springs and then Saint Pete, and down to the pricey heaven of Captiva and Sanibel and then that swampy alligator cross-country to Leisure City, and the high-rise route out to the Keys.

"It was fun," I told Chantal. "It was like running away from home and staying home at the same time. Maybe dangerous here and there."

"Yeah, but not for a kid who loves fried food, trashy motels, and girls that hang out in cheesy nightclubs."

"Well, I didn't take the girls too seriously. I figured I could run faster than most. Even the all-out ratty joints seemed safe by the time I got to them. I thought I'd get tired of the tacky crap, the minigolf and souvenirs and franchise restaurants, but I never did. Not for years."

"You going to eat that?" she said, her fork poised over a small oyster in my basket.

"Nah. He's all yours," I said. I tossed a chunk of bread out the unzipped plastic window, and immediately it was hit by a couple of passing gulls. "It wasn't all shantytowns and pearly fish scales," I said. "Used-car lots with colored spinners on long wires overhead, but those were the places I liked best. I kept a diary of the trip, wrote down what I saw, all the junk architecture—I was still planning on studying architecture at that point."

She nodded. "You might have been a good architect," she said. "You've got an architectural look about you."

I took a minute to figure that out, got nowhere, continued my report. "I liked everything from beach dives to peach-colored stilt houses. I looked at what I figured was overlooked—lumber, seasonings on dive tables, wall colors, electric light. I thought you might be able to build junk for people and make it work. Houses like yours, for example."

"I don't really call that a house," Chantal said.

"Whatever you call it, that's what I was thinking," I said. "I was sure that everything was already trash, garbage, artifice and mimicry, remake, rerun, for better or for worse, and that try as we might to change it we only made new layers of waste. That suggested we should embrace this line as the future of building. There were already guys working the territory, I'd read about 'em. I figured I was getting set to join 'em."

"And so you did, sort of," she said.

"Before I got religion," I said.

"Religion?"

"Art. Takes you over, leaves you gasping. Like religion."

"I guess," she said.

"Well, not seagull art."

"I figured you'd like seagull art," she said.

"You got me," I said. "I'm a little inconsistent. Still gasping after all these years."

"I see that," Chantal said. "Coming out around the edges."

"I like the coast," I said. "Peppered with crap, the too-tired-to-fix-it kind, the wait'll-it-breaks kind. Where the too-lazy-to-perform end up because it's easy enough, and there's still something purely rewarding about spending another inessential day next to the unwashed. The Gulf is a neglected animal in a zoo, an animal nobody wants to see, on display so deep in the property no one ever goes back there."

"Look at you," she said. "You poet."

"I apologize. I regret it all. Take me back and lock me up again."

"I will do that," she said.

All this talk was fun for me, and Chantal was the perfect foil, she being more authentic and about twice as beat down as me, hard as nails, apparently, and skating with her on the surface of things was good therapy and heartwarming to boot. I was interested in the surfaces, the reflection of bright light, the appearance of things, the society of strangers. Surfaces are kind of final, kind of real in a way nothing else is. You can't really take it back once it's out there. I figured what I was doing with Chantal was taking the temperature of the patient, me, postdivorce, laying my palm across my forehead. I was already a fan of junk culture, every excess, every heartbreakingly bad idea some fool came up with, every pathetic effort we made to clean up our act and our lives, every crummy joke, every dumb gesture, every pretense to profound thought, deep spirituality, or, going the other way, low self-loathing. We were blockheads and ninnies, and I liked that about us, even the grand and miraculous, who knew not this rarefied enlightenment.

"I wrote in my diary that a parking lot in Bear Claw, Alabama, was exquisite, and I meant it heart and soul. I was a kid then. Life by television, for television. I did this monster drive given over to motels, fast food, tourist joints, gas stations, flying fish, bad signage, seaweed, short people, and fierce suntans. And all I wanted was to run into one person as marvelous as any one of those guys in the movie *Vernon, Florida,* which I'd just seen. That guy with the five balls of brains was my hero for a while."

"Pay the bill, hotshot," Chantal said. "I'm headed for the Land of Mystery." She swung out of her chair and went to find the ladies'. I was left at the table waving at the woman who was wiping her pen off on her apron.

"Everything good?" she said when she got to the table with the check.

"The best," I said. "I loved it."

"Huh," she said. "That's good news. If you ask me, there are many things to love in this world, and if you don't love something, your life's probably not worth the napkin it's printed on."

"You got that right," I said.

"Yessir," she said. "Love is lucky. You see our gorilla?"

"What gorilla?" I said.

"We got a new gorilla out front," she said. "I always wanted one and we picked one up at a place down the coast. It's only about ten feet, a ten-foot gorilla, but we like it. Needs paint. Check it out when you leave. I don't know how you missed it coming in."

"We were talking," I said. "Probably not paying attention."

# 8

# COWARDICE

My incarceration at Chantal's ended shortly, and I returned to Forgetful Bay, where Chantal and I still saw a fair amount of each other. We were at my condo one afternoon when she noted that I had my ex-wife's things in one of the bedrooms, which she found odd years after the divorce.

"It's a den," I said. "She jammed it in there for storage. I never said anything about it."

Chantal said, "I see," and changed the subject. "So when did you turn into an artist? You always want to be an artist?"

"Everybody wants to be an artist," I said. "My brother said that."

"Not really," she said. "I wanted to be a swimming actress, like Esther Williams. Sit around poolside in Hawaii and such."

"There's an art to that," I said.

I explained that I had started painting in my twenties, in Houston, showing in local galleries. It was an accident, really. I got tired of architecture school, and it seemed you could catch up on art quick reading the magazines, so I did that ceaselessly and got way too much attention for my trouble—group shows, one-man shows, invitations to museum shows. "I won a few prizes at regional shows—Tulsa, Oklahoma City—and I was always in the art section of the newspapers in pieces about Houston art. I'd be in there promoting some exhibition. I was young. It was fun. There I'd be at an automobile graveyard or in a gallery alongside a ten-foot sculpture of stacked-up tubes from huge truck tires."

"Your sculpture?" she said.

"Uh-huh. Tire tubes were an important part of my work. Along with tape on walls, dirt on the floor, and so on."

"And cars, too, no doubt," she said.

I told her I made up stuff about my pictures being a demonstration of respect for cowardice, something I said had afflicted me since childhood, and I started writing on the paintings about the life of a coward. "It was interesting. Something people hadn't done too much back then, defining yourself in negative ways. So that was the story. It was maybe half true."

"My daughter's an artist," Chantal said.

She'd told me about her daughter who was a crazy child, the kind you can't control but can't give up on, either. A terror who was 90 percent hardship. "I want to hear more about her," I said.

She shook her head. "Sometime, some other time."

"Whenever," I said.

"You're not a big listener, Wallace," she said. "I miss her, though, but it's not like every day. I remember her when she was a pleasant kid. She was funny. She liked me."

"Probably still does," I said.

"Probably still missing," Chantal said. "Like always."

She went silent then, and I didn't know what to do, ask her questions or let it alone. I decided to let it go, so we sat up in bed and watched TV, and pretty soon she had the sound low and the closed captions on, and when I looked over, her eyes were shut down.

I stared at the screen and considered how much of a coward I had been, as a child, as a teen, as a young man, and what it meant to be a coward, how it fit into adult life. I didn't have answers and I didn't care that much anymore, anyway, though it had been confounding at the time. It was more than just made up, and I was surprised that it had come up with Chantal so readily. I had not always been intrigued by cowardice. As a kid a coward was the worst thing you could be. Kids taunted one another about it, like it was the measure of something. I was never brave or much interested in bravery, and I'd always weaseled out of every confrontation I could, which made good sense to me then. I had a few fights as a kid, but only when my imagination failed me and I couldn't beg or explain my way out. I didn't see the percentage in fighting, at least that's what I told myself, and maybe that was the problem. I mean, you knew a fight was going to be over quick, each fighter would cause some damage, usually not a lot, and most of the time nothing else would come of it. We lived in the suburbs; we weren't in gang country or anything. There were girls to impress, reputations to build, but that could be done other ways, so where was the payoff? Anyway, that was my interest in cowardice. My memories were littered with examples of little things that didn't amount to much but always had something in common, a discomfort with throwing and taking punches, fear of being caught doing something that would bring punishment. I was afraid of my teachers catching me without the homework, girls catching me doing stuff that was uncool. I guess it was a little cyclone of fear, my adolescence. I navigated grade school and high school using a battery of poses. I was the profoundly sorry offender, the guy who would apologize for anything, whether or not an apology was warranted. I could also do the puffed-up victim who seemed wild with barely contained rage, but that one was risky, even if it was a good setup for the elaborate apology if rage wasn't working. Sometimes I was a devil-may-care guy, or a deliverer of grace, or a font of good sense and kindness, or a temple of reason. All these were postures.

This coward angle was an art game, an idea about which I talked with other artists, gallery owners, newspaper art critics. It worked for me.

After a time I started taking the project seriously myself, thinking that I might begin a set of paintings as memoir, with scrawled notes about my father, who was not a coward but a bully, a small man physically but wickedly smart, with a nasty mouth on him, who had used wit and something like charm to find a wife and start a career as a renegade architect, very early setting himself apart as a modernist when modernism was not yet in middle age, and who built a successful practice outwitting and out-arguing more conventional men, until his practice of demanding perfection on the building site in matters of dubious importance earned him a reputation as a foolish pedant whose demands on tradesmen so often cost them money that in the end they would not bid his jobs. This left him with no one to build his remarkably modern designs—a flaw in the program, architecturally speaking.

At home my father was distant, busy, a clumsy parent who was at once demanding and unforgiving. For my older brother Raleigh, our father was a terrifying great figure on a hill, an oracle, a hander-down of tablets on which were written the unwritten rules by which we lived. A horrible tyrant. For the later child the father was less a threatening figure than an annoying one, always requiring work when play was wanted, always starting a project on a precious Saturday, always ranting in a minor key about the ignorance of the fools he had to contend with, this last becoming a well-worked shtick both of us children learned and which served us in later life, along with sci-fi X-ray eyes and the power of contempt not quite expressed.

As a kid in the Catholic grade schools, I was already adept at posing as the offended, the embarrassed, the wielder of ridicule, the victim of misunderstanding. But when I actually got into a fistfight with a guy named Michael Bono on the playground, got him eventually into a headlock, I couldn't bear to throw him into a convenient truck-sized hole filled with rainwater for fear that he would report to the nuns that I had started the ruckus by flipping him off. The damage from such a report quickly calculated as more profound than fighting only to a draw, I threw him not into the hole but to the soft dry grass alongside the hole, just as Sister Mary Grace arrived on the scene.

"It's a good thing you did not throw him into that water, Wallace," the nun said.

In fifth grade I got into an argument with a teacher who detained me after the final bell. She threw an eraser at me. I picked it up and threw it back at her. This was the error of bravado, for she embellished her report somewhat, adding that I had called her a "cocksucking slut," which I had not called her. And yet this became the heart of the matter in the eyes of the nuns who streamed out of the convent like so many ants the better to look me over and tsk and tsk and click their little black beads. Quite naturally, the nuns believed the teacher, and thus I received the stereotypical Catholic-school punishment of being placed in the convent, in solitary but air-conditioned confinement, in a dark room off the convent entrance, alone from eight-thirty in the morning until three in the afternoon every day for six weeks.

"Ah-ha!" Chantal said when she heard this. "All is revealed."

"My assignments given to me each morning," I said. "My parents accepted my guilt as fact, though I told them otherwise."

"Brutal reality," she said.

"Years later I made a tentative entrance into the world of young women," I said. "Marked by playful grabbings in the pool, gropings in the dark garage, until—"

"Yes?" she said.

"Until at long last, in high school I first found home with a putatively promiscuous Italian girl from Sacred Heart Academy, an all-girls high school of poor repute near the railroad station downtown. At the conclusion of a sexual act which found me so busy retracting myself from the scene of the crime that when the moment of moments arrived I whistled Dixie into the green plaid of her school uniform, my first partner, the sweet Valerie d'Angelo, berated me for an extremely safe but somewhat unsatisfying experience. I swore to her that this was intelligent design, not anxiety."

"That's a big hello," Chantal said. "Absolutely."

Chantal stayed over that night, sleeping on top of the bedspread fully dressed, with a beach towel as a blanket. That's the way she rolled, she told me the next morning when I commented on it. I was up at seven with her, having slept all of two hours by that time. We had coffee on the deck.

"I'm sorry I faded on you," she said. "It's not that I'm not interested, I get tired early."

"Not a problem," I said.

"Where's your daughter? I thought she came to see you. Didn't you tell me that?"

"She's in Houston, in the Heights someplace. I've never been there. I should go."

"You should," Chantal said. "Is she studying architecture?"

"Yes, but it's early yet," I said. "It's an odd course of study. Not much in the way of the liberal arts. I did almost four years and could not go on."

"You were at Houston?"

"I was at Washington University, Saint Louis, for the first year, but that summer I met this girl in Houston, and by the end of the summer I couldn't imagine living without her. I transferred."

"'Twas ever thus," Chantal said. "But you continued with the architecture."

"I did. Until the fourth year, when my professor thought it would be good for his students to do a parking garage—real world and all that. By that time I was more interested in art, so instead of designing a parking garage for six weeks, I prepared a multimedia presentation, a barrage of light, sound, image, a noisy catastrophe about sensory overload. Multimedia presentations in architectural school were decorous, quiet, and sulky, a single screen, stately transforming images, moving music, evocative shadows—the presentation of a mood being sought in the design. I had seen some good ones, art-house lyrical, but that wasn't my idea."

"You who went your own way."

"I wasn't much good at art-house lyrical. I was OK, not great, at ordinary drawing and painting. I mean, I could do that Chuck Close thing with the grid over a photo, where there are hundreds of little squares and if you get them approximately right, then your overall picture looks approximately right, but it took forever and what was the point?"

"Renaissance," she said. "Landscapes, the wonder of perspective."

"Yeah, and I thought those guys had great eyes."

"They had those, too. Didn't you listen to the museum recordings they give you?" she said.

"I didn't," I said.

"Didn't you read that Janson textbook, whatever it was?"

"I did not. Weighed too much."

"Cute. You weren't a figurative painter anyway, were you?"

"Too slow," I said. "When I started making paintings they were after some old pictures by Lester Johnson, big abstract heads, sloppy outlines in black, slapped on five-foot squares of Masonite. Day to day I played the role, dressed like painters whose pictures I'd seen—paint-spattered shoes, paint-dribbled shirts, paint-stained hands."

"A perfect replica," she said.

"So anyway, I did this multimedia deal with sounds—natural stuff, industrial sounds, jazz, sound collage, Steve Reich, Art Ensemble, Cage and Feldman, Ayler, Sun Ra, factory sounds, found sounds. I mixed a long piece with radio and television clips, the moon landing, assassinations, Cronkite, Wallenda falling, Elvis dying, *Rocky Horror,* Nixon in the helicopter door, and vocalizations of great beauty. Coupled with hundreds of slides of similarly miscellaneous origin, and that was it. I had the professor sit in the center of the classroom, shot the slides and film right at him from the corners, blasted him with the sound."

"Bet he loved that," Chantal said.

"He did not. The show lasted forty minutes. When it was done he left without a word. Days later I learned that he'd flunked me and I was out of the School of Architecture."

"Ta-da!" she said brightly. "Achieving a goal. The better to become a fine artist."

"I took a year of classes at the Museum of Fine Arts, and thereafter begged the university to let me into the art department, which was chaired by a delicate-handed older German still-life painter whose name was Schröder, a painter whose attitude toward contemporary art was something less than welcoming."

"The looming shadow of a German hand."

"OK," I said. "I'll quit. Thus ends 'The Story of Me.' Let's go somewhere, do something." I got up, headed for the door. "I think I need to go to the store. Target. You ready?"

"Way too early," she said. "It's a thrill a minute here. What could be as fun as this? C'mon. There you were, on the threshold of a great career. Very much of the moment, artwise, up to here with art magazines, art ideas, and the lengthy exposition of same that monthly graced the pages of the then-triumphant art journals."

"*Artforum* and beyond," I said.

"You toiled away, working on great heavy stones to produce unsatisfactory lithographs, working on small paintings and large, your clumsy hand an affront to the German master."

"Now you're having too much fun," I said.

"You pick it up from there."

"Did it again," I said.

"The multimedia?"

"Sort of. I set up a special problems course with the German master and turned in a four-hundred-page book of xeroxed articles and essays from art magazines, the selection of which I contended was a substantial scholarly essay on contemporary art, the required product of the course. The German master was not persuaded. I was excused from the Department of Fine Art."

Chantal clapped, slowly, lightly, rhythmically. "Bingo!" she said.

"Thereafter I sat in local bars drinking endless mugs of beer and talking with my fellow painters, and I was as happy as I'd ever been. Making art was immediate, soulful, satisfying in a way nothing was before. It was a revelation. Changed my life."

"And now," she said, waving her hand toward the sliding door behind us. "All the way from Wiesbaden, Germany, your old art professor Hans Jürgen-Jürgen! *Hier, kommen-zee, Professor Jürgen-Jürgen!*"

And then she would not stop laughing. Laughing and giggling, sort of intermittently, like the wiper blades once we got in the car and realized that it had started raining outside. Rain and fog all the way to Target, where we went to buy some Bounty paper towels. "Giant rolls," she said. "I am buying a twelve-pack of *rollos gigantes* equaling, as you may know, eighteen *rollos regulares.* The better to wipe this old egg off of your sweet artistic face."

# 9

# NY, NY

I KEPT thinking about the past. The past was, in many ways, more interesting than the present. I spent nights remembering people and events and circumstances, stuff that had happened, what I'd done and who I'd done it with in the years before I got settled at the design studio. It was all fragmented, came and went in a disjointed, now-you-see-it-now-you-don't way, but Chantal made me want to remember, not so much for enlightenment, but for the simple pleasure of recalling times that seemed gentler and richer.

At dinner one night in Galveston I told her about New York. How, kicked out of art school, I moved there planning on making art. I'd had fifty copies of a CD titled *Special Problems* pressed. This was the audio part of the architecture school fiasco, and I sent it to all the art magazine writers and critics I could find addresses for. I arrived at La Guardia, took a cab into the city. A friend from Texas was subletting a loft on Greene Street. The loft was small, grubby, and stocked everywhere with the owner's furry sculptures, which loomed in the space like Bigfoot penises. I set out to get a job in a gallery, since I'd done that work in Houston. I had another friend in New York, an ex-teacher, Zin Wang, who had made a small splash with his postsurrealist figurative painting, extraordinarily out of time but happily well received at a SoHo gallery where his pictures were often, but not always, painted on shoes and similar, displayed in ancient frames. Zin had a flat in the West Village and a wife from Brazil and wrote occasional articles for *Art 1,* an already failing art mag. I got a job at Sara Goldman Gallery, helping her hang shows, manning the desk when she was out, answering the phone, keeping the place tidy. Sara was a pleasant middle-aged woman with a taste for sixties art who thought I was cute, in a scruffy, out-of-town way.

"From this beginning," I said. "I waded through the New York of that moment, meeting some painters, showing in a few group shows at independent galleries."

Our food was delivered and we began to eat. Chantal motioned with her fork, rotating it in my direction. "Go on," she said.

I told her I was sitting in the front room of Sara's gallery late one afternoon and in walked this pretty blond woman, all Dick Tracy'd in suede head to toe. She looked rich and she looked young. We had on show a couple privately owned Flavins, an Alex Hay yellow pad, a Larry Zox piece, and a few second-tier concept pieces. Douglas Huebler, I think. It was summer in New York. Nobody was showing anything.

So the woman said, "Are you Webster?"

I thought I should call Sara, because this woman looked like she was married to two doctors and all three of them loved art a great deal.

So she said, "I'm looking for Wallace Webster." Instantly I switched from Wallace the Meek to Wallace the Bold, and I said, "Yes? And who might you be?" But I thought I should not be talking to this woman, whoever she was. She was from another planet.

"I am Plastique," she said, and there was an accent, not an extreme accent, but it took me a minute to get that this was *Plastique,* the art-pop singer, who was, at that time, very underground and hip, and she had come to find me. I was thinking: God is great.

So in a few minutes I had locked the gallery and we were in a cab headed downtown and she was telling me she had gotten my CD from a friend and she liked the noise. At the restaurant we ordered, we talked, and she proposed that I back her at some club where she had a gig the following week. I could not see how that was going to work, but I was so flattered that I was unable to say that. I was afraid her noise and my noise were not the same noise. We got through the meal, and when I was paying the bill I got some change from the waitress and left ten dollars and the silver on the table.

Before the waitress returned, Plastique snatched the change off the table. "Never leave this," she said to me. "It's uncouth. It's demeaning."

It was like eighty-four cents or something, and I hadn't

even thought about it. Outside the restaurant she dropped the change in a plant by the door and I could tell she had lost some respect already. We went to a loft off Houston belonging to a woman percussionist who introduced herself and handed me a guitar. A couple scabby-looking guys loitered in the background. They were clearly there for my audition. For about five minutes I scratched around on the guitar, which was plugged into an old Fender amp, trying to look serious about my scratching, but I knew this wasn't the noise I was good at. I thought about trying to explain that my noise was composition based, that it was produced by sifting hours of tapes and other sound sources, that there was a lot of dubbing and overdubbing involved, that I could prepare something for them in a few days, that this guitar scratching really wasn't *me.* But they were already, like, looking at each other, pushing their hair around mightily. Moments later Plastique signals me to stop and takes the guitar, then walks me to the door, her arm through mine.

"You had frozen under the harsh gaze of celebrity," Chantal said. "You did not measure up. But it was only the first test!"

"I had failed already."

"Let's get some dessert," Chantal said. She waved at the waiter, who came rushing at us as if we were on fire. "Could we have the dessert menu?"

"We have no dessert," the waiter said.

"Is that design or circumstance?" Chantal said.

"The first," the waiter said.

"Fruit?" Chantal said.

"Yes," he said.

"Well, that will do," she said. "A selection of your best fruit, please." And the waiter vanished. "Plastique did not remain long in the limelight, as I recall. Wasn't she Swedish or something?"

"Norwegian," I said. "Or Icelandic."

"Somewhere chilly," Chantal said. "Iceland, of course. It figures. They're always entertaining. Do go on with the story."

"There's not much more," I said.

"You were young at the time? Twenty-something?"

"Two," I said. "Maybe four."

"It was an embarrassing moment," Chantal said. "But these were not the keys to your future as a fine artist, certainly."

"I was wounded," I said.

"Still," she said. "The show must and all that."

"I began to take on a slightly jaundiced view of celebrity at this time," I said.

"Known to the trade as the Cornball Defense," Chantal said.

"Sort of, I guess. Jeering as denial of desire. I waved hello to Bob Dylan, who I saw on the street in the Village, as if we were the best of friends and Bob had forgotten, the plodder."

"Noble work," she said.

"I had an intimate interaction through a shopwindow on Madison Avenue with a very attractive actress whose black push-up brassiere was very much in evidence as she shopped for blouses. This involved pointing and other gestures."

"Well done!" Chantal said. "You were scoring at every turn."

"And then there was the thing with Paul McCartney," I said.

"Oh, ick," she said. "Don't tell me."

I explained that I felt odd about adopting this conflicted mode of interaction on the street but concluded it was better than slinking along in silent admiration of the celebrities that forever patrolled the town. This approach/avoidance, always making jest of the celebrities, fit exactly my view of myself as a coward, fleeing genuine expression of feeling, contact, intimacy, even friendship. Why must I jeer at them? Why must I make them the butt of my private jokes, jokes I was sure no one else would find humorous in the slightest?

"I wondered," I said to Chantal, "how I could become a famous artist in New York if I was always making embarrassing public jokes about the kinds of people New York was so proud of."

"And you determined then and there to stop such displays as unbecoming a young man with goals," she said. "Yes?"

"Exactly," I said. "I lived for several years with a young woman named Candy Roberts, a manager from another gallery, and continued showing in various exhibitions such that my name was always linked in articles about indie art with the other unheard-of people. What was clear was that New York was, for practical purposes, a small town, and the art world was tiny, powerful, and well financed. The world that I had imagined from reading art magazines was real, but more maquette than full-size sculpture."

At this point the fruit arrived at the table. It looked like Del Monte Mixed Fruit. We stared at it for a few moments. "It's, uh, fruit," Chantal said.

"Yes. I think so," I said.

There were two bowls of the fruit, one for each of us.

"If we only had some Oreos," she said.

"Exactly."

She fetched up her spoon and moved on the fruit. "Continue," she said, munching delicately.

"I got tired. Eventually I was asked to write a piece about the new art for a magazine, and at about fifteen thousand words I ran out of steam."

"Thank heavens," she said.

"That was the beginning of the end. Within weeks I discovered that Candy Roberts was sleeping with my old friend Zin Wang, and within days of that Candy and I agreed to terminate our arrangement. In short order I quit my job, packed my belongings, and left. One was surprised at the relief one felt looking from the bridge en route to La Guardia back at the city skyline in the lowering evening light. Knowing one would not return."

"The end of an era," Chantal said.

"I talked my way into a job at a junior college in Houston. Later I met my first wife, Lucy, at a store where I'd taken my boots to be repaired. She was a folksinger with a lovely voice.

We went to clubs; she sang. We entered that world, by good fortune produced Morgan, enjoyed life. I changed schools a few times, swapping up to universities, and I began showing work at Houston galleries, again. Notoriety, again, but no sales. The locals were still walking with knuckles firmly in the dirt. I talked the dean into letting me take a graduate degree with a minimum of hassle, giving me credit for time served, as it were, and made a side deal working with Point Blank. So things were going well, and I figured we were set."

"Not to be, I guess," she said.

"Lucy got sick and died. Bang. Six months door to door. I'd heard of it happening, but it was something to watch up close. We'd been married seven years when she died. Six and a half were splendid."

Chantal gave up on the fruit. "That's the worst story," she said. "That's awful."

"I kept putting one foot in front of the other. It was strange, her not being there, not on earth. I was on automatic for a year or two before I could even begin to function in the normal way. I shut down."

Leaving the fruit where it lay, we left the restaurant and went over the causeway and headed up the Gulf Freeway. It wasn't unpleasant out. We got off at Dickinson and stopped at a gas station for ice-cream bars, a quality dessert, got back on the freeway, and went all the way to the League City exit before cutting across to Kemah. On the drive I told Chantal about Diane. How I'd met and married Diane after she enrolled in my advanced painting class. We had an affair, which was not specifically precluded in the e-handbook at the very modern school where I was teaching. Soon I was more valuable to Point Blank if I worked full-time, so teaching went out the window. Eventually we got a house in southwest Houston. Our life got smaller and more routine, even with Morgan in tow. We rented a bay-front condo I found one rainy night when I wanted to get away and drove down to Kemah for no good reason. Eventually we bought the place and moved there, thinking to enjoy life on *Low.* But the sourness that was creeping into the marriage seemed to ramp up. The whole world seemed to have gotten cruder, uglier, and less satisfying. At home the days got longer. The marriage was strained. We knew each other too well. We kept up the routines for a while, but when even those began to break down we divorced.

"That's the short version," Chantal said. "I recognize that."

"It's enough," I said. "You get the picture. After the divorce people started looking strange to me. I worked at home. I was already keeping bad hours—up when everyone was asleep, asleep when everyone was up. Spent my spare time on the Net. The usual waste, though sometimes interesting. I joined Facebook, diligently reported my status, and made one thousand four hundred friends. I considered these things: When is thinking carefully the same as cowardice? When is avoidance cowardice? Is it cowardly to evade and dodge, to leave by the side door, to step out of the way? Is it fear that makes a person behave 'properly' and in accordance with one or another code of conduct? Must one seek always to attack and destroy an enemy? Must one regard the other as the enemy, always? Is 'settling for' something less than what you aspired to a kind of cowardice, or is it pragmatism or just good sense? Must one always pretend to be the hero? These and other questions preoccupied me as I motored through the second decade of the twenty-first century, widowed, divorced, alone."

# 10

# CROSLEY

My nights in Kemah were spent clicking around on the Internet, finding things that held my interest a few minutes at a time, sometimes longer—sort of like reading the paper was in olden times, except the range was wider and more colorful. I got sidetracked a lot, but I kept clicking most nights, link after link, and smoking the occasional cigarette, a vice I'd cultivated in spite of all good sense. I tried to keep it to a couple cigarettes a day, thinking I'd read somewhere that statistically a few cigarettes a day were the same as no cigarettes a day. The "few" was stretchable. The house at night was cleaner and more pristine than it ever was in the daylight, and since I always had most of the lights off, the place looked great—quiet and refined. It was magnificently straight. The pots and pans were polished, the silverware crisply sorted in its drawer, the curtains clean and flounced, the towels fine enough for hotel duty. Days were dreary, a time to work at something you didn't want to do, a waste, time spent waiting for evening, for darkness, and the window, the bay, the birds, the pretty little boats, the distant weather, watching as the night gathered it all up.

At five A.M. one day in April my ex-wife Diane called. She said, "Wallace. I have a problem. I have several problems and I am going to need some help."

"It's five in the morning," I said.

It wasn't unusual for her to call, though she usually did it around midnight. We still talked often, holidays, birthdays, other times when one of us felt like talking.

"Just listen," she said, and she told me a friend named Dan Crosley was killed in a one-car crash on a rainy highway seventy miles from her place in Woonsocket, Rhode Island. She learned this on the telephone when she got a call from the police. Dan was, she said, a publicity guy working freelance for cigarette companies. He ran a short route of outlets, where he managed promotions, delivered posters and punch-out promo boxes, supplied flyouts, and rode herd on the new age cigarettes—Saratoga, Misty, Sweet Dreams, Capri, Bailey Reds, a couple dozen others—in smaller mom-and-pop groceries, gas stations, nightspots all through his territory. In that world he was a powerhouse—a man with more friends than he knew what to do with.

The morning after the crash, after being bumped around most of the night by sheriffs, highway patrol guys, hospital aides who were too sweet or too clipped, Diane got back home in time to catch the video of Dan's car twisted around a little concrete bridge on the local TV morning news. It was a picture more horrible than she had imagined.

"Sounds awful," I said. "Are you OK now?"

"From that moment I pay attention to tiny things," she said. "Details and only details, because that's relief. Wallace, I'm older and I'm alone. I have nothing to do. I have plenty of money, but I don't know anyone and I am alone."

"What happened with Cal?" I said.

"He's around," she said. "But I don't know about Cal. He's a whisper in the dark, something flying past the window. Dan was another deal entirely. Dan is why you haven't heard so much from me recently."

"I haven't heard much from you?"

"Oh, stop," she said. "I need to talk about this. With Dan I was fine. The move, divorce, everything. But now this town up here looks like a foreign country to me. I might as well be in Yugoslavia, which doesn't even exist anymore."

It hit me at this point that there was risk in continuing this phone conversation and that, if we did continue, the call was going to be long. "Let me get up and get some coffee and call you right back."

"You're not up?" Diane said. "What time is it? I thought you were up till six."

"Usually," I said. "But I fell asleep a bit ago. I'll call you in ten minutes, OK?"

"Thanks," she said. "Thanks, Wallace."

We hung up, and I went into the bathroom for a shower. Then I had three pancakes microwaved back to life from a package Jilly had left. It was getting light out, and the world outside my windows looked like a toy world—one of the reasons I liked living there. I called Diane back. "Thank God," she said. "I was beginning to think you'd ditched me."

"I was getting set up."

"I met Dan at the pet store. They say pet stores are great places to meet people if you're a pet person. Anyway, he was this nice guy. He was a couple years younger. Thick necked, bristle haired, quick to smile. He smelled like something in a barbershop bottle. Vitalis—you remember Vitalis?" She didn't wait for me to answer. "We went to a restaurant and talked for a couple hours. His name was Dan Crosley and he was from New Orleans."

"Let me Google him," I said, clicking randomly on the keyboard in front of me.

"Stop it," she said. "We get some odd people up here, you know, tourists and guys passing through, but he was a straight shooter." Diane didn't pause there, went right on with her story, telling me that she took Dan home and slept with him.

"Thrilled to hear it," I said.

"I mean, he wasn't Michael-damn-Douglas, but he paid attention. We had dinner at my house and after that we drove through Woonsocket. He showed me some places I'd never seen before, showed me around. He'd been up here since college."

"How much of this do I really want to know?" I said. "You met your boyfriend in a pet store, went to a bar, took him home and screwed, then took the Woonsocket tour."

"Pay attention," she said. "I'm getting to it. So he showed

me his place. This gorgeous little cottage nestled back in the woods."

"Whoops," I said. "Getting scary."

"Not at all. It was lovely. We stayed there awhile, a few days, and I was, like, perfectly content. I was happy for the first time in a long while. It was, like, out of my hands. Do you get that, Wallace? I can't really tell you how relieved I was. I was hanging with Dan, and I started seeing the future. I mean, how the future could be. I was on cloud nine. It was sort of like the old days," she said. "You and me in the old days."

I remembered that, those days, that feeling, that comfort, the sense of everything in its place, the rightness of it all, when the winter is loved and the summer is all the sun there is. When you want that specific moment, that time, that place, that situation, forever. You can't force it or wish it, and praying doesn't help. You wait, you keep going, you hope maybe it'll come around again. That flawless equilibrium.

"I get that," I said. "That way of things."

"I was comfortable for the first time since the divorce," she said. "I had something that worked for me, that made everything balance. And it was strange but amazing and satisfying—I mean, I figured I was in for the duration, know what I'm saying? Dan was going to be it for me. I was one hundred percent with the program. Do you know that feeling, Wallace? Do you remember it? Everything slipping into place?"

"I do," I said.

"And then bam! He's gone. The whole thing's gone. Like

that. Snapped away." She paused for a minute, as if that was the end of what she had to tell me, that was the reason for the five o'clock call. "I did all the stuff after that. Talked to the people, arranged stuff. Dan didn't have anybody else, so I took care of it. I was kind of in shock. I walked through it."

"I am sorry," I said. "Really."

"I know you are," she said. "But now I really miss him. I miss everything about him."

I could hear her voice break on the phone, like I'd heard it break scores of times before in calls since the divorce. It didn't always happen, but I'd heard it often enough. It made me feel dreadful, like I'd destroyed her life, and nothing could be done. I hated hearing it but couldn't bear to say anything.

"See, I had this whole new world, I was finally home again in that tiny cottage with a man who needed me. It was us, day after day, fooling around more than seemed healthy. He was striking in that dark way. He was a little bit sullen, theatrically, as if life had disappointed him. We were like children together."

I raised some eyebrows she couldn't see, and said, "I got nothing. I'm on empty here."

"I know that, Wallace," she said. "Of course I know that. But this is what's happening with me, and that's why I'm reassessing everything, feeling everything again—a richness that I have not felt in a while, and I wanted to tell you. The world is fresh again, it's all bits and pieces of a thing I had forgotten, that had all but disappeared, something I rediscovered. And I thought you would want to know about it, I thought it was something you should know. This thing is possible, this new thing—"

I made some guttural noise and held on to the phone there at my desk, stayed silent and heard Diane crying, and after a while, after a few minutes, I heard her place the receiver softly back in its cradle.

# 11

# iPHONE

The neighborhood settled down some. The police were always around, and so it seemed things were safer than ever. People figured the cops would leave, so that's what they were worried about. Parker kept sending e-mails to the residents "updating" us on the developments, of which there were none, apparently. Chantal had recovered completely from her "incident," and we were all "sorry" to learn of the departure of Forest Ng's family following on his "tragic" accident. The rest of the Ngs, it turned out, were going back to Florida and California, whence they had come, and their home had been purchased by the Changs, a local family who already owned one house in Forgetful Bay and needed another, apparently for their relatives who were about to join the family business, a po'boy sandwich shop they ran in town. A new location was to be opened, staffed by this new wing of the family.

Morgan came to visit, and I reported the whole of the conversation with Diane, the life and death of true love, which I did not report in a skeptical light, rather the contrary. Morgan scolded me anyway for making light of her stepmother's love affair. "It's easy for you," she said. "Not so easy for women at her age."

"I'm not making light," I said. "And it's not easy for me, either. What are you talking about?"

"Jilly," she said.

I handed her the box of pretzels we were both eating out of. "That's something else. It's not like I'm making a move on her," I said. "You guys, for heaven's sake."

"A move?"

"You know what I mean," I said. "Gimme one." I pushed a broken half pretzel back at her and waited for her to fish a full-grown pretzel from the box. "Besides, Jilly's been there one way or another for years."

Morgan leaned into me, close, playfully getting up in my face. "Yeah, and what is the deal with you two, anyway?"

"You don't know? You're around, like, all the time when she's here, you see everything, and you have to ask? For years now, since the divorce, maybe before the divorce, you've watched us, and you never once asked."

"I know," Morgan said. "Aren't I strange?"

"You are a strange daughter," I said.

"She's old enough to be my mother."

"If she had you at thirteen, maybe."

"Happens," Morgan said.

"Are you taking me out to dinner or somewhere?" I said. "To the store? You want to go to the store? I have to go to Best Buy and get a new iPhone case." This was a little bit of a sore point with Morgan, since I already had two dozen iPhone cases.

"Great," she said. "You've spent more on cases than the phone."

"Free country," I said. "It's my fortune and I'll et cetera."

"Quit that," she said.

"What?"

"Never mind. Let's go." She shouldered her purse, which was gigantic, and headed for the door. "We'll get dinner. I'll let you buy me some new running shoes."

So we went out. It was near sundown, and the wind was up, cool. I watched her go down the stairs in front of me and thought how lovely she was, how graceful. Seeing her made me happy.

At dinner we talked about her classes, about Diane's troubles, my meds, the TV shows we were watching, the crap on the news—all the usual, all worn out, of course, but we could eat and nod at each other about these subjects.

She asked, as she often did, about my father, who had practiced architecture in Houston for years. Morgan had not known him when he was alive but knew him through things I'd kept—renderings, models, drawing equipment, articles in *Texas Architect* and other magazines. So she started toying with architecture early, way before she was old enough to think about what she wanted to do as an adult. She liked playing with the tools of the trade, the drawing tools, and as a kid she would go into my office and make drawings using his old equipment. I showed her how to use a T square and triangle, how to use French curves, the different kinds of pencils for different kinds of drawings. I taught her to print like an architect, those precise, boxy letters, striking and evocative, which she still used all these years later, for everything from checks to grocery lists. I had learned lettering from my father, but mine had long since gone to seed. I envied her hand. I was proud and envious in equal measures. I suppose that's common with fathers and daughters.

"There haven't been any more rude events out here?" she asked.

"Not that I've heard of," I said. "Chantal is the strangest. The dancing woman was a Parker misadventure. No one ever said anything else about it, but the whispers are that he and the wife are duking it out these days."

"Where did the security people take that woman?"

"Nobody knows. He knows, of course. They work for him, so sweeping her away is an indication of something."

"So what about Chantal?"

"I like her. She's nice, funny. Easy to be with. I never got the whole story about the break-in and all. I'm guessing it was a one-nighter gone wrong, but she's not talking."

"Bad romance," Morgan said.

"If I were a betting man," I said.

We were eating at a gas-station-turned-Mexican-restaurant. The conversion was well done. All those big windows in the interior, the wall opened up into the two automobile bays, those, too, having new all-glass overhead doors that could be opened up onto a patio. The food was nicely grimy, too, which was a break from the usual franchise stuff. This was Tex-Mex, but made by a hearty crew not afraid to push the envelope greasewise, even though they went easy on the name—it was called Old Mexico, which I remembered was a restaurant in Houston when I was growing up.

"I love this place," Morgan said. "They ought to call it Pulque Mi Dedo."

"What's that mean?" I said.

"Look it up," she said, and went on eating. "The thing with Chantal could be scary. I mean, even if it was a lover it's not a good thing in the neighborhood. Mr. What's'isname wouldn't approve."

"Mr. Green Jeans? Mr. Who?"

"I forget his name. Lovely day in the neighborhood," she said.

"Rogers," I said. "And it's a beautiful day."

"That's a mistake. Anyway, you ought to ask around, you know? Interview the folks? Give you something new to do. You can be like a PI, like Mangum."

"Magnum, I think," I said.

"What I meant," Morgan said, waving a heavily laden tortilla chip at me. "You could do that, yes? Wheedle around and get the lowdown?"

"You figure that's a good use of my time, do you?"

"Well, it's something. You could do worse. I'm not criticizing—"

"Of course not."

"Jilly could be your sidekick. Something you guys could do together while you're not doing other things that you aren't doing anyway."

"Are you staying at the house tonight, or are you returning to your high-class university?"

"I'm with you for the duration," she said. "I need to stop at Target on the way home, though, pick up a few necessities."

"Maybe I can find a bumper case there," I said. "I'm thinking of changing the color of my phone from black to white with this .4-millimeter 9H bulletproof-glass screen protector I found, but I need a case that wraps a little over the front edge so that the edge of the glass isn't exposed."

"You are a sick lizard," she said. "Why not buy a white phone?"

"Well, what color is yours? Maybe we could swap. I can't tell what color yours is in that monster case you use, what's that called?"

"OtterBox," she said. "Defender."

"Can't even tell what color your phone is in that full enclosure."

"White," she said. "It's pearly white."

"Fancy that," I said.

12

# COPS

CHANTAL AND I were up in the apartment over the restaurant. It was nearly two in the afternoon, and she'd been working on whatever she worked on for the restaurant while I slept. She looked fresh and clean, bright eyed. I didn't. We were at the table, sitting on opposite sides of the table, which was Knoll—Saarinen, maybe. Or maybe that sculptor whose name I never could remember—Bertoia. Harry Bertoia. No, it was the tulip table. I was right the first time.

Two police cars turned into the drive and pulled to a stop. Four cops emerged, two in suits, two in uniforms. We could see them from the kitchen windows. The cars were marked. We watched the four men rearrange themselves. They were leaning back into their cars to get things, one fellow twisting into his jacket, the uniformed guys spitting and adjusting their gun belts, straightening out their too-tight policemen's trousers.

"What do you figure they're here for?" I said.

"Never can tell," Chantal said. She went down the hall to

the little space she used as an upstairs office, then came back. "I don't want you to be surprised," she said. "You should know that my name isn't really Chantal."

I was surprised. Plenty. But I said, "Your name is not Chantal."

"It is now, but it wasn't always," she said. "I changed it. I've lived here awhile, in Texas, but before that I was in Mississippi. Biloxi, there along the coast."

"You're from Mississippi," I repeated.

"Not from there, but I lived there."

"So what do the police want?" I said. "Is there something I should know?"

"Always," she said. She seemed a little rattled. I hadn't seen her like that before. "I used to live louder, I guess you'd say, but now it's slow and easy, and being quiet, stick to the shadows. Suits me best these days. I gotta change these clothes."

She left the kitchen and went to her bedroom and I buttoned my shirt and thought about getting my shoes but decided to do without and went into the front hall where I could get a better look outside. A minute later she came out of the bedroom straightening her hair. She looked thin, coming toward me, real thin, even gaunt. She reached my side and looked out the window at the four men below. One of the suits was finishing a smoke and shot the butt into the air toward the coast road. The four of them exchanged a look and some remarks, and three headed for the door. The fourth, one of the uniforms, went under the house.

"This looks like no fun," I said, which was the truth. Unvarnished. I was not a fan of the police, or, more accurately, I was a fan of them out doing their duty but not visiting me and mine.

"They look businesslike," Chantal said. "Don't they look businesslike?"

"Maybe they're just here to go over the attack again," I said.

"I don't think so," she said. "I had some trouble in Mississippi years ago. Whenever they show up like this it takes me back."

"So, what was the trouble?" I was rebuttoning my shirt because I'd gotten it wrong the first time. It was a striped shirt from Ralph Lauren, blue. Heavily wrinkled at that moment.

She put her arm around my shoulder, pulled me to her. "Tell you later," she said. "It's a long story." She had that Chantal smell in her hair, her skin, that scent I'd become attached to. We stood together at the edge of the window until the knock hit the door.

We welcomed the police inside, and they were very polite. They wanted to talk to Chantal about the "gangland style" murder of her late husband, Bo Del Mar. Chantal made coffee, and we sat with them in the living room of the apartment over the Velodrome. We were forthcoming, at least Chantal was. I was quiet and scattered, sat there fiddling with my hands.

She'd married an army guy named Bo Del Mar, who, it turned out, accused her of endless infidelities, which, according to her, were imagined, but that, apparently, made no difference to him when he was beating her. She would flee the house in the middle of the night and he would follow, catch her, bring her home, and beat her more. One night he pressed a steam iron into her back, leaving a scar still visible all these years later. I'd seen it. She'd said it was an accident. She went over all this with the officers. What they knew was that her second husband had been killed in his sleep in their bedroom. Chantal, who was then Greta Del Mar, was a suspect, as spouses are when the mate is killed, and after an investigation she was arrested and charged. Then, once the trial started, the DA suddenly withdrew the charges and asked that the case be dismissed with prejudice, meaning she could not be charged again. So much time had passed by now that she hoped she'd heard the last of it, but here they were again.

What she told me later, but did not discuss with the cops, was that she had eventually decided she needed to defend herself. It made sense that she would do that, but for me it was frightening. She told me she got a twenty-two-caliber pistol from a guy who worked odd jobs for her, a Gulf War vet named Dave Roberts, and she shot her husband in the temple while he slept, drunk and passed out, in their bed. With good reason, she thought. Self-defense. After years of beatings, drunken rages, hiding from him in and under neighbors' houses, of trying to divorce him and being threatened with everything from strangulation to being washed in gas and set on fire—a method Bo Del Mar said was a common punishment for bad women in the Middle East—she had done the unthinkable. "I shot him," she said. "I put him to sleep for good."

Her lawyer, she told me, was an ex-prosecutor who was so successful in that job that the street in front of the courthouse was named for him, and he was every bit as good as his reputation. He was later implicated in a Dixie Mafia multiple-murder case but was eventually absolved of any connection to the scandal that ensued.

As Chantal told the story, after her charges were dropped she changed her name and worked as a low-level executive for one of the Biloxi casinos when the casinos there were still relatively new, dodging the hangers-on and fourth-tier TV personalities who seemed to drift through the neon-lit gambling palaces and weather-vulnerable condos that dotted the beach. It was after one of the big storms that hit Biloxi every few years, so it was a whole new coast, empty by day, fog ridden by night, splashed with blistered light, silly white limos endlessly trailing up and down the beach highway, a place overgrown with and much in love with any new Gulf Coast celebrity, among which Chantal was often counted most notorious because of the publicity of her case. After the arrest there had been support parties in penthouse condominiums, gambling binges in which Chantal and her friends hit the blackjack tables with more money than seemed reasonable; there had been boating parties and too many mornings seen from dark to light. TV people called, networks wanting interviews for the likes of *20/20* and *Dateline.* And the case became stupidly famous, so that some nights Chantal remained hidden in her place and watched herself on program after program. The discussions of the case on television were wildly off, but that didn't seem to bother anyone, and all skated on, the case on television looking nothing like the case in the court, the crime nothing like the crime that occurred, the horror more inane and less complicated than a woman pushed to extremes taking a pistol and standing over her husband in their barely lit bedroom late one night, squeezing the trigger.

That was the story she told me later, after the police had come and gone that afternoon. Their project was routine, they said, and they asked a few questions, jotted a note or two in their various notebooks, thanked her for her time, and moved on.

She spent the remainder of that day and night telling and retelling the story, adding bits of detail, trying to get what she called the most accurate rendering of events, so that I would understand. I did understand. Chantal was not Chantal, she was this other woman who, in another lifetime, had shot and killed her husband, a serial abuser. And she had gotten away with it. I was with a woman who had murdered her husband. With reason to be sure, if she was to be believed, and I had reason to believe her, but the act itself was so large, so real and present, that it redefined her for me. My feeling for her changed in an instant. I tried not to show it, not to reveal myself, but I was sure she could see it plain as day. She frightened me.

13

# MODERN WORLD

JILLY WAS down for the weekend and I was glad to have her back. She was all energy, thinking of things to do, places to go, goofy projects that were easy and pleasant to dispatch. This time she wanted new T-shirts, but she had to have women's T-shirts, which were different from men's T-shirts. I suggested that she'd look great in regular T-shirts, but that involved defining regular T-shirts as men's T-shirts, plus it intimated that the women's T-shirts she was interested in were somehow inferior, which didn't seem like a great idea, so I backed away from my position quite readily. She also wanted some boy clothes, like dress shirts, but was horrified at the price, so we thought the best deal would be to drive to the outlet mall in Texas City. It was a nice drive, coastal part of the way and lots of those huge high power lines strung on the tall T-shaped steel towers that look like giant Japanese war poems, warriors marching across the landscape. She did some voices for the warriors, fake Japanese movie talk, which was funny. I told her I was working through all this stuff that had happened to me over the years, it was all coming back to me. It seemed like since I crossed fifty I spent about half my time remembering the crap that happened way back. I was wandering around in memory.

"Oh?" she said. "Like what?"

"People and places, stuff I did or didn't do, the way the world was then."

"Dark ages," she said. "Pre–Johnny Depp."

"Not at all. Anyway, he's about my age."

"I thought he was about twenty," she said. "And prettier, no disrespect. Has more hair. How did you lose this much hair?"

"Sold it," I said.

We were driving on Camber Road, which was a recently refinished four-lane running into town. She was driving; I was manning the map. She couldn't read anything when the car was moving without getting seasick, so whenever we hit the road I was navigator.

"So what things are you thinking about? Are you thinking about God again?" She said this like I was hitting the booze. "Remember," she said, "we're scheduled to go to church."

"I'm thinking the world has passed me by," I said.

"Duh," she said. "Is news?"

"Wasn't always the way," I said.

"It's passed me by, and I'm still in my teens," Jilly said. "So, what else?"

"My mother, I'm thinking about. She was funny and wry, mysterious to us kids, at least until the late going, when she got a little addled. We have these people around, parents, and then they go south on us. And they vanish. I hate that."

"I know. I went to a funeral last week, this kid at the office. I stood there at the casket and looked at him, and all I could think was here was this body, and it was not working anymore. I mean, I was this close to him," she said, waving a hand between us. "And the week before I'd talked to him, and we planned a thing for a deal we were working on. And he was all there. And then, suddenly, he wasn't."

"How'd he die?"

"Some weird medical thing. His heart started racing and sort of exploded. That's how they explained it to us. What bothered me was the casket. The thing inside there, the body, seemed utilitarian, like something you'd order from Amazon. A rug-shampoo device. I guess that sounds stupid, but that's what it was. Another busted machine and the guy, Ricky Lipper, was gone. The body had nothing to do with him, it was a thing, there, on display." She shook her head. "I'm not explaining this well."

"I get it," I said.

She turned down toward the bay, a little street that went past where a lot of shrimp boats tied up, and she ran the windows down so we could get the full effect, the smell of the place. It was overcast and reasonably cool for late spring, and the rain clouds looked as if they could do some damage. Breezes whipped through the car.

"I haven't thought much about church," I said.

"Morgan said you hit her up about it," she said. "Thing is,

I'm tired of all these Tea Party church people, and as tired of the other end of the deal. Like that British wiseguy who died and his hard-boiled atheist bullshit. Like who really knows what is going on? How we got here? What other 'people' are out there? How it started—all that shit. It's fucking unknowable. Why is that not good enough? Let's say *Who the fuck knows?* and let it go."

"Religions are built on that stuff, so they gotta know."

"That's crap," Jilly said. "Hokum. Made-up mumbo jumbo. I'm sure, these apostles really did that Jack Webb thing and reported just the facts. Or the other guy, or—" She pulled up in front of a two-story restaurant that had a deck overlooking a harbor. "You want to eat something?"

We went inside, through the room, got a table on the deck. "I like going around with you," I said. "You improve my life."

She eyed me.

Her energy turned the lights back on for me. I wanted to say something about that, but I didn't want her getting the wrong idea. I didn't know what the right idea was, but I didn't want to look like I was going overboard.

"You haven't been around much recently," she said. "I've called a few times."

"I've been hanging out with Chantal," I said.

"You going vintage?"

"Meow," I said.

"Didn't mean it that way," she said. "On the other hand—"

"You're chilly today," I said.

"What're we having here?" she said. "Looks like it might be good for oysters."

The waitress arrived and looked familiar, but I couldn't place her at all. She did the waitress thing, standing there with pad and pencil, looking off in the distance to give us a little extra time. It was clear she wasn't leaving the table without an order, so we gave her one, and she strode away.

Next to the restaurant there were a couple wood-plank piers running out into the bay. They were chockablock with pelicans, maybe fifty pelicans in various states of disarray, some with tucked beaks, others with twisted necks in service of underwing cleaning, others stretching and waddling, throwing their heads all the way back until their necks showed up in the cavernous bottom halves of their open beaks, some so buttoned down they looked as if they had no heads at all.

"I saw this special on TV," Jilly said. "They were doing religions, a two-hour special on world religions, contrasting them and that sort of thing. People in church—Catholics, Jews, Protestants, Muslims, Holy Rollers, all the way to snake handlers."

"TV loves it some snake handlers," I said.

"God, the author of famine, plague, blindness, and decapitation," she said.

"And flambé," I said.

The waitress brought our salads, and I cherry-picked Jilly's for the croutons. She didn't like croutons. "Religion always gets to me," she said. "I don't hate it, but I kind of hate it, you know? I'm a little negative when it comes to religion."

"We're better at plumbing," I said.

She shook her head and straightened up in her chair. "I guess I shouldn't be going on. What's with you and Chantal? You guys hooking up?"

"We're not altar-bound," I said. "But, on the other hand, when you're not around—"

"Reflect," she said. "Meditate. Stroll quietly through the great apses, footsteps echoing, flying buttresses flying overhead."

"The buttresses would be outside," I said. "But I will start tomorrow if it pleases you."

"Picky, picky," Jilly said. "Should I conclude there is still a chance?"

"You are unnaturally direct this weekend," I said.

"I missed you," she said. "You know. When you didn't call back immediately, when I got nothing in my e-mail, no clever text messages, nothing on my Facebook page, nary a tweet. I felt, like, abandoned. In a minor key, of course."

"What other key is there?"

I worked on my salad, ate some lettuce and chopped bacon, more croutons, some honey mustard dressing. I felt lucky to have her to spend time with, drive the coast roads, eat at local dives, someone who hadn't killed anybody. I kind of gazed at her. I smiled at her. In the harbor the boats rocked and splashed in the water, their moorings and riggings and ropes stretching and clanking in that lovely way they do.

* * *

When Jilly visited she was always cleaning some part of the house, and she seemed to enjoy being there, making it up as she went along. I spent a lot of time thinking back on things, remembering bits and pieces, but Jilly didn't do much of that. She'd mention something, hint at it, but rarely elaborate.

One night I tried pressing her, and she started telling me about a time when she was working at an antique shop in New Orleans. "I was living there," she said. "I went to work for an older guy in his forties named Simon Color, keeping books, selling some things when he was out of the store, being a personal assistant. He had a son, a good-looking kid, sharp dresser, sort of a mix between a jock and a geek. Like that idiot actor, what's his face? Anyway, this kid was finishing at NOCCA in New Orleans. This is years ago. I was twentyish, still in school, and between boyfriends. Pre-Cal."

We were in the kitchen at the condo. I was putting butter on premium saltines, lightly, for a premium saltine indulgence, one of my favorite late-night indulgences. Jilly wanted nothing to do with the saltine thing but got herself a beer from the refrigerator. She said she was planning on staying up all night with me.

"You couldn't be more welcome," I said.

"So this kid was pretty, direct, and since my duties involved being at the house sometimes, ferrying stuff from the shop, like that, we got to be friendly, probably more friendly than I'd anticipated. After a while it was clear we wanted to have sex."

"You're scorching my ears," I said. "I thought you'd never had sex, to this day."

"We'd go out and park, and talk, and get along great, and after a bit, we started making out some."

"Heaven forfend."

"Simon didn't know about this. I figured I was going to end up selling something for a living, so I was glad to have the antiques job, even though I didn't know fuck-all about antiques. I worked as a gofer, really, I was the head gofer."

"I want to hear it," I said, chewing my premium saltines.

"I'd get Matthew at his house and we'd drive out somewhere, a parking lot, someplace out by the lake, anywhere, really. Matthew was sexy and a tease. I was questionable then, a rat girl. I had pink and blue swans on my Pontiac, behind the front wheel wells. This was before Pontiac went belly-up, but my Pontiac was old even then."

"Enough with the Pontiac," I said. "And then—"

"Matthew was, uh, Mediterranean, maybe, medium thin with big shoulders. I was only a few years older than he was anyway. We were both kids, sort of, was what I thought."

"So did you *consummate* with him or not?"

"I want a premium saltine after all," Jilly said, so I gave her one. "Mmm. One more," she said, holding out her hand. I gave her two more and waited for her to chew through them.

"In the Clinton sense, I did not have sexual relations with that young man," she said.

I squinted at her, suggesting, I thought, disbelief.

"Not intercourse," she said. "Everything but, every way to avoid it, every option, the whole show. We had our moments in the house, in motels, in the car, but I dodged that one single bullet. He didn't seem to mind. I didn't, either. He was a good boy, fast learner. Eventually Simon sort of caught on, though I don't think he ever discovered the length and breadth of the thing, I think he thought we were just a little too friendly. So I was gently out of a job. And the other thing is I never really regretted it."

"A scalding memoir," I said. I was cleaning up the crumbs on the kitchen counter, sweeping them into the sink where the water was running strong.

"That's one I never told anybody before. You're the first."

"You did what you did. You're a regular what's her face."

"Who?" Jilly said.

"You know. That Oregon woman. The teacher."

So then we had to look up female teachers who had sexual relations with their students, and we found a list of the top-fifty female-teacher sex scandals on a site that included pictures and links to news stories. The list began with Mary Kay Letourneau—"A love story," Jilly said—and included Abbie Jane Swogger, Traci Tapp, Autumn Leathers, Cameo Patch, and Deanna Bobo among others.

We stared at the pictures on the MacBook's screen for what seemed like a very long time. Finally, I said, "You want to click the links?"

"These women are all pretty good looking," Jilly said.

"This modern world," I said.

# 14

# LULLABY

CHANTAL AND I were up in the Airstream and she was telling me about her daughter, Tinker, a wild child. Tinker had lived with her grandmother, left for California after a stint at a boarding school, lived on the streets panhandling out there. We were meeting Tinker downstairs. I'd seen a picture of her in a book of photos Chantal had by some Memphis photographer, not the famous guy, somebody else. Tinker was nineteen in the picture, and she was all rags and mascara, skanky clothes that were too big for her, bidirectional hair, and punctures all over her face. You could have done a photo essay and sold it to a fashion rag. Name your year. "Go easy on her," Chantal said. "It's her first time home since then."

I asked why things had gone this way, the daughter fleeing and staying away, and Chantal sighed. "I don't know what to tell you. There was trouble with my first husband. He was a rough customer. Yeah, I know how to pick 'em. Anyway, I didn't have control and then I was alone, and

I couldn't handle her. I feel bad because I sent her to my mother's and that was the last I saw of her until she came back at nineteen."

We met at a corner table in the Velodrome. The place was empty otherwise. The daughter was lean and deep eyed, wearing black tights and a black T-shirt, a half-dozen scarves, a few strings of beads, a couple of chains at her neck and more at her wrists, a dozen bracelets, tattoos peeking out on her neck, shoulders, wrists, and legs, studs in her face, and more rings than I could count. She hugged her mother when we got there, said hello to me.

"Pleasure to meet you," I said, offering my hand.

"So, what are you—Corrections?" she said.

I shrugged at her, recalled my hand. "A pleasure is one of the broad class of mental states that humans and other animals experience as positive, enjoyable, or worth seeking," I said.

"I could have spoken too soon," she said.

"So, how are you, dear?" Chantal said.

"Good," Tinker said. "I'm doing art now. I'm here awhile, if that's OK. I'm tired of wandering around. I've been everywhere since I saw you last. All over. Nonstop."

"Pascal?" Chantal said.

"Still functional, far as I know," Tinker said.

"Who's Pascal?" I said.

"This guy, years ago, wanted to get married and I didn't. I spent months with him trying things out, but pretty soon I was leaving."

"She attracts the guys," Chantal said.

"They love me out there," Tinker said. "God knows why."

"When she was eleven her father sort of died in a bank robbery," Chantal said, filling me in. "He didn't really die, just died in spirit. Roy worked at the bank in Quantum, Florida, on the Gulf in that deserted stretch south of Tallahassee where nobody arrived, nobody left, and people kept opossums for pets. In hurricane season the water ran right up into town and stayed. Mostly Roy watched the girls and I watched him, because you had to."

"That's not fair," Tinker said.

"We had no business being together in the first place," Chantal said. "He was a southern boy from Plaquemines Parish and I was Miss America, metaphorically speaking. Two kids came to rob the bank, and Roy decided he was finished being on the bottom rung. He pulled an aluminum bat from under his desk and, you know, that ticked off the boys. Eventually one gun goes off, then another, and pretty soon Roy is on the floor bleeding substantially."

"The perps flee with beaucoup loot," Tinker said.

"Things changed after that," Chantal said. "Daddy got meaner and less daddy-like during his recuperation. He bought a pistol for twenty dollars from a guy in town."

"He wasn't that bad," Tinker said.

Chantal arched her eyebrows and squinted at her daughter. "She was twelve and he was nasty as a rat with cabin fever. He smacked her around; smacked both of us. I couldn't protect her or myself. He wouldn't let up, and when I came home early one day and found her crazy bruised I got the pistol and shot Roy right in the chest. Pop. Just like that."

"Him too, huh?" I said.

"Too?" Tinker said. She turned to Chantal.

"Was a little gun," Chantal said. "I felt bad, figured he was dying. Things get a little rough sometimes."

"Roy was fine," Tinker said.

"We called emergency, and they took him to the ER, and he was saved. I missed the heart and everything else that mattered, clean as a whistle. I wasn't even close. Thereafter I sent Tinker to her grandmother's in Lovine, Alabama, for her safety and for my sanity. Roy was in and out of the hospital in short order, and on a bus heading west. Permanently."

"As for me," Tinker said, "Grandma had the habit of tapping me with her cane, sticking me with it, poking me, and she kept saying I needed to behave myself or I'd never find a decent man."

They were feeding on each other, Chantal and her daughter, and Chantal, who previously passed as ordinary people, now sounded like a long-in-tooth version of the street-tough daughter. It bugged me.

Tinker picked up the story. "After a while there were too many boys and too much trouble, and eventually I was scheduled for three years at the Certification School for Troubled Youth near Birmingham. Grandma had a friend there. It was a warehouse building on the site of a chemical factory. I did my schoolwork in some woman's office and made my grade-school diploma in record time, and then, one night, I managed to wiggle out through a concrete pipe in the cellar of the main building, and I never looked back. Hitched my way around until I was all the way to Cali."

"When I saw her last she was nineteen," Chantal said. "I was going on forty."

"When I came back Quantum was still a backwater, but like everywhere else the kids had taken over, frightening their parents, so I had a natural crowd. I climbed their water tower, smoked in their abandoned depot, swam in a couple of creeks, laid out on the beach with them. There was an old Ford dealership, a snowball stand, a quadplex and the Gerald R. Ford High School, where all my new pals gathered for drug sales and fistfights."

"She was queen of the May with that bunch," Chantal said.

"So one day I took a walk to see the famous bank where my father took his stand, which was by then a slab of concrete littered with glass and four-foot weeds. North of the place there were these tall Cyclone fences peppered with KEEP OUT and MILITARY INSTALLATION signs."

"That was months later," Chantal said. "I'd already moved to Houston with Bert."

"Third time's a charm," Tinker said.

"We were good, Bert and me," Chantal said.

"What? Are you kidding?" Tinker said. "For a year?"

"I loved that one with all my heart," Chantal said.

"Sure," Tinker said. "So I had a room at the motel in

Quantum and pretty quick landed a job at a toy store called Bigger Models."

"Owned by Pascal Lullaby," Chantal said. "He was real nice to her, but he was thirty and looked like the kind of guy who might try to pay a pretty girl for one thing or another."

"How vivid," Tinker said.

"I'm adding color," Chantal said. "You go ahead."

"So one night I'm finishing my shift and Pascal was in there being as sweet as pie and I figured why not, so I shared a soft drink with him and sat and listened to his story, all about his ex-wife, his toy store, the rest of his life. That got to be a habit at closing. The clientele was old guys who sat like stones at the checkout counter, drinking beer and talking model airplanes, HO-gauge trains, about the tiny people they put on their layouts. I felt bad for Pascal because his story seemed about like mine. One day Pascal says to me that he likes me pretty much, and he reaches out and rests a baseball-glove-sized hand on my thigh."

"Didn't see that coming," Chantal said.

"So I swatted the hand off my knee in a friendly way, like I was being playful, which was mixed signals, I guess, but Pascal backed away quick."

"Hallelujah," Chantal said.

"The store was in a nice spot across from the beach and we closed at one every night. I asked why we were open so late—OPEN 'TIL ONE, the sign said—and he said modelers need glue all hours. He said I needed a better place than the motel, and I told him he had that right. So when he said he had an extra room I figured it would be OK. Pascal himself was only like the tenth-worst guy on the planet, and I'd already visited with the other nine, so I had nothing to lose. We crawled down the highway one night about a week into my employment, his convertible's exhaust hammering and thudding, the sky big and black, and he told me he was ready to be whatever I wanted him to be, and when he asked me how I felt about that, I said, 'So soon?'"

"She always was a smart aleck," Chantal said.

"But then I felt maybe I wasn't taking him seriously enough and told him I liked him OK, too. He was touched, he said, and I felt even worse. I was getting cold feet and I hadn't even got in the door. When we went upstairs to the apartment I could only imagine my future, Mama and Roy all over again. But the place was clean and straight, and from my room I could see the white ridges of the surf across the way, and I figured it was worth a try. I told him there was only the one rule, and it was that I was not dealing with his needs, and asked him if we still had a deal, and he shot out his hand to shake on it. Then we went to the motel, got my things, stopped at the convenience store for Cokes and chocolate bars and pork rinds, and moved me right on in. When bedtime rolled around that first night he appeared in my doorway to say good night, outfitted in solid-brown pajamas, white piping. He blew me a kiss, and that was it. I slept like a baby."

"Sounds familiar," I said.

"He was a mystery," Tinker said, turning her head sideways that way some dogs do when something is not quite right. "He was fatherly. Full of instructions and directives and lectures, all of which made good sense, and this aspect of our relationship was magic for me. I liked it. Everything seemed settled. I was working at Bigger Models and teasing Pascal in front of his customers, and he got a kick out of that, got mileage with his regulars for having the teenage live-in. I'd tease him and he'd do his sweet grin while they all rolled their eyes and reset themselves on the stools, continuing to meditate on the niceties of modeling. We got weeks into it, then months, and we had fun together, watched some TV, ate take-out food, drove around aimlessly in his convertible car."

"We still do that here," Chantal said. "Don't we, Wallace?"

"We do," I said. "Often I say to your mother, 'Why don't we go out and drive around aimlessly for a time?' And she agrees, and we do. Enjoying it completely."

"Uh-huh," Tinker said. "Anyway, that's the story. I liked walking the beach, going down there around closing time, standing there in the middle of the dark night, the wind pushing at me and the water coughing up on the beach and then sliding across the road like some mutant organism."

"Like some new science fiction show that was almost as good as some old science fiction show they'd pulled after running it into the ground?" I said.

She didn't notice me being clever. "It was not too bad," she said. "Watching. Standing there, a couple of flood lamps on the top corners of the store spraying all the light there was except maybe the blinking red a half mile down toward the center of town."

"So I come to visit, get a room at her Motel 6," Chantal said. "We meet at a restaurant in town, Mulvahill's, and I meet Pascal, and Pascal has this giant head. I mean, huge. Massive. Basketball sized."

"It was not," Tinker said.

"Was," Chantal said. "Gigantic head, and the setup with herself had gone to it. He tells me Tinker makes him feel like a kid again, and he starts pawing her right there."

"That's true. He wouldn't stop," Tinker said. "There was something about Mom being there that made him need to fondle me, wrap his arms around me, touch me."

"I told her he wasn't a keeper," Chantal said.

"She said he seemed like a meatball I would rather not have rolling around on my plate," Tinker said. "Those were her exact words."

"He was fine as long as he stayed in his cage," Chantal said. "But when he went all Romeo and Juliet, told her she was the sun and the moon and the stars, well, it made my baby feel poorly."

Chantal and Tinker were having too much fun telling this story, performing for each other, and seemed about two times too seasoned for me to be messing with in the first place. Right then I wished I had stayed at home and gone to jail for stealing the hogs of Curl Trenary, as we loved to say back in the eighth grade. I wished for a quiet evening with Jilly, maybe watching a Netflix movie or a nice *Wallander* episode, in Swedish, subtitled.

"That's a heck of a story," I said.

"Wait, there's more," Chantal said. "Isn't there, sweetie?" She petted her daughter then, by which I mean she touched her daughter's shoulder and back in a manner that was exactly the manner in which you would pet a dog.

Tinker said, "Get off me, will you?"

"It's OK, baby," Chantal said.

"I like being an afterthought," Tinker said. "You know? Not too much is expected, things remain on an even keel, and every time you manage to smell nice it's a big accomplishment. I'd been that girl and I was OK with that, it was familiar. Finally Pascal said he wanted to marry me. I told him he was a lovely man, a kind man, a generous man, and a good man, but no."

"And then he raped her," Chantal said.

"Well. Almost," Tinker said. "Sorta."

"Jesus," I said.

"That was a bad night," she said. "He was turned all the way up to deranged zombie. He knew he was in trouble. When I got free I got the twenty-two Mama used on Roy, which I had inherited and gotten repaired, and I gave Pascal a couple of flesh wounds to remember me by. Nothing too serious. Nicks and bruises, really, and he looked startled by that. So I told him I was taking the car, and he said to me, 'You can have the car.' I told him if he squealed about the car I'd come back and testify. He nodded, wouldn't say a word, stared at the floor. I gave him a chocolate bar to cheer him up. He looked at me and did that monkey thing where you say *I love you* by pointing to yourself, rocking an imaginary baby in your arms, and pointing at the other person. That was something. I gave him a kiss on the forehead for that. Took the car and split. I've been driving around ever since. Almost ten years. All over this damn country. I've been going continuous. I'm ready to quit that, to do better."

"And she's an artist now," Chantal said. "Ain't that something?"

# 15

# THE OFFER

On July 1, my late brother Raleigh's birthday, I got a visit from Cal, Jilly's ex and the gentleman who was most recently sleeping with my ex, setting aside the Crosley fellow who died in the car crash up north. Cal was in cowboy regalia, no doubt in honor of his return to Texas, including a cowboy hat and a cowboy shirt and a pair of highly decorated cowboy boots, and he was standing on my front step. I looked at him for a long time before I spoke.

"Hello," I said. "What are you doing here?"

"I've got very special things to discuss with you, Wallace," he said.

I figured I knew what he wanted to talk about, but I said, "Like what?"

"Diane," he said. "I think we're getting serious, and I wanted to talk to you about that."

I didn't want to talk to Cal about Diane. Cal looked positively greasy. He looked worn and tired, red around the eyes like one of those hyenas you always see in nighttime pictures of Africa.

"You're walking dead, Cal," I said. "You're under arrest on the minors charge, there's the thing with Jilly, there's Morgan—I don't know what makes you think you can talk to me about anything."

"We've got a lot in common," Cal said.

This was where I closed the door. I knew I'd open it again if he knocked again, and I knew he would. Could have saved myself the trouble if I'd let him come inside in the first place.

Sure enough, he rang the bell. I opened the door. He followed me to the kitchen where I offered him a beer. He accepted. I pulled a beer out for myself, asked him to follow me out to the deck, then waved at a chair.

"You gotta know I'm not happy about being the man I've been all this time," Cal said. "I got started wrong, went wickeder after that, and didn't get it until years later. Jilly got the worst."

"That's her sense of it," I said.

"She's dead right. I was a mess then. I'm better than that now."

"That's a song, Cal."

"I know. Sorry. I didn't mean to say it that way."

"What way did you mean to say it?"

"Some better way," he said. "I'm over myself, I'm finished stalking the kids, I've grown up some since this thing with the girl. I mean, it wasn't like they said, anyway, but I was probably wrong to be working in that vein, if you know what I mean."

"OK," I said. I squinted at Cal because I was carrying on a conversation with myself about what the fuck he did want. He didn't need anything from me. If Diane was willing to take him on, I had nothing to say about it. Maybe he was angling to get a character reference for his trial. Maybe he was on the level, feeling lousy and thinking I was the therapy that would clear up all the bad juju.

There was a fly buzzing around his head and he didn't even notice, or if he did, he didn't try to evade it in any way. I'd never seen anyone not react to a fly buzzing around his head. It was astonishing, really. Could have made an act out of that. Put some monkey grease on his head, let out a bunch of flies, watch 'em circle like bees to honey, he wouldn't even flinch.

I was getting off track. "So, what about Diane?"

"We are serious, a little bit," Cal said.

"Well, that's good, I guess," I said. "How's her place up there? Nice? You just came back, right?"

"She's not very happy there."

"Yeah, she told this horror story about a friend of hers."

"Dan Crosley," Cal said. "She liked him a good bit."

"I felt bad when she told me about it," I said.

"She doesn't want to stay up there," he said.

This was it, the news, the reason for his visit. He was on a mission for Diane, sent to inform me that she was coming back. She was finished with Rhode Island.

I said, "Doesn't she? What's she thinking of doing?"

"Not sure yet," he said. "Looking over some options. I don't think money's a problem, so she can go wherever she wants."

"Her father set her up pretty good," I said.

"That's what I understand," Cal said.

"She could go anywhere," I said. "Watch those *House Hunters International* shows and find a nice beach someplace. *Buying Hawaii.* That'd be good."

"Nope," he said. "Thing is, I think she wants to move back here."

"Here?" I said. "As in Houston?"

"Kemah," he said. "She was looking at places online. She's got a couple Realtors hooked up, sending her stuff."

"Uh-huh," I said. "Well, she doesn't need my permission."

"She wasn't sure how you'd feel," Cal said.

"I'd feel fine. We're pals. It would be nice to have her around. We get along since the divorce."

"Yeah, she said that. But . . . I don't know how to say this exactly."

"Say," I said. "Don't worry."

"Well, she wondered where you were on this place," Cal said. "She was wondering how attached you were to it."

"You mean here? The condo? My house? Pretty attached," I said.

"She said you were pretty easygoing about where you lived. Said there were a lot of nice places here and you might want to trade up or something."

"I hadn't given it any thought," I said.

"It's an idea," he said. "Diane was thinking top dollar, no special arrangements. A straight-out cash deal if you were interested. And if not, well, she'll get some other place."

"Hmm," I said, nodding. "I get the picture. It's an idea, I get that. Be easy, wouldn't it? You're going to have to let me reflect on this for a while, Cal. It's a weird idea but has some aspects. I'll think on it."

"Let me give you my number," he said. "We can talk it out." Here he, for the first time, lifted his hat and brushed a hand back over his hair, which I noticed was newly dyed a rusty red-brown.

"Nice hair," I said, pointing toward his head.

"Yeah," he said. "Got it done in Houston. Close to natural."

"I see that," I said. "Looks good." I waited a minute looking out at the bay, then stood up. "So, that's about the extent of it?" I said. "You going to be staying down here for a time?"

"No, I'm headed back. There's a lot of packing and such, and I promised Diane I'd pitch in. Then I have to be back here for legal stuff."

"Pitch in," I said. "Good. Well, I'll tell Jilly you said hello, next time she's down."

"She doing all right?" he said.

"Seems to be doing great," I said. "I don't see her as much as I'd like, but she's always pleasant when she comes. I guess she's got a lot of work."

"Good, good," he said. "Give her my best, will you? She's a great gal."

"She is a great gal," I said.

"OK then," Cal said, getting out of his chair. "I'll leave it with you. And I appreciate you giving me this opportunity to talk a little. I hope we'll have a chance to do more."

"Hell yes," I said. "I'm sure it's going to work out, one way or another." I grabbed his elbow in the friendliest possible way and steered him back through the house and down to the front door. "You have a safe trip now," I said. I patted his shoulder a couple times for good measure.

I didn't know who to call first. Jilly won the toss and I rang her immediately. "Guess who just left the house?" I said.

"Malcolm X," she said.

"Cal and Cal alone, in cowboy duds. That boy got a tin ear and tin eye and tin brain, you ask me."

"Cal? I thought he was up north interfering with your wife?"

"Now, Jilly," I said.

"Sorry. What did Cal want? I mean, is he here to stay? Do I have to lock my doors?"

"Took him a bit of time to get it out, but he was apparently sent by my ex-wife, with whom he is interfering, to tell me that he and Diane are a 'serious' item and that they are moving back here from Rhode Island and that she wants to buy this house from me for 'top dollar.' Get that? Top dollar."

"Top dollar," Jilly said. "That's great. You being poor as a church mouse and all. Her being rich as Croesus. A sad truth."

"He was all cowboyed up," I repeated. "Hat, shirt, boots. I don't remember that being the Cal way, was it?"

"Don't think so," Jilly said. "But I better get in my crappy car and get down there right now before you fall into the slough of despond."

"'*Slew,*'" I said. "I looked it up."

"You're always doing that," she said. "Whatev. I arrive presently."

"OK. That'll be good. Call for landing instructions."

"Will do," she said.

I wasn't ready to talk to Diane, so I started to call Chantal when the doorbell rang again. I figured it was Cal, back with one last thought, and considered ignoring it, but then I answered. It was Duncan Parker.

"Can we talk?" he said. "I need a minute."

I was startled. Duncan Parker had never been to my house in the years I'd owned the place. I rarely saw him and then not usually to speak. We did wave, but that was it. I asked him in. "You want something to drink?" I said. "It is hot out there, isn't it?"

"Not too hot, no," Duncan Parker said. "And I'll have a soft drink if you have one."

"Diet Coke?"

"Perfect," he said, following me to the kitchen. "I need some information about Chantal White," he said. "I understand that you have made her acquaintance?"

I stood at the refrigerator a minute, feeling the cool breeze coming out. "Yep. We're friends, new friends since her situation. I went to her restaurant one time and we started talking. I didn't know her at all previous to that."

"Right, right. That's what I understood. Your wife knew her, correct?"

"My ex-wife Diane, yes. They occasionally chatted when my ex was still here, some time ago."

"Correct," he said. "So, what can you tell me about Miss White? I understand she has recovered from the incident. I gather there's no progress on apprehending the perpetrator. There is some suggestion among the neighbors that this may have been a prearranged event that went bad somehow—have you heard that?"

"I have," I said. "But not from Chantal, if that's what you're asking."

"Well, the police are always asking me and I don't have squat to tell them, so I'm, you know, looking around a little bit to see what folks know."

"You could tell the police what *you* know and leave it at that," I said. "That's what I did."

"You didn't tell them you knew her and all," Duncan Parker said.

"I did not know her when they talked to me," I said.

He shook his head and put an expression on his face that I interpreted to be friendly and intended to put me at ease. "Right, that's right. I know that," he said. "But you know her now. I understand that you've been spending some time with her down at her restaurant? She has an apartment where she's been staying recently and not in her place here. And you've been down there with her sometimes?"

At this point I considered ending the conversation, as I think I would have been within my rights to do. But instead I said, "Yes. I've been hanging out, but I don't know anything about the attack. We've only talked about it briefly, and only to say it was awful."

"You meet the daughter?" Parker said.

"Yes, I did."

"She's been staying here, at their condo. Kind of a hippie girl?"

"Well, yeah. Sure. You could say that."

"So you got nothing for me on the perpetrator," he said. "She has no idea, or she hasn't said anything to you that would suggest she knew the perpetrator."

"That's correct."

"Which is correct?" he said. "She has no idea? Or she's said nothing suggesting she knew him? If it was a him."

"She told me she has no idea who it was, what it was about, or why it happened. She's a little frightened about it, but grateful it wasn't worse."

"OK," Parker said. "OK. That's something. That's clear and direct, I can forward that information to the detective."

"Sure," I said. "Be my guest. If they want to talk to me I am available."

"You will make yourself available?" Parker said, apparently writing that down in a small notebook not unlike the ones the police were using when they talked to me earlier.

"Absolutely," I said.

"I don't think that'll be necessary," he said. "But I will advise them."

"Good."

"I think that's all I need."

We'd been in the kitchen the whole time. He left his Coke on the counter and I could see the line of condensation around the middle of it, showing how little he'd drunk. He started for the front door and I followed him out. "Thanks, Wilson," he said. "You've been a help. Not everybody can say that, you know."

I nodded, shut the door behind him, then leaned into the peephole to watch him walking away.

I met Chantal for dinner at the Half Shell, an oyster house down by the marina. She looked terrific. "I was up in Houston today," she said. "It's lawyer day. This is one of my best getups, reserved for those times I need to look like a serious person on serious ground."

"Convinced me," I said as we weaved through the place to a window table. We were eating early, so there were plenty of prime tables available. This had become a norm for me, eating early. I liked restaurants best when they were empty. They were quiet then, oddly pleasant, something about preparation, all being in readiness, anticipation.

"You were on Parker's mind today," I said.

"So you said earlier. Via the very modern text you sent."

"I worked on that," I said.

"It showed," Chantal said. "So what was on Mr. Parker's busy little mind?"

I went over my meeting with Parker, repeating it something like verbatim, doing a dopey southern voice for the officious Parker.

"What is that voice you're doing? Is that... What is that?"

"Sorry," I said, returning to my regular voice. "I was being interesting again."

"What did he want?"

"Basically, he wanted me to rat you out," I said. "But I stood tall and true."

"Rat me out? What about, I mean, what were you supposed to tell him?"

"He seemed to think that I might have known, as a consequence of our recent companionship, about which he seemed to know practically everything, by the way, seemed to think you may have known your assailant prior to the incident. He wondered aloud whether the incident, as he called it, might have been an engagement gone awry."

"Ah," she said. "I hear that is rumored. Didn't I say something like that to you last week or sometime? That people thought that?"

"Don't remember," I said. "You could have. I told him you didn't understand the cause, nature, or context of the attack, and that you were still nervous about it."

"All true," she said.

"He told me that Tinker, whom he did not know by name,

but did know was your daughter, had been staying in your place up here recently."

"She has," Chantal said. "Have you seen her?"

"No, I haven't," I said.

"She's at work on some art thing," Chantal said. "Some video performance where she sits in front of a camera and reads something, I don't know what. Nude. She's nude when she reads the thing. It's terribly important that she be nude, apparently."

"Art wants what art wants," I said.

"Cute," Chantal said. "She's preparing the piece for a New Artists Show at the Texas Gallery in Houston. You know that gallery?"

"Sure. Know the people, too. Knew 'em when. I dream about them to this day."

"Tinker's never had much success with art." Chantal dipped a corner of her napkin in her water glass and used the napkin to wipe away a small spot on the window that was apparently bothering her view. "So Parker thinks I knew the perp?"

"The very word he used," I said. "Other than that I don't know what he thinks, but he was eager to get some ideas to report to the cops. They call him all the time, he says."

"Roll my eyes," she said, sighing. "So, what else is new?"

"Diane is moving back and wants to buy my house." I stopped there, surprised to see Duncan Parker and Cal walk into the restaurant together. They stood at the bar. "Don't look now," I said, "but Parker is here with Diane's latest lover, the one who delivered the news of her offer."

"Small-town blues," Chantal said. "You want to leave?"

"Do I want to? Or will I?"

"Either one," she said. "We don't need the publicity."

"I will if you want to. I don't really care."

"We can stay," she said. "Hang on here a minute."

With that she got up and walked across the room toward the two at the bar. Her heels, I noted, were tall, shiny, and a nice lemon color, and they made a satisfying click on the hardwood floor as she strode across the restaurant. This reminded me of a student I had in a painting class once. Hello, good-bye.

By some miracle Cal and Parker didn't see Chantal coming. She tapped Parker's shoulder, and when he turned she crooked a finger and backed away from the bar. He followed, puppy-like. I watched as he leaned forward, hanging on her every word, and she said whatever she was saying in a pleasant but direct manner. After a minute it seemed she was asking if he understood what she had said and he was answering in the affirmative. She smiled then, extended a hand for him to shake, which he did. Daintily. Then she returned to our table, sat down, and motioned for the waiter.

Parker and Cal glanced our way a couple times while paying their check, left bottles sweating on the bar.

* * *

Diane called that night to still the waters, or so she said. "It was an idea," she said on the phone. "You're always looking to move on, start over, something."

"I am? News to me."

"You talk about it," she said. "Used to, anyway. And I thought if I'm throwing in the towel up here, I could take the house, you know, easy deal, market price, asking price, whatever, and free you up for whatever you're looking to do next."

It was late when she called—three my time, four hers. I was in the office with all the lights off, the computer screen illuminating the place, waiting for the moon to slip into view. Maybe three was a little early, but I had time.

"Took me by surprise, I guess. And Cal delivering was a bit much."

"Cal's a soldier," she said.

"So you told me."

"No, I mean he does as he's told. Well, you know what I mean—he's reliable. And I figured you knew him—I don't know. Probably a bad move. I apologize."

"Not necessary," I said. "I didn't know you were planning on coming back."

"I tried to tell you in that other call? You know? But it didn't quite get out. I'm completely finished here. Can't stand it. It was all right when, you know, Dan was around, but it's a compendium of beasts now. Get me outta here, you know?"

"Got it," I said. I felt a little pissed, really. It took balls to talk about buying my place when it used to be hers, too. And how it figured in the divorce. All that.

"So you want to forget about that? Would that be best?" she said.

"Well, for now, yeah," I said. "I will think about it, though. If you want me to."

"Sure," she said. "But don't make it a thing. Don't worry about it."

"Keep it in mind?" I said.

"Exactly," she said. "A thought. Anyway, I'm coming down myself in a week or two. Hope we can have dinner or something?"

"Sure," I said. "It'll be good to see you and catch up."

"I think we're pretty well caught up," she said. "Except I didn't tell you about my TENS machine."

"Tens?"

"An acronym," she said. "Transcutaneous electrical nerve stimulation. This little thing you sort of shock yourself with and it's supposed to alleviate the pain."

"What pain?" I said.

"Any," she said. "There's a lot of history and such. Dan had a broken foot once and his doctor suggested it. You buy it over the counter. There are lots of theories about how it works. One is endorphins. One is called gate theory, which is about sending a stronger signal to the brain than the pain signal, thus sort of blocking the pain signal, know what I mean?"

"Uh, sure. Like distracting you."

"Yes, sort of. 'Masking' is the preferred way of describing it, I guess. It's a real thing, and I started using it after Dan died. It worked for him, not so much for me, really. Rattles me."

"Sort of electroshock on the Triple-A level," I said.

"Did you know they got electroshock from pig butchers? It made the pigs feel comfortable so they were easier to cut. Anyway, I'll be visiting you soon."

"I look forward to it," I said. "Bring the zapper. I want to give it a try."

"I will, Wallace," she said.

# 16

# HOUSE WEAR

A WEEK or more later I was taking it easy on the deck when somebody called up from down below. I got up and looked over the railing. It was Parker, back for more. I said hello.

"Hey, Wilson," Parker said.

"It's Wallace," I said. "Hey yourself."

"It's Wallace?" he said. "Your name is Wallace?"

"Yes," I said. "What can I do for you?"

"I need to talk. Can I come up?"

I waved at him and went down to the door. Then we were back on the deck, staring at huge storm clouds rolling in. From where we sat it looked like three-quarters of the sky was blotted out. "So the deal is," Parker said. "You know the woman, dancing woman?"

I nodded. I don't know why, but I saw this coming.

"Well, I'm involved with her. Don't ask, but there it is." Then, as if he'd embarrassed himself, he pointed to the clouds. "It's always raining here, what's with that?"

"Time of year," I said. "Squalls. Besides, they're great looking."

"Long as they don't turn into tornadoes," he said. "So anyway, what I want to do is talk to you about my wife. I want to be rid of my wife, but I can't get it done. She's a giant of a woman, sprawling gray hair and more than six feet tall. There was a time when all the height excited me, but it's long gone now, now she's a memory getting in the way of good times. Like I remember good times. Doesn't matter, though. I'm sixty-one, maybe months into it with this new woman, and it's a mess. I'm telling her to go easy, let it, you know, happen, but nah, she's gotta pull the dancing thing. Ella went nuts. Ella's the wife. You met the wife?"

I shrugged. He drove straight ahead.

"So I'm looking forward to Social Security, know what I'm saying, and I run into this woman in the hardware store. She's buying a set of wrenches, good ones, too. So she asks me a couple questions, and I act like I know from wrenches, which I oughta, and maybe I even did at one time, back in the old days, but the thing is I'm thinking sixty-one is not much different from fifty-nine, even fifty-five, but it's night and day to fifty. Fifty you're still alive, still a functioning cog in the system. There are parts to play, deals to make, women to bed. You can still sell yourself to the ones that remind you what pretty women look like, what good skin is, and the rest. But it goes downhill after that. Some guys keep up the pretense, but I never could. I get stuck over there where we've been for a million years, seems like. The wife likes it, she says. It's cheap,

I says. It's cheap and tacky and perfect for a couple of losers like us. Two bedrooms, two baths, a living room, and a furry kitchen. It's not really furry, but that's what it feels like, like the walls are covered with fur. They're sticky, grease from the stove, the range, she fries a lot of beef for me. Twenty years and we've got this crap furniture that came with the place, shitty bedspreads, bad towels, lamps from Walmart. I mean, for me Walmart lamps aren't that bad, I mean they work, but then you see some lamps on TV and you realize where you are in the lamp pecking order. So we're in at six-thirty every night, we're into our house wear, which is like sloppy seconds all over the place, T-shirts, shorts—it's not pretty. We try to keep our eyes on the screen, that's the only way to get around the mess."

"I don't know about all that," I said. "My first wife died of cancer, and the other, well, we reached an agreement before it got that bad."

"You got a beer?" Parker said. I tell him I do and go get him one. When I get back he's pulled out a big cigar and he's mouthing that, and the butt end of it looks like he's chewing it. What I can't figure out is why we're best buddies suddenly, I mean, me being Wilson and all.

He starts up. "Look, I'm on a pension from the oil company where I worked after I left the United States Marines. Worked until my forties and was blessed with a plant explosion that took out an eye. Wasn't my best eye, but I miss it anyway. Still, you can see as much with one eye as you can with two, it just takes twice as long. And you're always swinging your head around, which gets uncomfortable. You get used to it, but it's still a pain, and lots of times it makes you feel like you're in two places at once, like the overall scene never comes into focus. So Ella and me, we have some money—the settlement, the pension, the money I get for being counted among the disfigured. She says it's the second-best thing that ever happened to us, losing the eye, but she's got no imagination, she's not interested in France, or beautiful young women with ocean-like hair, skin like custom paintwork."

"I never knew you had a bad eye," I said.

"We don't broadcast it," he said. "This one." He tapped his right cheekbone. I could hear the thump. He had the big fingers.

"Sorry to hear that," I said. "That one there is, uh—"

"Glass," he said. "We're old-fashioned. I can take it out if you want."

I wagged a forefinger at him. "Not required."

He rubbed his right eye, made the pupil bob around in some crazy ways to give me a taste of the thing.

"That's something," I said.

"It's nothin'," he said. "It don't feel like nothin'."

"You seem a lot younger than sixty-one," I said. "I'm mid-fifties, and I always thought you were younger than me."

"I try to keep it going," Parker said. "I'd be a lot better off if I could get rid of Ella. I mean, sometimes we go to the bakery together and she buys trays of doughnuts, bear claws, the rest of those things. She can't stop herself and I don't try anymore."

"I don't blame anybody for what they eat," I said. "Me, I love that white icing on cinnamon buns, you know, the kind you get in the all-night gas station? I could eat that forever. And that yellow spongy bun. I may be getting some tonight."

"You and Ella would get on great," he said. "Why don't you take a look at her? Take a load off me?" It was like he was selling me his car.

"I got too much love on my plate already," I said.

He didn't laugh. "Yeah, I hear that."

"Now you got the dancing woman," I said.

"Well, I had her, but with the showboating I had to put her on ice for a while. Gotta figure out this Ella thing."

"What about a divorce?" I said. "Isn't that the usual way? Clean, civilized, the well-worn path."

"Can't," he said. "She's money. Her family is. That pension of mine? It's shit. It's something, but it's for shit. Ella is the ride and I'm the rider. Been that way for all these years. Sometimes she's OK, you can't trash her all the time, but at my age what's left?"

"Not much, I guess. Goes for both of us," I said.

"What are you talking about?" he said. "You got the girl from Houston, this White woman, her daughter, and who else? I mean, you are loaded, good buddy. You are covered."

"I've got some friends," I said. "And that's something."

"Damn straight," Parker said.

I backed my chair away from the railing. The rain had started to fall in earnest. There was thunder and lightning. I was ready for Parker to make an exit. "So, what do you figure to do? I mean, what's the endgame?"

He drained his bottle and stood up. "I gotta run," he said. "Ella's waiting on me. We're going to Costco. You like Costco? I love it. Buy shit and take it back six months later and they don't even blink. It's terrific."

"Yeah, but—"

"Nothin's happening. I mean, I may try some shit, but in the end I'll die in Ella's arms. In her lap is more like it. She's good to me. I'm a crap husband, though, and we both know it. She and I both know it. But I think she loved me once and that's the whole story. She loved me and I loved her. What am I gonna do, start over? Never happen. I envy you, man," Duncan Parker said. "You got all the aces."

## 17

# PERFORMANCE ART

CHANTAL'S CONDO at Forgetful Bay was all dressed up in mid-century modern, Eames stuff, Aalto, Risom, some stuff I didn't recognize except to notice that it was in the same ballpark as the stuff I did recognize. Most interesting was that nothing looked like a replica. "Great house," I said. We were gathered there to preview Tinker's video project.

"In which I have lived for many years," Chantal said. "My late husband was a collector."

"Late husband," I repeated.

"Bert," she said. "He died right upstairs." Here she pointed straight up at the ceiling.

"Good to know," I said.

"I've still got the body outline on the floor," Chantal said.

"That's a joke, I recognize that," I said.

"We're going up to Tinker's room for the preview," she said. "You want something on the way up? Some cake?"

"You have cake?" I said.

"I do," she said.

"Maybe later," I said. I wanted the cake right then and there, but I didn't quite trust her. It might have been some abnormal kind of cake. She still made me nervous.

Tinker was on the bed attending her phone when we got upstairs. She was wearing black tights, a black T-shirt, various other things including tattoos and jewelry and so on. A video camera was set up pointing at a straight-back chair in front of a bare wall. There was a large flat-screen TV on the floor, showing the chair and wall, two other chairs in front of the windows opposite. "Want me to roll this shit?" she said, sliding off the bed to retrieve the remote.

"Sure," I said.

Chantal and I took the two chairs, Tinker took the one in front of the wall. She appeared on the large TV sitting in the chair. The picture was sort of distorted, like it was run through a Lomo filter, or a set of such filters, making the image much less clear and much more visually evocative, like those filters are supposed to do. Make pictures more interesting than they are. There was a second flat screen on a table beside her. "I'm doing this nude," she said. "I'll let you imagine that, OK?"

"OK," we said.

Tinker sat in the chair onscreen and started reading from what looked like a diary.

"I spend my days at the university's I. A. Pung Primary Lessons Center doing work with giant roster apes, the 'reds' as researchers are inclined to call them. I am feeding the apes treated paper, in particular, the pages of some of this century's greatest works of fiction, as part of a continuing thirteen-year study on the effects of printing inks on the digestive systems of mammals. Here I read pages I am preparing to feed Rector, a four-year-old female red."

I did not know exactly how to parse this. I was not unfamiliar with performances of this kind, though it had been years since I'd seen one in a gallery or museum. But in Chantal's condo, in the bedroom, with Chantal's daughter, well, it was a little wacky.

Tinker kept on reading some text that I couldn't follow, and which I eventually figured out I wasn't supposed to follow, and I sat there with Chantal, my hand on my chin, ridiculously, watching the proceedings.

"Some urban liberals hope the spread of new sources of information through the kingdom will bring a modest flowering of tolerance and pluralism to postwar society," Tinker said. "However, many feel that is not likely. Dahar al Daza, for example, the first virgin-born ruler, believes that her people 'jumped the gun' in their rejection of Western societal models for the family, and she is on record with this sentiment. There is no way to be certain that even the former Crown Prince of Efficacies would approve this casual dismissal of progressive values. Daza spoke in an on-the-record session at her celebrated Eastern Retreat. She noted that state-controlled television had stopped its experimental broadcasts and had returned to programming prayer and separations of a physical object, or a portion of a physical object, into two or more portions, through the application of an acutely directed force by government ministers. She said she was not going to encourage or entertain any 'weird' happenings, that hers were a people who looked at technology, but also looked at religion and morality."

I nodded, occasionally brushed back my hair, switched which leg I was crossing over the other, attempted to appear engaged with the show. I noticed that Tinker's eyes were not entirely, or even closely, symmetrical. I noticed that whenever she moved her jewelry chimed a little. I noticed that her legs were shapely and that her arms were cut with muscles. I noticed that there was a mosquito hawk in the room, swerving about, landing sometimes within the frame of the video.

"The collapse of the American family in the past few decades is historically unprecedented in the US, and possibly in the world. Daza, who has spent much of her adult life studying the American familial unit as an alternative to the Otareen model, remarked of her former companion, Naziri, that he grew more puzzling the more she tried to study him. She only emerged from this despair when she found that others, including his wife, were equally bewildered."

Her teeth were very nice, I noticed. I thought that was odd, given the hardscrabble background, that her teeth would be near perfect, and bright white. Once I had noticed this it was impossible to look away, to see anything else, at least for a few minutes.

"Our team excavated the front half of a large skeleton, recovering a skull, a two-foot shoulder blade, and limb bones two feet to three feet long and six inches in diameter. The group also uncovered a three-inch tooth. The find is being preserved in freezers in prisons, libraries, colleges—all sites visited during her education in the country."

Chantal touched my arm, and it shocked me. I jumped. I turned to her and she made some face that seemed to ask if I was all right, and I made some face back to indicate I was, and added a shallow nod in case the face I'd made was misinterpreted.

All this time Tinker was reading the notes in her book, diary, or whatever, without ever looking at us. I guessed that was part of the program, ignoring the audience. I assumed she meant to sit in the gallery and read material like this while it was also being recorded and displayed on an accompanying television screen. I wondered why the material was so opaque. What was the point of this opacity? Was that cultural comment? All remarks are opaque or some such? The nudity of the real performance, I figured, would model the stance of the work toward the audience, that is, open, lacking artifice, but also challenging.

There was a rip in Tinker's tights at her left thigh, two inches. Skin was visible there.

"Asked about the prosperous isolation and a return to the austere, both tenants of individuation theory, she reported that the Commerce Department report (which she is charged with leaking) does specify the universities and institutes later targeted because they were believed to be engaged in biological and chemical research believed damaging (or possibly damaging) to the prospect of peace. When queried about her capture, one of the scientists, an Algerian, who said he once worked as a taxi driver in Los Angeles for a year, recalled that there were one hundred nine victims in the hideaway."

Here Tinker paused and closed her book or diary and then began slapping herself with it, mostly about the shoulders and arms, her legs, her chest, in a way that seemed random. The book wasn't a big thing like a dictionary; it was leather covered, similar to a small missal you might find in a pew at church, a book of hymns, perhaps, you'd need if you were to sing along. I was afraid of what might come next, with the diary, but after a few minutes of slapping she suddenly got up and left the room, leaving us there with the TV displaying the chair and the wall alone. That was a huge relief; I was stunned how relieved I was at being left there with this placid video of a single chair against a wall. I noticed its shadow, cast diagonally behind and away from the chair by the light from the lamp on the dresser. It was a soft shadow, softer on the video than in real life. From outside the room Tinker started reading again, but in a weak voice, so quiet that I couldn't really hear what she was saying. She must have gone slowly down the stairs because the reading got progressively softer until you could hear only the muffled sound of a voice in another room. Then Tinker stopped speaking altogether. Chantal and I remained in the bedroom staring at the empty chair and at the image of the empty chair for a while. I was happy to do that longer, but Chantal tapped me again, and we went downstairs.

* * *

The postmortem was in the kitchen. I started with "I liked it. I liked it especially when you got up and walked out, leaving us there with the chair."

"Yeah," she said. "That's what I was aiming for."

"Relief," I said.

"Free from the threat."

"Not a threat, exactly," Chantal said. "Discomfort, maybe."

"Same thing, same area," Tinker said.

"The text was, I don't know," I said. "Unintelligible? Like I couldn't make sense of it. Was I supposed to be processing all that?"

"It's up to the observer. It's there to distract," Tinker said. "You expect it to make sense so it mobs your brain for a few minutes, puts some smudges in there, while you're sitting right in front of me and I'm, like, really naked. I want the people to be that close to me at the gallery."

"Is that, like, legal?" Chantal said. "I guess it is or the gallery wouldn't do it."

"Dunno," Tinker said.

"The texts are about stuff, though," I said. "Conflict, truth, convoluted references, rhetorical stories of a kind we're used to. Some sounded like TV reports."

"It's all copped off the Net here and there, news reports, wiki entries, some of it chopped up and reassembled. Something for me to read. I don't want to make too much of it.

Usually it's stuff I like the sound of. Can you 'understand' the text, decode it? Sure. Surfaces are everything, the only thing, interpretation is required here as anywhere. Note the text is filled with the rhetoric of insurrection, of sensibility setting itself over against an established mode, a special sympathy for so-called third-world peoples, a commitment to spiritual values as well as humanistic ones, a voice constantly aware of the otherworldly, the larger-than-life, the place beyond the pines, so to say, and primary positions afforded women, perhaps a suggestion of discontent with leaders and a preference for woman leaders, with the perceived inclusion in their worldviews of more diverse value systems, particularly as to getting and spending and such. You will see that the text traffics in language systems that seek out from the assembled diverse modalities new ideas and opinions, freshness of view being highly regarded, and that there is in the text a willingness to try to reveal complex subjects via reduction, even if, as might be supposed from your reaction itself, the complete unpacking of the content is not necessarily expected or required; in other words, a premium is put not upon complete understanding but upon some understanding—catch as much as you can, being the concept, perhaps. There is also the mystical dimension, which can be teased out and laid bare, further demonstrating the willingness of the text to entertain concepts largely disallowed by more conventional political systems, except in the way of 'talking points' such as always pressed forward in current political systems."

"I see that," I said, and turned to her mother.

"So the work is about you being naked?" Chantal said.

"That's important, someone being there naked," Tinker said. "Could be anybody. Intrusion, violation of the standard protocols, implicit threat, crossing personal boundaries, that shit."

"And then releasing us," I said.

"Exactly," she said. "I got it from this guy I hung out with in Denver. He used to walk around naked all the time. We weren't lovers. I was living in his place, and I felt this powerful aggression in the way he did that. It was like he was stabbing me with his junk all the time. Every time he left the room I felt better."

"Hmm," I said. "I see that."

"If you got that, you got the thing."

"Was terrific," I said.

## 18

# BAPTISM

JILLY TOLD me about her baptism. "I was three or four when I was baptized, only we called it christened, that was our name for it. I was three or four and I still remember it. It was at the river, more of a creek, really, that ran through our farm and then down past the church, which was a Quonset hut with some plants around it dropped in the middle of a parking lot. There was a leggy oak down beyond the parking lot, actually several of them, so there was shade over the water, and that's where the Parson Bob did the baptisms. He was an old guy, much older than my daddy who got himself rebaptized the same day. Anyway, I was scared about being baptized, but not of the water. I was scared of the parson's teeth, which were big and square and loose. They looked like they were made of wood or something. They had bad color, and everything he said took on a strange sound, like the words were slipping and sliding in his mouth. Clicking around. He was leaning over me real hard, had a big hairy hand on my back to keep me from drowning, and his face was real close to mine as he dunked me. I had nightmares about it later. The creek was muddy from all the baptizing he'd been doing, so I held my nose when I went under, and spewed a little when I came up. People thought that was funny. Daddy went in after me, and the parson had a little trouble holding Daddy up when he laid back into the water, so he had an accident and had to get up out of the water on his own steam. Parson Bob lost control of him when he was performing the ritual. I remember we left pretty fast afterward, jumped in the car, which was a Buick that Daddy got from his parents before they died, and we shot down the highway toward our place. Daddy drove all the way home barefoot, which I never forgot, I was so surprised. I'd never seen his feet before. They were big and white and veiny. Hairs on his toes. I can still see them down around the pedals, dripping wet, I can see those feet like it was yesterday."

19

# FIREWORKS

MONDAY I was up early. I went out for a walk hoping to refresh my aging muscles, feeling bad that I hadn't been exercising. I was planning to go once around Forgetful Bay and then stop at Chantal's for coffee on my second tour, assuming she was there and receiving, but when I got to the extreme north end of the development there were three police cars at the Parker house. A small group of neighbors had gathered outside.

I found my brainy next-door neighbor Bruce and asked, "What's up?"

"Parker's dead," Bruce said.

Another woman from the development, whom I recognized but did not know by name, said, "Suicide," and shook her head.

"Jesus," I said. "You sure?"

"Ella Maria's up in Houston," Bruce said. "The police have called her and she's on her way back."

"You know the wife?" I said. "I never met her. I don't even know if I've seen her."

"You've seen her," the unknown woman neighbor said. "She's hard to miss. Gigantic."

Bruce said, "We've been to dinner a couple times. They were great together. She is big, like an Amazon woman, you know? Remember that thing when big women were calling themselves Amazons back in the day? She's one of those. And he was a small guy." Here he held out his hand at an exaggeratedly low level, as if Parker were belt-buckle high.

"Cute," I said. "Parker was strong as an ox. Marine, wasn't he?"

"Was," Bruce said. "Been out a good while. But I guess marines are never really out."

"This is crazy. They sure it's suicide?"

"Gun," the unknown woman said. "He must have been a lot less happy than the rest of us."

"We're having a bad year in the neighborhood," Bruce said.

"Say that again," I said.

I hung around for a few minutes, then headed for Chantal's, hoping she was up and around. I hadn't heard from her for a few days and she hadn't returned a couple calls. I was shaken by Parker. Dead. Bang, like that. I mean, with what he told me about the dancing woman, and the true-crime TV shows I'd watched, I thought the usual things—murder, multiple murder, suicide pact. I hoped his wife wasn't dead somewhere. Who knew if she was really in Houston to begin with? People in the murder shows are forever setting up alibis before they kill their spouses. I guessed it wasn't odd to hope he had committed suicide when the alternative was worse.

I texted Chantal "Parker's dead. Prob suicide. Coming yr way" and continued my walk to her house at the far end of our development. Before I got there a neighbor with no hair at all stopped me in front of a tan house and asked what was happening at that condo with the cop cars. He said he'd been watching out the window for half an hour.

I introduced myself, and he did likewise, telling me his name was Oscar Peterson. "Like the piano player," he said.

"I think Duncan Parker's had some trouble," I said. "Nobody knows anything, really, not yet. His wife's coming back from a business trip is what they say."

"I knew it," Peterson said. "It's that woman, you know, the woman they found there? My wife said that was trouble. Damn."

"Could be," I said. I gave him a facial expression I imagined was "who knows?" and moved on.

At Chantal's I rang the doorbell and waited, taking a couple steps back from the door so I wouldn't be too close when she opened it. I hate it when people ring my doorbell and then stand right up close to the door.

"Look who's here," she said, the door cracked less than three inches.

"Pedestrian crossing," I said, pointing at the crack she was peering through.

"Yes, sir," she said, swinging it full wide. "Get inside the house."

I went straight to the kitchen for a paper towel. I felt a little sweaty.

"You all right?" Chantal asked, following me. "Want coffee? Want bacon?"

"You got bacon?"

"I am baking some bacon right now," she said.

Then I smelled it. It was there all along and I'd missed it. It was in the oven. We'd had some before when she had me sequestered. She cooked it on a rack sitting on a cookie sheet—the bacon. The grease falls and the bacon gets crisp.

"Sure," I said. "I came around the bend down there by Parker's. There are cops and apparently he's dead inside. Plus gawkers. They think it's suicide, that's what some woman said. I didn't know who she was. She was talking to Bruce."

"Are you kidding me? Parker? When?" she said. "How do they know it's suicide?"

"Don't know. This morning, last night? I don't know how they found out, either. Bruce said the wife was in Houston."

"I thought she was a homebody. The wife."

"Parker was over at my place a few days ago telling me how he wanted to get rid of her. I mean, he didn't want to hurt her, just wanted to be free of her so he could make time with the woman who danced in his driveway a couple months ago. Back when you got roughed up. Told me this woman was his piece of cake. A new woman, a new start."

"He said that?"

"Well, approximately."

"Fool," she said. "Jesus."

"I know. I was thinking on the way over I hope he didn't, you know, get her, too."

"Get her?"

"The wife, the girlfriend, either one. Murder-suicide."

"You're a nut. You don't know the wife, do you?"

"I know of her. Parker said she was really big, you know, like, big around. And tall. I mean she was already tall, like, man-tall, NFL-tall, and recently she ballooned through love of doughnuts."

"I think I've seen her," Chantal said. "There can't be two women that size around here, can there? She used to walk sometimes, I think. She's huge. I mean, like bug-your-eyes-out huge. It's wonderful, really. I mean, from the point of view of something you don't see every day." She paused and stirred her coffee, looking over her shoulder out the window. "I guess that's not what I should be saying, huh?"

"It's our secret," I said.

"It was inappropriate," she said.

"You meant it as a compliment."

"Yeah. I did. You know, the wonder of things," she said. "Everlasting."

Under a photo of a young and more attractive Duncan Parker in the next day's paper was the caption:

*Duncan William Parker was found dead in his home at Forgetful Bay Condominiums on Monday morning by his neighbor Constance Whiting. He was discovered in a walk-*

*in closet with a small-caliber pistol with which he had apparently shot himself to death. A note was found with the body but its contents have not been made public. He is survived by his wife, Ella Maria Parker, and no others.*

Morgan was in town for a few days, and we were at my place. She was upset by the news. "That's awful," she said. "I always liked that guy, especially when I was younger."

"What?" I said.

"I had a crush on him a couple years ago," she said.

"Great," I said.

"Things are getting kind of derailed down here, aren't they? Ng, Chantal, the dancer, now Parker."

"It is adding up. We had a deal last week where a guy was having a fight with his girlfriend. They were throwing shit around and screaming. They were over by Chantal's and she called the cops, then somebody else showed up, maybe the girl's father or something, and the girl was pounding on the guy's door, trying to get her phone, which she'd apparently left inside, and he wouldn't open up, and that's when the cops cruised up in their cruisers, blue lights wailing, radios crackling, police chatter—"

"She get the phone?" Morgan said.

"Yeah, but what was funny was these kids staying across from this guy's condo, renters, I guess, threw open their doors and played that old TV cops song—'who you gonna call' et cetera—at full volume right out into the floodlit night. It was terrific."

“These kids,” Morgan said. “Where’s Jilly?”

“She’s coming later,” I said. “It’ll be nice having you both here.”

“I’ll bet,” Morgan said. “Should we invite Chantal, too? Maybe her daughter, Vacuum, or whatever her name is. Maybe some other neighbor ladies.”

“All right, OK, chill, will you? How’s school?”

Morgan draped herself from one end of the sofa to the other, eating sea-salt-and-black-pepper Triscuits out of the box. She was wearing leggings and wedges and a thin scoop-neck tee that was way too long. By design, I assumed. “I’m not having a great time,” she said. “It is possible that architecture is no longer the dream of beauty I imagined.”

“Oh yeah? You mean you’re changing?”

“Not sure,” she said. “This woman I know has a little house, and she asked me if I could give her some ideas about how she might renovate it, add a room, so I worked every night for two weeks drawing things for her, and, you know, I wasn’t really thrilled by what I had.”

“Well, you’re getting started.”

“I know, but even if I had come up with something, it would be crap, essentially this cute, slightly interesting, crappy little house addition in a sea of tract houses.”

“You have to earn the right to do the big things, I guess.”

“You never did,” she said.

“Gee, thanks,” I said. “Anyway, I quit before I began. Architecturally.”

"You worked for architects, though, didn't you?"

"A little, not much. One was pretty good. One wasn't. I certainly wasn't."

"Me neither," Morgan said. "The stuff I do sucks. My answer to everything is a corrugated metal building. I love those."

"The moment came and went, I think, didn't it? For a while everybody was doing those."

"Yeah. Before my time," she said. "Maybe I can bring 'em back."

"Or maybe the idea was, I don't know, exhausted."

"Thanks, Dad. That's what I'm talking about. Even if I did it brilliantly now it would be shit. That's what I mean. That's what I'm saying."

"Sorry," I said. "I guess I made a mistake there."

It was getting toward four in the afternoon and I felt tired so I said I was going to take a rest and invited Morgan to make herself at home. I went to my bedroom and got in the bed. It was cool and wonderfully refreshing and dark in the bedroom. The windows faced west, but I had blackout curtains, a gift from God, given my sleeping schedule. I lay on my back with my hands at my sides flat on the sheet, two down pillows under my head, a light cotton summer blanket pulled up to my chin. Years ago I always slept with a CD of rainfall on Long Island playing on my compact stereo, a gorgeous CD called *Winter Light.* Maybe that was the photo on the CD cover, I can't recall. I thought maybe I'd buy a new player, since I didn't have one anymore. I'd tried to find the CD on

Amazon once, but no luck. I liked the photographer who did the cover, I remember that. Joel somebody. Very pretty, very calm. I had bought a dozen CDs of rain, but that was the only one that was any good. In the bed I practiced the art of remaining perfectly still. I listened to the lovely thrum of the air-conditioning system.

Jilly showed up later than expected, and the three of us went to the All Star Room for a late meal. It was nearing ten when we got there, and service was dwindling. Jilly and Morgan took turns making fun of me the whole time. I liked that because it meant what it meant, it was reassuring, which was all good fortune for me. I was feeling lucky to have two charming women to have dinner with. Sometimes, when nobody was around—no Jilly, no Morgan, no Chantal, no Diane—I got a glimpse of what a lonely life would be like, and it wasn't pretty. It was frightening, really. You see people who live in complete isolation, move a certain hesitating way, look like they are on rails going through the motions, and you can sort of figure what that's like, gray and repetitive and endless. And then you're thankful there is somebody—anybody—in the car with you, at dinner with you, across the table or in the room, somebody else there breathing. It makes a big difference. But then maybe most people have lives that are so full and rich they can't even imagine having lives that empty.

"What, you zoning out?" Morgan said. "Didn't get enough sleep this afternoon?"

"I was thinking how much I enjoyed your company. Both of you."

"That's sweet," Morgan said. "Isn't that sweet, Jilly?"

"That is damn sweet. You're right."

"I was also thinking about *Wallander*," I said. "In the Scandinavian version that guy is exactly the right amount of depressed, wised up, existentially damaged, et cetera."

"Existentially," Morgan said.

"Amen to that," Jilly said. "Get me a plate of whatever he's having."

"You know what I mean."

"I've only watched about two of them," she said.

"He has the whole set on DVD," Morgan said.

"I think I knew that," Jilly said to her. "But whenever he puts on the Swedish stuff I fall asleep because I am so existentially wearied." She did some a cappella snoring for us then, a few quick snorts.

"OK, all right," I said. "I like him. I'm old and tired like he is, and most of the time I feel about like he looks."

"Identifies heavily with the protagonist," Jilly said.

"Identifies heavily with a white swayback horse standing in a lonely grove nearby," Morgan said.

"With a solitary silhouette in a fifth-floor window late in the evening," Jilly said.

"Fine. Fine, thanks," I said. "Let's move along. Let's talk suicide."

"Great concept. Why didn't I think of that?" Morgan said.

"I'm talking about the Parker suicide," I said.

"What about it?" Jilly said. "Are there developments?"

"There's talk among the natives," I said.

"Foul play?" Morgan said. She was spearing her shrimp with a man-size toothpick that had, apparently, come with her dinner.

"Something like that."

"Have you talked to the surviving spouse?"

"I have, finally. I expressed my condolences. She appeared to be in a state of shock. Or maybe . . . *acting.*"

"Should happen to more men," Morgan said.

"Hmm," I said.

"Men are pigs," Jilly said. "Present company excepted."

"Thank you, darling," I said.

She nodded at me. Morgan rolled an eye. Somehow she could do one eye at a time. When I first saw it, a hundred years ago, I didn't believe it was humanly possible.

"You figure something's fishy with the suicide?" Jilly said.

"I don't know. It's possible. There was another piece in the paper, but it was circumspect. Said the death was 'thought to be' a suicide. Very tentative."

"No threat to Mrs. Parker, then," she said.

"I don't think so," I said.

"Has the dancing girl made an appearance?" Morgan asked. "Like at the funeral? That would be a solid clue."

"I have not seen her," I said. "No one has mentioned her to me."

"Uh-huh," she said. "Interesting."

"Does anyone know anything about her?" Jilly said. "I

mean, from the first dance in the driveway? Was there ever any report on that?"

"No," I said. "Security took her away and that was the end of it."

"Well, there you go," she said. "Find out."

"What, I'm going to ask Parker?"

"Well, where is she? Doesn't live here, right?"

"Not that I know of. But what difference does it make? We know from the horse's mouth she was diddling Parker."

"Diddling?" Jilly said.

"A term of art," Morgan said. "Among shamuses like Dad." Here she tap-pointed at me.

"Sorry," I said.

"We'll ignore it," Morgan said. "We'll be graceful for you. You can count on us."

"Girl's a fucking skank-ho," Jilly said.

They kept after me for a bit, eventually settling down some. Jilly was curious about Morgan's interest in school and got Morgan to tell her pretty much the same thing Morgan had told me. Jilly was still working at Point Blank but was starting an online business she wanted to develop. She was also working with the coder she'd told me about, though they didn't have an app yet.

"You could move down here," Morgan said. "Shack up with Dad."

"Not sure that's happening," Jilly said.

"Aw, c'mon," Morgan said. "You've been working up to it lo these many years."

"He's seeing someone," Jilly said.

"Well, no wonder he hasn't been calling every five minutes," Morgan said. "Who you seeing, buster? Somebody I know?"

"Ms. Chantal Chinese White," Jilly said. "Lives on-site, mostly."

"Oops," Morgan said.

"I feel repelled," Jilly said. "Crushed with repellent."

"You are repellent," I said. "And I'm not 'seeing' her anyway. You'd like her."

"How come she wasn't invited to this meal then?" Jilly said.

"Please," I said. "She runs a business. We can go down there if you want. It's close enough. I'll take you there. Lay bare my highly controversial and deeply personal life."

"Me so tired," Morgan said.

It was closing on midnight when we got back to the house. Jilly and Morgan sat up for a few minutes chatting in the living room while I repaired to my home office and cranked up the computer. I did my e-mail, which included a note from Diane reporting her scheduled arrival, twenty-six identical inexplicably late-arriving press releases from an unknown source about the merger of two publishing powerhouses, e-mail ads for a few apps, diverse speculative Twitter notifications, a "nothing happening" note from Chantal, and assorted chocolates. Also an e-mail from Bernadette Loo and the HOA board entitled EXPLODING FIREWORKS that set out the rules for same in our little development, including that only sparklers approved by the Texas State Fire Marshal were legal for consumer usage; that it was illegal to use exploding and flying fireworks in Texas, which included shells and mortars, multiple tube devices, Roman candles, rockets, and firecrackers; that, as a general guideline, anything that flew through the air or exploded was not allowed for consumer use and Texans should not sign "waivers" in order to purchase fireworks, because signing a waiver would not clear a consumer of responsibility should one be caught illegally using fireworks, a first-degree misdemeanor punishable by up to one year in jail and a ten-thousand-dollar fine; that there was still a risk of injury with the use of legal sparklers, as, when lit, some sparklers could reach temperatures between thirteen hundred and eighteen hundred degrees—at least two hundred degrees hotter than standard butane lighters; that a list of hundreds of sparklers legal to use in our area was available at the State Fire Marshal's website; that we should use sparklers and other legal novelties on a flat, hard surface and not light them on grass; that we should light only one item at a time and never attempt to relight a "dud"; that it was a good idea to drop used sparklers in a bucket of water; that we should never carry sparklers in our pockets or shoot them off in metal or glass containers; and that we should never have any portion of our body over a firework device when lighting the fuse.

# 20

# AIRSTREAM

In the days that followed the police decided the suicide was most certainly a suicide, and the veil of suspicion, which I had not known to be lowered, was lifted from Mrs. Parker, who promptly decided to travel somewhere, Alaska or northern Canada, or both, on one or more of those boat excursions you see advertised everywhere, beautiful scenery, lots of ice in the water, snug cabins, and quaint ports of call. I got that from Bruce Spores, who had become my ideal friend in the wake of recent events.

Bernadette Loo, who had now taken over from Mr. Parker as permanent president of the HOA, was delightfully quiet, apparently understanding her role in the community to be a leader who was seen and not heard. This was much appreciated by some of us, and a significant change. Roberta Spores was not happy about missing out on the presidency but cozied up to Bernadette, and they became fast friends, or so Bruce reported.

I was busy making small pictures, collages, postcards, and

other almost miniature objects, mostly flat and drawn but often printed after a lot of manipulation on the computer. I'm not sure I thought these were actual works of art. In fact, they seemed something short of that, insufficiently dense, maybe, not resonant enough to earn the name. Still, I was making them at a good clip, so much so that I quickly had a bit of a storage problem in my home office. The condo had four bedrooms, but three were allotted on a permanent basis, to me, Morgan, and Jilly, and the fourth—the den—was still cluttered with Diane's leftovers, three years after the fact, which I was sure she'd want to clean up when she returned, which was scheduled for any minute.

I saw less of Chantal, though she occasionally came for dinner or for an evening of television, which was OK. Things were a bit restless when we were together. I had tried to put aside the anxiety about her past. She had a new manager at the Velodrome and was spending less time there, but it wasn't clear where she was spending *more* time. Once or twice I drove down to the restaurant, stayed up in the Airstream. It was still a favorite, like a tree house a person might have had as a kid. The interior had been refurbished to resemble a much older trailer. I found a book about it in one of the cabinets. It was a 1958 Flying Cloud 22 but inside was redone to look like something out of the thirties or forties. It had that industrial modern look, flat colors, some aluminum-faced cabinetry, pastel panels in sky blue, a few weird curves in the built-in stuff giving it that 1939 World's Fair look. On the whole it was endearing and seductive. I'd studied the World's Fair in architecture school, where much was made of industrial modernism by my professors—the future as Zeppelin. They were retro way before retro. We weren't encouraged to replicate the clichés in our design problems, but the occasional nod to one or another past motif was always appreciated.

Chantal joined me up in the trailer late one night. She was a little drunk. "You think they got it right? The Parker thing? I don't. I don't think they did. I think she killed him and she's getting away with it, that's what I think."

"That's what you think, eh?"

She sat at the linoleum-topped foldaway table built into the front of the trailer holding her drink with both hands and looking out the windows there at the lights down by the harbor. "You?" she said.

"No idea," I said. "He was in my house telling me about how he wanted to get away, but it's too grisly to think she killed him."

"Would make more sense if he killed her," she said. "You ever know people who killed some people? It's hard. Especially if they're close. Like you have to look at them a lot and you never forget what they did, I mean, if you know for a fact."

"Ah," I said. "I can only think of the one person."

She ignored it. "I guess there's a chance she did it," Chantal said, rubbing her eyes. "Guy can go out in the middle of the night and shoot somebody in the head in a parking lot. And he's a regular guy, seems like, I mean, like Parker. So if she kills him and makes it look like suicide and everybody agrees that's what it is, that's it. It's shit, really. Could happen to any of us at any time."

"This girl held a gun on me one time. Her name was Fatima and she thought I screwed her sister. I was supposed to be screwing her and she had this other idea because her sister was always around the house. What was I going to do, cover my eyes? So one night Fatima came at me with a pistol and was saying how she could shoot me in the face. We were drinking some, I guess. So we're in her den, or her family's den, and she comes with the gun, and, you know, I didn't have any idea whether or not she would pull the trigger. No clue. You don't believe she will, but you know it's possible."

"I know," Chantal said.

"I was afraid to move. She could have made a mistake, held it too tight, whatever. It could go off. This went on for a while, like half an hour, a little more. It was dark in that den, there were a couple table lamps in there, and a pass-through to the kitchen where some light was on. I remember looking at the barrel of the gun. She wasn't that far away, it's not like she was across the room or something. She was on a stool and I was on a stool; we were at the bar she had in the den. I couldn't do anything and I didn't want to—too risky."

"Would have been stupid. Good thing you didn't."

"She was blond," I said. "Sixty percent pretty. A little pasty, maybe. Too much jaw. I remember she looked too white, light colored, with that dark wood paneling behind her."

"So what happened?"

"She was talking and asking me if I'd slept with Lorraine,

the sister. Saying stuff like 'You like her?' and 'You think she's pretty?' and smiling that smile that's not a smile at all, that's all about anger and heartbreak. Mocking me, sneering that way that gives you away."

I opened the door of the Airstream then, stood in the rounded doorway, and looked out over the odd rock-like roof of the Velodrome at the dark sky, the stars. There was a breeze and the breeze was cool, like there was a front blowing through.

"I'm guessing she didn't shoot," Chantal said.

"No. Kept waving the gun and talking about me being interested in Lorraine. I think she was trying to gauge how much interest I had, and I figured if that was what she was doing I would probably end up OK because I didn't really have much interest."

"Some, but not much," Chantal said.

I looked at her and she looked back, and I couldn't quite read her. I said, "The hole in the barrel was small. I remember that. It was dark, too. There was a front sight on the top of the barrel, like cap guns I'd had as a kid, only those were always chrome looking, and this barrel was near black. Anyway"—I backed away from the Airstream door and got my beer off the countertop—"anyway, she didn't shoot. Eventually she stopped pointing it at me and told me she wasn't going to shoot. She was a little crazy, this girl, which is why the thing was scary. Some girls you wouldn't even give it a thought, you'd know you were safe even if they pointed a gun at you. Not Fatima. I had no clue what she might do. She ended up committing suicide. I was long gone by that time, but Lorraine, the sister, told me, sent a clipping."

"That was so sweet," Chantal said, without looking at me. Threw the line away.

"Anyway," I said. "That's probably as close as I come to knowing somebody. Fatima, I mean. Kind of takes one to know one, doesn't it?"

"Would you kill yourself?" she asked. "Can you imagine it?"

"I think about it. I've been here long enough—you know that idea? On the planet. Letting it all go. Sometimes I think I'm ready."

"The thrill is gone," she said.

"Sure, but also after a while the end is a lot closer than the beginning, and you've spent all your time planning for the future, and suddenly there's only about thirty minutes of future left, and while it's not ghastly, it's not a delight, either. And the idea of doing stuff, planning stuff, looking forward to stuff, all of it is out the fucking window, isn't it? You're watching the clock wind down."

"Whoa," she said. "Did we go over a cliff or something?" She was sitting back, lounging on the fold-out, looking like her pictures downstairs but much older. "You sound like you need twenty milligrams of something by mouth PRN. Man, you're darkly dark right now."

"Tired. We get swapped out, all of us. The replacements run the world, let a few folks stick around, but most go to storage for the concluding years. It's like at work, they don't really care what you've done, what you can do, how the work is or isn't, all they care about is getting you out the door, replacing you and starting over. The company lives forever."

"Where's that guy who liked being locked up?"

"Still with you," I said. "At your service. Maybe we ought to break for snacks downstairs or something. Maybe we ought to go get some cinnamon rolls, huh?"

"I could do a cinnamon roll," she said. "Close that door, will you?"

So we shut the Flying Cloud and went down the stairs into her apartment, and then down to the restaurant and out into the parking lot. It was a relief to be out in the open, suddenly. There were bright lights on tall poles, and we could hear the boats jostling one another across the street in the Small Craft Harbor, ropes and riggings banging against masts, water slapping the pier, spraying, half-unwrapped sails snapping in the gusts of wind. We headed for the car and rolled down the windows the minute we were inside. She pointed toward the coast road and I pointed the car in that direction, rubbed a hand over my scalp, and wondered where Ella Maria Parker was at that exact moment, wondered what she was thinking about, wondered what was next.

21

# NIGHT MOVES

Cal and Jilly were sitting on the deck at my condo when we got back. I hadn't seen them when we drove in, but they must have been watching us because when we got out of the car I heard Jilly call out, "Hey now!" in that *Larry Sanders Show* way, and I knew it was her because of her voice, and she was the only person who still did that *Hey now!* thing that everybody did for about ten minutes when the guy was doing it on the show.

Jilly said, "The return of *The Lost Patrol.* Come on up and have a nightcap."

"What are we doing up there?" I said, craning to see her leaning on the railing. "You alone?"

"Not hardly," she said. "I've got your close personal friend and my ex-husband, Calvin R. Molester, up here. He was here when I returned from town."

Chantal and I went upstairs, collected a couple of beers, and went straight out onto the deck. After the introductions, which were perfunctory, I said to Jilly, "What did you mean he was here when you got here?"

"He was here," she said, pointing straight down toward the deck.

"How did he get in?" I asked her, but I was looking at Cal.

"Key," Cal said, holding up a bright silver key.

"Oh," I said. "Our friend Diane."

Cal nodded, raised his glass. "Good guess," he said.

"Why don't you give that to me?" I said. "She doesn't need a key."

"I probably can't do that," Cal said, pocketing the key. "She sent it to me and I have to return it to her."

"Give it to him, will you?" Jilly said. "Don't be Cal for once."

"We've been talking old times," Cal said. He turned to Chantal and explained, "We were young marrieds for a while years ago. She was my first wife and I her first husband, I believe. Isn't that right, Jilly? I think that's right."

"Give me strength," Jilly said. She turned and shook hands with Chantal for the second time. "It's nice to meet you," Jilly said. "But now I think I will go to my room. Good night."

"Good night, Jilly," Chantal said.

"Don't leave on my account," Cal said, waving his glass in the air.

"I'm thinking maybe you'd better move along," I said to Cal. "Is there some reason you're here? Or is it a friendly key-brandishing visit?"

"I hear you talked to Diane," he said. "She said you weren't friendly."

"I was perfectly friendly," I said. "Then. Now, not so much."

"I get it," Cal said. "Don't get your trousers in an uproar."

"I want the key," I said. I was counting on him being pretty drunk, figuring he wouldn't want to get into any monkey business under the circumstances.

He stared at me, then said, "Sure," and reached in his pocket and pulled out the key, handed it over. "Whatever. Keys are available." He turned to Chantal and said, "Nice to meet you again, ma'am. I've heard about you. I ate at your place once a couple weeks ago. I was going to intro myself then, but I got shy about it."

"My lousy luck," she said.

"Yes, ma'am," he said. "But new opportunities present themselves all the time, don't they?"

"They do," Chantal said. "Like raindrops."

Cal was out of his chair and headed for the sliding door, leaving his drink behind on the wide deck railing. " 'Night, folks," he said. "See you soon."

I followed him inside the condo and down to the front door, where I let him out. "Listen," I said. "I don't want to be unfriendly or anything, but I don't think there's much reason for us to see each other again, do you?"

"We shall see, Rodrigo," Cal said. "The future will be what it will be."

"Good-bye, Cal." I closed the door and locked it. A reflex. Then I went to Jilly's room and knocked lightly on the door.

"Yes?" she said from inside.

"He's gone," I said. "Coast is clear."

"Maybe I'll stay put," she said. "I'm tired."

I decided to let it rest. "Sure. Sleep tight." I started to leave, and the door opened a little.

"It's the first time I've seen him in a long while. It wasn't fun. But I don't want to be rude to Chantal. Will you explain?"

"Sure," I said.

"She seems nice," Jilly said.

"She is. And so are you," I said.

"I know," she said.

Chantal wanted to go home about a half hour later, so I walked with her to her condo and sat there with her for a few minutes while she microwaved a tiny cup of some strange-looking soup she said she'd made earlier in the day. Green. It was greenish, but not pea. Spinach, maybe. I didn't know.

After the soup I was ready to get home and resume my routine. Finding Cal at the house had been distracting and uncomfortable, so I figured I'd write a note to Diane asking her to chill on the Cal thing, at least insofar as it involved him coming to the house. Maybe he was flying blind, without instructions, which I thought might be the case, since Diane was usually less confrontational. She wanted the house, but I thought we'd solved that, at least for the moment, in our telephone call.

"Jilly is nice," Chantal said. "Pretty."

"All young people are pretty," I said. "It's a universal truth. Even unattractive young people are pretty at my age."

"I get that impression when we're out and about. You keep a close eye on the field."

"What are you saying?"

"Girls. You watch the girls. All the time. Without cease. You are a girl watcher. At grocery stores, drugstores, shoe stores, the seafood place, restaurants, my place, wherever." She held her hand up to her face as if holding a camera. "Click, click," she said. "You take brain pictures."

"Not at all," I said. "Scanning the horizon for potential dangers. Protecting you, my dear."

"I don't need to be protected from girls in sports bras."

"Never can tell. Concealed weapons, et cetera."

"You always done that?"

"I'm keeping an eye out, you know. It's all about style."

"You are all about style," Chantal said. "But tell me about Jilly. What's your arrangement?"

I didn't want to get into it. I said, "I don't have a good answer for that. She worked for me when I was at the studio. She was an artist, did layouts and design for print, mostly, some TV later. She's good, gifted. We became close when we were working together, closer when Diane and I split up."

"Uh-huh," Chantal said, getting a bottle of wine and two glasses.

"None for me," I said. "Anyway, we get along very well. Morgan likes her, too, so sometimes all three of us do stuff."

"She's another daughter?"

I hemmed and hawed about that. "Sort of, but there's always been this ambiguity about it. We worked together and so we had that setup as a beginning where we were unequal partners in a job, but partners anyway. So that's not so daughter-like, is it?"

"Not usually, no," she said.

"I don't know," I said. "It's a vexed thing. She was screwed up being married to Cal, even though it only lasted a couple years. I don't know the whole story, but apparently it was grim."

"He seemed swell," Chantal said. "Lacking only the pencil mustache."

"A peach," I said. "Incidentally, Jilly asked me to explain she left to get away from him. She was worried about being rude."

"That's nice of her."

"So that's Jilly," I said.

"Fine," she said. "I was curious. Scanning the horizon for dangers."

"Hmm," I said. "Sure."

"Yeah," she said. "I gotta go to bed now. Should we meet up soonish? We still have work on the Parker case."

"We can do that," I said. Then I slid off the stool and gave Chantal a proper peck on the cheek, which she returned in kind.

## 22

# JEAN DARLING

DETECTIVE JEAN DARLING came around to meet the residents and to discuss the death of Duncan Parker. She was a good-looking woman about Jilly's age who lived in one of the semidetached cottages that bordered the lake on the property, though why the property needed a lake with Galveston Bay right across the street I never understood. Developers will be developers is the answer, I guess. I'd said hello to her a couple of times on my walks and nodded at her more often. She took her walks outfitted in black shorts and black T-shirt, which I always thought peculiar, and she had a dog, a German shepherd she called Big Dog. In fact, on one occasion I had been sitting on the curb taking a breather when Jean came by with the dog, and he came quite close to me and I petted him. His head was large. He was one hundred percent friendly, but the size of his head at close range was enough to scare me. I worried that he'd sense that I was frightened, because I remembered something from childhood about how you are not supposed to let on that you're scared by an animal, a dog in particular, lest the dog get upset about it. Something like that, anyway.

When she came to see me, unannounced, she was with Bernadette Loo, newly crowned HOA president, who introduced us in my doorway but begged off when I invited them both inside, saying she was going to drop in on Roberta Spores next door.

It was early for me, a bit before noon, and I had recently gotten up after a fitful sleep, having gone to bed that morning after six.

"What can I get you?" I asked Detective Darling. "Coffee, Coke, tea?"

"Water," she said. "If that's convenient."

"Perfectly," I said.

"No ice," she said.

"Gets easier," I said, poking the glass into the water dispenser on the refrigerator, which was, unfortunately, set to dispense ice. "How about ice?" I said, waving the ice-filled glass at her.

"Ice would be lovely," she said.

"Are you here on official business? Or what?"

"I'm doing a little reconnaissance for the department but also for Bernadette," she said. "Two birds, one stone. That kind of thing."

"OK," I said. "How can I help?" We sat in my living room, which was less spare than I would have liked because I still had some of Diane's furniture, rather a lot of Diane's furniture, as a matter of fact.

"I'm talking with folks about what they know about Duncan Parker and his wife, and so on," she said. She had a notebook, like the police that had come around after Chantal's trouble. "You knew Mr. Parker, is that correct?"

"Sure," I said. "We were not friends, but I spoke to him on the street sometimes. Complained about the HOA fees, you know."

"The fees are high?"

"Stupefying," I said. "You pay them, too, yes?"

"Not so bad in the cottages," she said. She referred to a loose sheet tucked into her notebook. "But you are not one of the derelicts, so to speak. You are very good, I'm told, about keeping up with the payments. Some people, as you may know, are less conscientious."

"I hear that," I said. "There's always a note in there pleading with the 'derelicts' to act responsibly and pay their bills."

"As for Mrs. Parker," the detective said, "I gather from Bernadette that she intends to return soon and take up residence in the unit where her husband passed?"

"I don't know that," I said. "If Bernadette says it she knows more than I do."

"Yes," Jean Darling said. "She had thought originally that Mrs. Parker was going to move on, perhaps leave the area, but that turns out not to be true, apparently."

"I see. Well, she has every right, I guess. I'm not sure I'd want to come back, were I she, but not my call."

"Though apparently some residents don't feel good about her return. A group has been formed, sort of beneath the radar, to explore the possibility of heading her off at the pass."

"The language of my childhood," I said. "Is that legal?"

She shook her head and raised her pen from her pad. "I really don't know the particulars. I suppose there are condominium covenants or similar. I imagine if a sufficient number of owners agreed that someone should be discouraged . . ."

"I don't know," I said. "Sounds strange. What grounds?"

"Beats me," she said. "The department, as far as I know, is satisfied with the investigation of the husband's death, and even if it weren't, that might not provide a sufficient cause for action. I guess some people here think the suspicions surrounding her attach to the community itself, which is not good for property values, sales, the rental market, and so on."

"Do you have suspicions?"

"Me? No. I was repeating what I've heard."

I scratched my head at this point. "I suspect it's illegal to exclude a property owner, or try to oust a property owner, based on the things you cited. I mean, people might want to get rid of anybody, but I'm not sure discomfort is sufficient reason."

"I understand that," she said. "I was reporting that I gather that many residents would rather Mrs. Parker seek other arrangements."

"I don't really follow, Ms. Darling," I said.

"It's Mrs.," she said. "But my husband passed some time ago."

"I'm sorry to hear that," I said. "My condolences."

"Thank you. Please do not misconstrue my mentioning this," she said. "I'm sort of the messenger here."

"Let me ask you," I said. "Do people imagine she figured in his death?"

"I don't really feel as though I can discuss that," she said. "As a friend of Bernadette's I gather that Mrs. Parker is not well liked, and there are some residents who feel she may know more about his death than she let on."

"Ah," I said. "And the police?"

"As I said, the police are satisfied that it was what it appeared to be," she said. "But we are always on alert. We make mistakes. When we do, we like to catch them early and repair them. Mend and repair, that's our game."

"We don't want to be known as the deadliest condos in Kemah."

"Right," she said. "Now, was Mr. Parker a particular close friend? Of yours? Bernadette said you sometimes talked to him and that he was at your place a few weeks ago."

"Did she?" I said. "Well, yes, I talked to Mr. Parker from time to time. He kept a nice yard, seemed to have a way with the grass, as you may know. Always had the good grass, so I got tips from him sometimes. And yes, he came by recently."

"Could you tell me a little more about that meeting?" Darling said. "Was there some specific reason he selected you?"

"Wanted to chat," I said. "He hadn't made a practice of visiting. I don't think he had a lot of friends, and he wanted to talk."

"What did he want to talk about?" she asked.

“Is that an official question or a neighborly question?” I said.

She did a theatrically awkward face. “Hadn’t given it any thought,” she said. “I was just wondering.”

“Ah,” I said. “Well, he was upset because of some difficulty in his marriage, and I have no idea why he picked me to discuss it with, maybe he thought I would be especially sympathetic.”

“And were you?”

“No.”

“I wonder if he had anything to say about his wife, Ella Maria Parker? Did you get some impression of how things were between them?”

“I’m not sure I’m comfortable discussing that,” I said. “It’s hard to figure how I’m supposed to deal with you.”

“Because I’m police?”

“Right. I mean, if you want to talk formally as part of an ongoing investigation where it’s my duty and responsibility to report as accurately as possible my conversations with people, that would be fine. I’d be fine with that. But here we’re like neighbors and this is like gossip.”

“And you don’t gossip?” she said.

“No, I do. I do. A lot. But it’s with friends, people I’ve known awhile, with whom I have a certain relationship, usually, mutual understanding. That sort of thing.”

“And usually they are not police,” she said.

“They are never police,” I said. “I stay as far away from police as humanly possible.”

"Did you have a problem with the police?"

At this point I wanted out of the conversation and Jean Darling out of the house. So I said something like that, and she flipped a page in her notebook and said, "Why don't you give me an overview of your conversation with Mr. Parker? I'm asking formally now, as police."

"OK," I said. "He talked about being smitten with the woman who was dancing at his house one morning. I'm sure you heard about that?"

"Yes," she said. "He said 'smitten'?"

"Something like that. And she was hotheaded and turned up in his driveway that morning because she wasn't happy with the way things were going between them."

"She intended to embarrass him? Confront the wife?"

"I got that impression, yes," I said.

"And did he say anything else about the wife?"

"No," I said. "Well, yes. That he would rather be, you know, sort of apart from her. Sort of single again."

"So he could pursue other romantic interests?" the detective said.

"Correct," I said. "That was the sense I got."

"And was there more? Did he make any remarks about pursuing this goal? Was he going to get a separation? A divorce?"

"Divorce was a nonstarter," I said. "I mentioned it. He said I was fortunate to be divorced and to have new friends."

"New friends?"

"Women friends," I said. "I have a grown daughter, and

I also have a woman with whom I worked in Houston, and she comes down and stays sometimes. And I also see Chantal White socially."

"Chantal White is the woman who was attacked, covered with paint, and so forth? Isn't that right?"

"Correct," I said.

"And you started seeing her after that?" Jean Darling said.

"Correct," I said. "She owns a restaurant and bar on the way to Texas City."

"The Velodrome?"

"Correct," I said.

"I've been there," the detective said.

She smiled at me here and I smiled right back at her. "The food's pretty good," I said. "I like the shrimp, particularly, but then I never met a shrimp I didn't like."

"I'm sure they feel the same," she said.

Jean Darling gave me a look, a police-officer look, something they must teach them at the academy, and it seemed to express in a split second decades of police distaste for ordinary citizens, of which I was at that moment the primary representative.

She folded her notebook and stood up without another word.

23

# THE LETTER

DIANE CALLED. "I'm not coming," she said. "If you don't want me there I'm not coming. Simple as that. It's up to you, Wallace." Diane was changing her plans again. I didn't care. I wasn't selling the condo and she wasn't going to hound me, so it made no difference. I said something like that to her, smoothing the edges where I could.

"Have you found other places here?" I said. "Your pal said you had a Realtor."

"I do and she sends me stuff all the time. I look at it. Can't really tell much. I gotta get down there and look at 'em in person. Cal is useless for that."

"He was at the house," I said. "I came home and he was on the deck with Jilly. He'd let himself in, apparently."

"I'm sorry about that," she said. "He doesn't follow instructions as well as I had hoped."

"What were the instructions?"

"Don't use the key," Diane said.

"So why give it to him?"

"Didn't think about it. He asked, I supplied. Never occurred to me he'd use it."

"Why? He's your guy, figures whatever he does is OK with you."

"I get that now," Diane said. "I apologize. My mistake."

"I got the key from him," I said.

"I heard. So there you go," she said. "All is well."

I didn't want to let her off the hook, but at the same time it looked like a lost cause, so I said, "Whatever. Are you guys back on?"

"I see him," she said. "Not overmuch, but we're friends. He's down there to plead out. I'm afraid he's going to have to go away for a time."

"Are you kidding? I thought the lawyer said the charges would wither and die."

"The lawyer was wrong and is gone now, anyway. The new lawyer says plead and take a couple years. I don't know how they do this stuff, but the new woman says he could be out in eighteen months."

"Jesus," I said. "I should have been nicer to him."

"He wanted to straighten out some stuff with Jilly. He said it didn't go well."

"I got that from her," I said. "She didn't say anything about it, but she was unhappy."

"Cal's not that bad, really. I don't know—maybe everything will get better in time."

"He's an ass," I said. "He's not going to turn into a nice guy in prison, is he?"

"Probably not, I guess."

"So the future doesn't look that rosy," I said.

We were quiet on the phone a minute, as if things had reached a point where we were being friendly, and we were both realizing it at the same time and unsure about what was next.

"I'm going to have to split here in a minute," I said.

"Company?" she said.

"No, just the usual. Must make my rounds."

"Hmm," Diane said. "OK. Before you go, though, can you tell me whether or not it's going to bother you if I move back down there? I could move somewhere else—Galveston, for example. One of the other towns. Seabrook, Freeport. It's that I know that area right there really well and I was always comfortable there."

"The condo was the only thing that bothered me," I said.

"I'm sorry about that," she said. "That was a bad move."

"That and having Cal deliver the news. But apart from that, wherever you want to move is good with me. I'd be happy to have you in town, or nearby—wherever you want to be. Please don't hesitate on my account."

"You sure?"

"Yeah," I said. "I am sure." And I was. That was a good moment between us, gave me hope for patching up our friendship.

Bruce Spores was working in his garage on his perpetual-motion machine when I started my walk. He had his garage set up as a workshop and was always in there with his electric tools wailing away, with his radio cranked up and blasting Rush Limbaugh for all passersby. Bruce kept his cars outside, in the drive, which was explicitly disallowed in the covenants, but nobody paid that much attention to the covenants anyway, so it didn't matter. People used the wrong colors on their condominiums, but it didn't bother anyone on the HOA board. I didn't mind the rules. They weren't that restrictive. I didn't have to think about what color to repaint when I had to repaint. But others always stretched things, redid their yards without reference to the covenants, added knickknacks and gazing balls, dwarfs and trolls, miscellaneous reindeer, fountains, swans, biblical scenes, trellises, flamingos, concrete rabbits—all these profoundly personal expressions of self. I was good with rabbits up to actual size and, of course, giant rabbits, four feet and above, but for the rest, well, some seemed to elasticize the borderline. Forgetful Bay was ruled with a droopy hand.

Bruce cocked his goggles up on his forehead, shouted for me to come in, and waved in my direction with a bright yellow electric drill he had in his hand.

I started up his short drive, and he came out of the garage, still carrying the drill. "Hey, Wallace," he said. "You hear?"

"Hear what?" I said.

"More trouble," he said, standing the drill carefully on the roof of his car. It was a portable drill, one of those with the battery in the butt of the handle. "There was a police bust over on the far end, past Parker's place. Some people over there were apparently running a business, a girl business."

I figured he was in on the gossip. "What business, exactly?" I asked.

"Modeling and massage. Escorts. Three young women live there, and there were several gentlemen present when the bust went down. They have a four-bedroom place. Like yours, I guess, I don't know. Anyway, they were booked on solicitation and so on. They've been given thirty days to get lost."

"There's still time," I said.

"No one died," Bruce said.

"That's a breakthrough," I said.

"Mrs. Parker remains MIA," he said. "Looks like she's taking a permanent vacation up there in Canada. Was it Canada? Or Alaska? I get them mixed up."

"One of those," I said. "They're hunting her now?"

"Yeah, apparently. Bernadette told Roberta about it. She got it from that Jean Darling."

"I talked to her," I said. "I told her Parker came over and yakked about wanting out. I didn't know what else I could do. I mean, she was police."

"I expect she knew, just wanted to hear it from you."

"Well, I don't know where she got it," I said.

"Bernadette. Maybe he told her, too. They had some talk when she took over the HOA thing, so probably it was in there."

"I was the corroborating witness."

"Something like that, yeah," he said.

"So you think Mrs. Parker is not coming back? What, did she actually, like, whack him?"

"Beats me," Bruce said. "The cops want to talk to her. They say otherwise, but they're not so sure about suicide."

"And now we have escorts, too. I like it," I said.

"I've seen those gals at the pool a couple of times. They weren't bad."

He grinned, his eyes sparkling behind gold-rimmed glasses. I was looking at the gray stubble on his cheeks and chin, flickering in the early afternoon sunlight. He would not have gone into a sex shop or massage parlor in a zillion years, and the big grin was a giveaway. I didn't blame him. I wouldn't have gone in, either.

"Entrepreneurial spirit at Forgetful Bay," he said.

"You go to Parker's funeral?" I asked.

"Nope," he said. "Roberta did. I stayed away. She said it was small and funereal, in that church on Bayside. Know that place?"

"What denomination?" I said.

"Nonspecific. Episcopal or something. They had music and readings and such, she said. Par for the course. I don't like funerals, generally."

"I probably should have gone," I said.

"I don't imagine anyone expected you."

I was struck by that. What did he mean? Did he mean something, or was he saying the next thing that had come to him? Did he mean nobody expected any particular person, or was it me that no one expected? Then I figured it was the first. Still—

"Any other weirdness happening?" I asked. "You seem to have your thumb on the throat of things."

"Nah," he said. "One of the Everly Brothers is ill again. So I heard."

"Those damn Everly Brothers," I said.

"The new people on the other side of you? They've requested permission to add two rooms under their place, off the garage, I guess. Board is going to OK it, apparently. Vote was close."

"Not a great idea to build on the ground down here, is it?"

"No, but, you know, they've got a lot of folks to house. You meet 'em?"

"No. I knew Ng, but haven't met the Changs."

He nodded at me. "That's all right, I guess. They keep to themselves, like good neighbors, right?" Bruce clapped me on the shoulder and reached for his drill.

"The best ones," I said, smiling at him. "The very best."

Bernadette Loo arrived at my door at eight in the morning a few days later with a worried look on her face and a FedEx mailing envelope in her hand, one of the cardboard ones for small documents. "May I come in?" she said, and, without waiting for an answer, she came in.

"Come in," I said. I was not awake, straight out of bed, wearing tan shorts and T-shirt. Not my best look.

"Sorry about busting in on you in the morning," she said. "I know you sleep in the morning, right? That's what I was told."

"Ordinarily," I said.

"Well, I apologize," she said. "But I had to show you this." She wagged the FedEx at me.

"What's that?"

"It's from Mrs. Parker," she said. "Sent from Saskatchewan. Yesterday."

"What does she say?"

Bernadette handed me the envelope. I pushed apart the lips where the "pull here" strip had been pulled and fished out several sheets of paper containing a lengthy handwritten note. I was struck at once by the wonder of the penmanship. The writing was beautiful, very old school and very fine, not at all what I would have expected of Mrs. Parker, the giant. "It's handwritten," I said, fetching the reading glasses from my home-office alcove.

"I assume it's her hand," Bernadette said.

I nodded and clicked on the light. Then I read the letter.

"I, Ella Maria Parker, have commenced a new life as a single woman, a widow, a survivor, and a person of the not-impoverished class, going on with my life following a series of misadventures that have left me transformed, a person unlike any I have been before in my fifty-odd years on this green earth, a frightened woman of reduced means, a woman with four pairs of blue jeans, all of which were purchased at TJMaxx in the last years of my marriage to Duncan William Parker, now deceased, my husband of twenty-some years, a man of accomplishment and character who suffered for many of those years as a result of my own limited ambition, confidence, and effort, but who nevertheless himself prospered in his public life as President of Forgetful Bay Condominium Homeowners Association, a member of the United States Marine Corps, and an honored member of the Kemah City Council in Kemah, Texas, the town in which we spent the better part of our marriage, and from which I recently fled. I am writing to you today this message to put down in writing those events and circumstances that led to the untimely and unnecessary passing of Duncan Parker from this life into the next, in a form and format in which I will have the opportunity to render those events and circumstances in their fullest and most comprehensive arrangement so that all might know the particulars, the ins and outs, as it were, of dear Duncan's many trials over the last years of our marriage, and may understand thus the fine details which permeated that marriage in which I operated as a partially functioning partner along with my beautiful husband who has now predeceased me through means unknown, a trick of fate to which I was not a party and in which I was not an actor in any capacity. I was, nevertheless, for the entirety of our marriage up to that point a constant companion to Duncan Parker in many things, and in particular to his wish to remain happily married, a fact not known to all, known, in fact, to only a few, to include myself and his surviving sister Bianca Del Toro Parker for these many years, up until the recent events to which I herein refer."

I stopped at this point and invited Bernadette to join me in the living room where we might be more comfortable.

"We should get the police," Bernadette said.

"Yes," I said. "You haven't called them yet?"

"I wanted you to see it," she said. "Since you were his friend."

I shook my head. "Why does everybody think we were friends? I barely knew the man."

"Well, he wasn't friends with anybody else," she said.

"Call the police. Tell them you got this letter from Mrs. Parker and that we're reading it now."

"It's not a confession," she said.

"I guess not," I said.

"It's a declaration of innocence."

"We should call that Jean Darling woman," I said. "She is police. She in your phone?"

"I think so." Bernadette already had her phone out and was looking through her contacts. "Yes, I have it here," she said.

While she talked to Detective Darling I looked over the rest of the letter. It was more of the same, that unlikely language in that pretty black script. It reported that they had some discussion about the marriage, about alternative resolutions to their divergent views, and she was "a little bit" despondent to learn that Duncan was not completely happy. She threatened suicide with a pistol and, when they struggled over possession of the pistol, the pistol discharged. "Ironically," she wrote, "no one was hurt."

I imagined her in Canada writing this letter reporting a disagreement that happened before his alleged suicide and noting, as she wrote, the irony of the gun going off and killing no one while he was preventing her suicide and then, presumably, using the same gun for his own suicide. I didn't feel so good about that. I mean, who thinks about irony when they are hurting, when a crisis is right on top of them? Irony is a luxury for individuals in big houses and expensive dressing gowns, not people at the mercy of events.

"She's coming over now," Bernadette said, getting off the phone. "Did you read the whole thing?"

"Skimmed it," I said. "I'd say it was not written in haste."

"Is that the way she talked, I mean, when you talked to her?"

"I never talked to her," I said. "I don't remember talking to her."

"Does she mention the woman?"

"The dancing girl, you mean? I didn't see her in the text."

"Her name's Olive Mars," Bernadette said. "There were some things of hers in the house, apparently. She's a high-school teacher in Baytown, well liked by the students, oversees the debate team and assists the cheerleaders. Police can't figure how she hooked up with Parker."

"Where'd you get all that?"

"Where do you think?" she said.

"Jean talks too much?"

"Sufficiently," Bernadette said.

# 24

# PRESENT COMPANY

JILLY AND I were back on the deck in our usual seats, only it was raining like crazy outside, blustery and crackling with lightning and thunder. We were backed up against the windows, deep under the overhang, so missing most of the downpour except the splashing stuff. "I thought of coming down to stay for a while," Jilly said. She had her face hidden behind a cup of coffee held in both hands, and the part of her face I could see, the eyes, had a serious look about them.

"I'd like that," I said. "Seeing more of you more of the time."

"You be OK with that?"

"Absolutely," I said. "We could move Diane's stuff to the storage place and you could have that room, too. A suite of your own. Turn it into a studio, sitting room, whatever."

"Could be too much competition around here," she said. "I might get a place."

"Oh yeah? Sure. OK. But you're welcome to stay, I mean, that would be my preference, if my preference were to be noted. Unless you think it might be an impediment."

She made a face. "To?"

"You know, whatever. Us," I said.

"We're all right," she said.

"We're great," I said. "I'm a pensioner dawdling at the bay, not much use to anybody, happy to have a friend for the heartbreaking future."

"That's pretty half empty, isn't it? You're a little young for that."

"Well, look what happened to my neighbor," I said. "Or my other neighbor who wrecked his car. Things happen to oldsters."

"What about the *other* other neighbor?" Jilly said.

"She's a pal," I said. "A property owner and an acquaintance."

"You don't think she'd mind if I moved in with you?"

I wanted to answer the question truthfully, so I took the time to stare out at the rain and consider what I might say. I didn't want to lie, or diminish my connection with Chantal, and I ran through a lot of alternatives in a short space of time. Nothing seemed right.

"Probably not," I finally said. "The ground has shifted some. She may be too, uh, progressive. We're friendly, but I see her less often. Things are different from what they were. I guess she'd be fine. I don't know how you'd be. I don't know what you would expect. I like you, though, and I like you enough to want you to stay here." I made some corny hand gesture, like a shrug, with hands. "That's my pitch."

It was Jilly's turn to stare at the rain, which she did for a good long while, sipping her coffee occasionally. Eventually she said, "This is pretty down here, isn't it? Rain or shine. That's really something."

That was the last word of the conversation. After that we sat on the deck, under the drippy overhang, and waited out the storm. There wasn't much reason to do anything else and staying out on the deck was the next best thing to actually being out in the weather, something I loved when I was a lot younger, and remembered still, though I expect I knew better than to try to recapture the experience now, in my midfifties, when time went so fast that I wouldn't have time, wouldn't, or couldn't, allow myself the time, to savor it. I counted that inability as another of the losses of getting older, which goes too slow at first, leaving you aching to speed things up, and then goes too fast when it's way too late to slow things down. And all the time, old or young, you're looking at people on the other side of the equation, riddled with envy.

We took Chantal to dinner that night at the Blind Captain's Table, a pretty good but touristy seafood joint built out over the water at the end of a pier. It had been there in one incarnation or another for years. The food was good enough, and it was usually crowded, but not so much that night. I said hello to the owner, whom I'd met before, and Chantal knew him, so he sat for a short while with us, chatting about her restaurant and his, and the season, and so on. It was an obligatory visit. When it was done, we ordered.

"So what's Mrs. Parker's letter about?" Chantal said.

"She denies it," I said. "Said they had a fight, but it was she who was considering suicide and he stopped her. She left for Houston and next she heard he was dead. The dancer is a high-school teacher from Baytown. Her name is Olive Mars. That's about all I know. I'm sure we'll get more as the police get into it."

"High-school teachers can be especially attractive to older men," Jilly said.

"This one is the worst," Chantal said. "He's always ogling. His head on a swivel."

"I know it," Jilly said. "We've tried to work on that, haven't we, Dad?"

This was a good lick. One thing to do it with Morgan, another with Chantal.

I said that I recalled this tendency having been called to my attention on a number of occasions by various female individuals, but that I was not myself aware of it as a part of my general practice.

That got a snort from Jilly and a smile from Chantal. Things were going to be civil.

We spent the evening talking about them. Chantal talking about her background, her daughter, her restaurant and bar, the way she ended up in Kemah. Jilly did the same. They got along better than I would have anticipated after the talk with Jilly, who seemed to open up to Chantal in a way that surprised me. Jilly was direct and pleasant, didn't make any nervous jokes, seemed genuinely interested in Tinker, especially. Made a certain sense. Tinker would be closer in age, sort of another Morgan, with a dose of ragamuffin. Or maybe more differences than those, but still in the ballpark.

The food showed up eventually, and we ate it.

For some reason, even though the restaurant was sparsely populated, they put a couple right next to us, perhaps because we were at a window seat, and those are always prized in waterfront restaurants. These two were young, brightly outfitted in upscale off-the-rack branded clothing, and having an intense argument about the Danish TV show *Borgen.* The girl, who looked thirty and ritzy, especially in the hair department, said it could not be very realistic because the politics seemed so amateurish. The prime minister, she said, lives in a two-bedroom apartment, for heaven's sake.

The guy, who was wearing one of those Brooks Brothers happy-summer shirts with Life Savers rainbow stripes, said Denmark was a tiny country and it made sense that the politics there would be amateurish. What was more interesting to him was that they had only, he said, "seven or eight" actors in Denmark, so that they showed up in all the Danish television programs. And he ticked off the other Danish shows in which actors from *Borgen* had appeared.

Chantal got my attention by tapping on my hand. "Would you leave them alone, please?" she whispered.

"Sorry," I said. "I was listening in."

"We know, Dad," Jilly said.

I smiled at her, a smile I thought might suggest that I didn't prefer her to call me Dad, then turned to Chantal. "Did you know we had this woman police person in Forgetful Bay? Name of Jean Darling?"

"Yes," Chantal said. "She talked to me after the guy painted me blue." She turned to Jilly. "You've heard about my blue period, I assume?"

"Yes, I have," Jilly said. "Wonderful work in that period. So essentially, profoundly...*blue.* Did we ever catch the artiste?"

"We did not," Chantal said. "We haven't a clue."

"You should ask Wallace to pierce this web of obscurity," Jilly said. "One of his favorite jobs, here in his dotage."

"Is true?" Chantal said to me.

"I'm a regular Mangum, PI," I said.

"Magnum," Chantal said.

"Right," I said. "What I meant."

And so the dinner went well, smoothly, comfortably for all concerned. It was fine. I was pleased they got along. Who knew what was going on under the surface, but up top all was well. A small triumph.

I got a call from Jean Darling but didn't take it because we were finishing dinner. Later, when Jilly and I got back to the condo, I listened to Jean Darling's message. She wanted to talk. Jean Darling was an odd kind of pretty, a little bleary eyed, with freckled skin and good blond hair. She looked a little like the actress on the American version of *The Killing,* almost as if she'd fashioned her appearance after the character. This recommended her, as I was a big fan. Linden and Holder together jingled all my bells, and Sarah Linden I could watch forever. I was spellbound. This did not happen often. Actresses and models looked like so much Photoshop, gorgeous and beautiful, but a little interchangeable. And, as a man of parts, once you've seen Lauren Bacall in *To Have and Have Not* or Grace Kelly in anything, there's not much room for improvement in the looks department. This actress who played Sarah Linden was from Houston, was about Jilly's age, and had something curious and stunning, like she'd changed the game somehow. She didn't say much, but that fit her. I looked her up on IMDB. Did some Google searches. I was taken.

Even though it was late when we got back, I called Jean Darling thinking I would leave a message saying I could meet anytime, but she answered the phone, which threw me off.

"Detective?" I said. "Detective Darling?"

"Mr. Webster," she said. "I'm glad you called me back tonight. I need to meet with you tomorrow, in the morning maybe? I want to talk about Parker and this letter."

"Would early afternoon be OK?" I said. "I tend to—"

"That's fine," she said. "I remember now. Late to bed, late to rise."

"Yeah," I said. "My body clock's gone haywire."

"It's fine. I'll come by around one? That work?"

"That's great," I said.

"See you then," she said. "Thanks." And she hung up the

phone before I could say OK myself, left me hanging on to the receiver ready to say good-bye.

Jilly was in her room watching television, so I joined her on the bed there. "What're we watching?" I said.

"*House Hunters International,*" she said. "These two women want to live in Bali. One of them, that one with her bra showing, she already lives there. Teaches yoga or something. This other one has moved to Bali to be her roommate."

"A romance?" I said.

"Probably," Jilly said. "I guess. They keep saying that this one who has been in Bali for a year got out of a destructive relationship, but they don't mention who the partner was."

"So mysterious," I said.

"Isn't it always?" she said.

We watched for a bit as these two women looked at what seemed to be wholly unsuitable accommodations with a hairy Realtor in Bermuda shorts and a flowery shirt. He kept saying, "You got to feel it, feel this room, feel this location." He wasn't exactly savory. He was sweaty and toothy, and his chest hair was unruly.

"I don't care for the Realtor," I said.

"Looks like a hot-dog guy at the ballpark," Jilly said. "Or a plumber from central casting."

"You're being unkind to plumbers, aren't you?"

"Yes, Daddy," she said. "OK, I take it back. He doesn't look like a plumber." She took the beer bottle out of my hand and helped herself to a drink. Then she palmed the bottle's mouth as if to clean it before handing the bottle back to me. "What about the hot-dog guy? Do I have to retract that, too?"

"He looks something like a vendor," I said, thinking I'd meant the first round of this as a joke. "Mostly he's a guy with more hair than he knows what to do with."

"Unlike, say, yourself."

"The detective is coming at one tomorrow to ask me about Mrs. Parker's letter. I don't know what I'm supposed to know about it."

"She acts like you and Mr. Parker were best buds," Jilly said.

"I already told her that was wrong. I guess she's in touch with the Canadian police about the missus, trying to corral her and get her back here."

"The Mounties," Jilly said.

We watched the rest of the show, and the two women picked the wrong place, we agreed, and then Jilly started cycling through the channels and I went out on the deck for a smoke. Not something I did all that often. I'd mostly quit smoking after Lucy died, but a couple years later two other people I knew got throat cancer. One died, the other didn't, at least not right away, but that was enough for me to pull the plug. One was an older woman who worked at Point Blank as a writer. She had moved from New York, where she worked for one of the big agencies, moved because she wanted out of the city and we paid well. Her cancer was well along when it was discovered, and I spent a lot of time with her after it had been found. She didn't actually get through it. She died on a fold-out bed in the dining room of her rented apartment in southwest Houston. I was there the morning she died. She was weak and refused to go to the hospital. She knew what was happening and how quickly it was going to happen, so the hospital didn't make a lot of sense to her. In the days leading up to her death I drove her around some evenings, we got ice cream, we stopped in to see some other friends from the office, I had to carry her up the stairs at one place. She was very light. She was funny, wry, not very pretty. And she was resigned to her fate. Having the cancer was another piece of lousy luck she chuckled about. She'd been on the lookout for death for a good while. The dining room where she died was small, with green wallpaper and a big rosewood table that we had shoved against the wall when she started sleeping in there. She did that because she couldn't climb the stairs to her bedroom. I called that morning, but she didn't answer, so I drove over.

Jilly had a miniature horse when she was a child. She was raised on a farm or something like it, outside of Houston, and her father bought her this tiny horse she called Chris. It was no bigger than a good-sized dog, a big Lab or a German shepherd, and she was crazy for that horse. She had pictures of it that her father had taken with some weird box camera, little four-by-four snapshots, sepia colored, that she kept in frames in her room. She had other pictures, or copies, in her wallet and at her place up in Houston. Every chance she got, when we were working together at Point Blank, she'd slip one of those pictures into some ad layout or some set decoration for a TV spot or an annual report for a bank or an oil company. Sometimes they got all the way through to the finished product; sometimes the client would catch the pictures and ask what they were. Usually we took them out then, but we regretted having to do it. Sometimes we made up stories about Chris and Jilly together in this one particular picture when Jilly could not have been more than three or four, saying it was an expression of the longevity of the company or product or organization and that it was important to the overall impression given to the target audience. Sometimes that worked.

# 25

# DETECTIVES

Bernadette Loo showed up with Detective Darling the next day. They were right on time and I was, too. Jilly had a lunch date with Morgan, no doubt to be debriefed about the dinner with Chantal. I invited Bernadette and Jean Darling inside and offered coffee and butter cookies, those Nabisco ones that look like flowers. They were the only cookies I had in the house.

"So look," the detective began. "I want to go over your last talk with Parker, and I'd like to get your sense of this letter, and then I may have some things I want to discuss."

"Fine," I said. "I don't know what I can tell you. I think I said it all last time."

So she asked a few questions and I answered much as before, trying to add details when I remembered details. I told her about the eye, his offer to remove it, the pastries his wife liked—I was at a loss, really. "He said she'd gotten huge, like it was a sudden thing, that there was no predicate that he knew about. He told me almost nothing about the other woman, but you've found out a good deal about her, right? High-school teacher and all that?"

"We've done some work on that," Darling said. "But what I need to know is whether he made a specific threat, or something that could be understood as a threat, to his wife's life."

"No, I can't say that," I said. "At the end he was saying he was going to die in her arms, in Ella Maria's arms."

"Said those words?" the detective said.

"Yes. It wasn't like he was happy about it, but he was resigned to it. Said she was good to him, I remember that. Said he was a bad husband and that they had loved each other once."

"So he was saying they didn't love each other any longer?"

"That was implied, but it was more like the reason to stay together was that they had been in love with each other once. That's more what he was saying."

Jean Darling had a few more questions, but I had about run out of memory, so we didn't get much further with that. All this time Bernadette Loo was sitting there stone-faced, nodding occasionally, making little noises as if in agreement, or acknowledgment. I couldn't figure out why she was there.

"So what about this letter?" Jean asked, presenting the letter, which was now dressed up in a large Ziploc bag. "What do you make of this?"

"How should I know?" I said. "I have no idea except what it says on its face. She says she was going to shoot herself, or threatening to do so, and he tried to stop her, to get the gun, but—you know—couldn't, and the gun went off, but no one was hurt. Then she left. Later he was found dead, an apparent suicide."

"If you take the letter at face value, that's a convenient truth, isn't it?"

"Yes. Convenient. But I didn't know the guy, really, so it could be anything. You need somebody who knew the guy."

"Do you think it's possible that Mr. Parker was in any way involved in the other incidents here at Forgetful Bay?" Darling asked.

"What?" I said. "What other incidents are you talking about?"

"The painting incident," she said. "Maybe the death of your neighbor the nail-salon owner. Anything else out of the ordinary that might have happened here recently. The mailbox robbery, the girls, whatever."

"It hadn't occurred to me," I said. "Chantal would have recognized him if he was her attacker, though I think he had a mask."

"Rabbit mask," Darling said.

"As for the Asian guy, Forest Ng, I figured he lost control of the car, ran off the road, crashed and burned."

"Was he a reckless driver, generally speaking?"

"How would I know?" I said.

"Well, he was your neighbor," she said. "Neighbors sometimes know things about each other."

"I like to keep that to a minimum," I said.

"I see," Detective Darling said. "Fine. We have people looking into his records, his business, his connections with Parker."

"Did he have any connections with Parker?"

"It seems as if he may have had such," she said. "As I say, we're looking into it. There is one more thing I'd like to go over with you."

"Fine," I said. I started eating the cookies. Nobody else had touched them, and I wanted a cookie, so I started eating them, one at a time.

"We wondered if you would be willing to take a slightly more active role in helping us get Mrs. Parker to return to Kemah. This would involve some travel, maybe a week or more of your time—you are a retiree, yes? So you are not restrained by a work schedule?"

What do you say to police asking for help? *No thanks?* I wasn't interested in volunteering. "I don't think that's likely," I said. "You have people. It's your job. I'm a bystander."

"Understood," she said. "But we thought she might be more responsive to someone she knows, or someone who knew her husband, especially in a friendly context. We were thinking a couple of us might go with you to Canada, try to get you a meeting with Mrs. Parker. You know, as a friend, a person Mr. Parker had opened up to before all this happened. You would be the carrot, more or less."

"I'm almost sure that'll be no," I said.

"Could you give it some thought?" Darling said. "Everything would be taken care of, of course, and you'd be in good hands." Here she smiled too much.

"I will," I said. "I will give it some thought. But don't bank on it, OK? I mean, it really doesn't seem like a thing I could comfortably do, for a thousand reasons."

# 26

# OSCAR PETERSON

DIANE SHOWED up unannounced a week later at three in the afternoon, with a suitcase and a dog. The dog was a liver-colored curly-haired spaniel. He was an active dog. He would chase a ball all day long, she said, and demonstrated this with about twenty minutes of tossing a tennis ball around the main floor of the condo. The dog ran at top speed to get the ball each time Diane threw it, slid across the hardwood floors as necessary in an often vain effort to stop, then usually bounced off a wall or a piece of furniture, grabbed the ball, and trotted back to her, apparently begging her to throw it again, which she did, over and over. It was amusing at first to see how much energy this dog had, but shortly the charm waned.

"What kind of dog is this?" I asked, not recognizing the breed.

"It's a Boykin," she said. "Boykin spaniel. Happiest dog in the world. I got it from a woman in Rhode Island who said she could not keep up."

"Got a name?" I asked.

"Leo," she said. "For da Vinci or DiCaprio, depending on your orientation. He's as smart as one and as pretty as the other. And trains easy."

Then the dog pissed on the kitchen floor.

"He missed out on some fundamentals," she said, snapping paper towels off a roll on the counter and clearing the mess.

"Thanks for that," I said, wiggling my forefinger in her direction. She bunched up the towels while looking under the sink for the garbage can, then washed her hands in the sink.

I figured a quick mop would finish the job, so went to the closet where the mop lived and got it out, took it to the laundry room, rinsed it in the sink there, and returned to the kitchen.

Diane held out her hand for the mop. "I'll get it," she said.

Truth was I liked the dog on sight and I immediately regretted not having a dog of my own. I thought that later I might look at the local rescue sites. "So, you decided to come after all. It's good to see you, really. You look great—healthy, cheerful, like old times."

"Not nearly," she said. "But thanks for the effort. I was hoping to stay a night or two, if that's OK. Who's bunking here now, anybody?"

"Now, right this minute, or now today?" I said.

"Are there rooms available is what I meant."

"Sure," I said. "Jilly's here. She's thinking of getting a place down here, too. I mean, like you said you were. I haven't seen

Morgan in a while. The woman I told you about, Chantal, she has a condo over at the other end of the development."

"So you got two bedrooms free, then, at the moment?"

"One free and one with all your things in it."

"That would be fine if it's OK with you," she said. "I'm here to look at places and to see Cal. He's in custody. There was some screwup with the new plea. He's going to jail anyway, so it's a question of how long. They're trying to arrange the new deal I mentioned for eighteen months."

I nodded. "That's not going to be fun," I said.

"Actually, he says it's not as bad as you imagine. Maybe jail's not that bad here, in the boonies, you know, compared to a big city or one of the grand institutions."

"That's good news."

"Yeah. I thought it was. He seems to like the solitude. He's got his own cell now, and he says he's got it fixed up as much as you can, I guess, and he's reading a lot."

"Who would have thought?" I said. "Brings out the monk in him."

Leo was surveying the house, trotting from room to room, coming back to see that we were still there, smelling everything there was to smell. "How old is he?" I asked.

"Almost two," she said. "He's real leggy right now, but that's supposed to work out in a while when he gets more meat on his bones."

"Maybe he'll settle down some as he gets older?"

"Maybe. I hear they're pretty active."

"That'll be fun," I said. I nodded and then nodded some

more. I was aware of how much nodding I was doing, but I did not have any idea what to do next. She saved me the trouble of worrying about it.

"Maybe I should put my stuff in the room, freshen up a little? Something like that? When are we expecting Jilly?"

"Anytime, really. I think she was going to lunch with her real-estate person."

"Oh. That's great. Maybe we can look together sometime."

"Not sure you're going to be looking at the same places," I said.

"Never can tell," she said. "Strange bedfellows and all."

Bernadette Loo came by to ask me what I thought of the detective's idea and I told her there was no way I was going to Canada to help find Mrs. Parker. "It's crazy," I said. "Is that woman a real detective? Is that what detectives do nowadays? Get the citizens involved? I don't think so. Doesn't she watch television? I didn't want to offend her, but there's no chance." We were standing in the doorway at the bottom of the stairs.

"Maybe they were trying to get outside the box," Bernadette said.

"I prefer being inside the box," I said. "Away from Mrs. Parker."

"I hear that," she said. "But Jean's not that bad, maybe a little idealistic or something? *Hey, kids, let's put on a show,* that kind of thing."

"She must be new, right?"

"I don't know," Bernadette said. "She has only been in her

place here six months, and I only met her recently, so I don't know if she transferred or got promoted or what."

"Kibosh the deal, will you? If you can?"

"We had a fire over the weekend down at the Ransoms' place. You know them?"

"No," I said.

"Electrical dysfunction—malfunction. Burned up one of their bathrooms pretty good. Scared Lydia. That's the wife. A barbecue setup was stolen from the Wenges' yard, one of those stainless-steel jobs the size of a pool table. He likes to barbecue, apparently. And there was that drive-by shooting..."

That was when Diane stuck her head in the stairwell and said to me, "Who you talking to down there?"

"Bernadette Loo," I said. "HOA president."

Diane came down the steps and introduced herself as my "estranged wife," shook Bernadette's hand vigorously.

"Pleased to meet you," Bernadette said. "So you're visiting our Wallace?"

"For a few days," Diane said. "Looking for property."

"We got some places, if you're interested," Bernadette said. "Happy to show them."

"Might be a little too close for my estranged wife," I said.

"Or him, maybe," Diane said.

"Nah," I said.

"Gotta run," Bernadette said. "Got errands." She turned to me. "Was a joke," she said. "The shooting."

"Got it," I said.

She shook Diane's hand again. "It's a pleasure to meet you.

I think I may have met you previously. You did live here awhile, yes?"

"Good while," Diane said. "Years ago. But some of us run a pretty cloistered ship, if you know what I mean. So I didn't know a lot of neighbors."

Just then Leo shot down the stairs and out the door with the yellow tennis ball in his mouth, then stopped suddenly in the driveway and sat looking at Diane.

"He wants me to throw the ball," she said.

Bernadette turned and smiled at the dog, then started across to her car. "Don't keep this boy waiting," she said, tousling the curly hair on Leo's head.

Chantal's neighbor two doors down was found dead in his garage that day. He was Oscar Peterson, the guy I'd met the day Parker was found. He was sitting in his car with the door open and one foot out on the concrete of the garage floor. There were no signs of violence of any kind. People in the neighborhood said they heard gunshots, three gunshots, two in quick succession, then a third a beat or two later. But Peterson had not been shot. The cause of death was not apparent at all. When the people who said they'd heard gunshots were asked they said the sounds could have been fireworks. A neighbor of Peterson's said she saw someone riding away on a motorcycle earlier in the day. She didn't remember having seen the motorcycle previously. People speculated that it might have been a suicide, one of those carbon monoxide suicides, except the garage was open in front and the car wasn't running and the car door was open and there was no hose setup from the exhaust. Otherwise it was a great theory. Except for one neighbor who said that the killer could have completed the killing with the car exhaust, binding Peterson in the car, running the car with the car closed and a hose attached, then unbinding Peterson and withdrawing the hose apparatus before leaving on his motorcycle. All agreed this could have happened, but few thought it likely. Most of us figured heart problem.

News of Peterson's death spread quickly. I got a call from Bernadette and, a few minutes later, one from Jean Darling. I was on the phone with her when I heard the sirens coming down from Kemah. "Another dead guy," Darling said. "This time nobody knows anything." She repeated the outline Bernadette had given me moments before—the car, the garage. "You know him?"

"Only vaguely," I said. "I met him. He's two houses from Chantal."

"Right," Darling said. "Chantal's not home. We already checked."

"Did you call her?"

"Bernadette did."

"Anybody else hurt? Anybody see anything?"

"Guy on a bike," she said. "Yellow motorcycle, black helmet, jeans, plaid shirt. Like fifty dozen other guys on bikes."

"Have the rest of your people arrived?"

"Some. Everything's moving quick. I'm at his house now, but this one is not mine. Another guy, Larry Weiner, is taking it."

"OK," I said. "I'm going to find Chantal. Maybe I'll get her to come over."

"That'll be good," Jean Darling said. "There's a mess here. We're turning people away."

We hung up and I called Chantal, but before it even started ringing I had an incoming call from her. I canceled my call and took hers. "You heard, I guess?" I said.

"Yes," she said. "You all right?"

"Yeah, but apparently that part of the development is off-limits. You can come here."

"I'm at the restaurant, but I should be there in a while. Bernadette said they'd get it cleared away before tonight, that I'd be able to get in the house."

"Diane is here," I said, looking at Diane, who had come out of her room as the phone calls came in. "She's staying over a few days. She's down to see Cal and look at property."

"Fun," Chantal said. "Where's Jilly?"

"On her way, I expect. I haven't talked to her since earlier."

"She know Diane's there?"

"No, not yet. Where's your daughter?"

"Houston. She has that show."

"Is that now?"

"It's soon," Chantal said. "They have any idea about Peterson? She didn't say anything except he's dead."

"No. Seems natural. But it's a little strange," I said.

"I know the guy," Chantal said. "Nice. Clean cut, has an ex who comes to visit. Has three kids or something. They visit, too. Sometimes a week or a weekend. You see them at the pool. Mostly they come with the wife, I guess. I thought he was a lawyer, but it's not like he goes to work a lot, so maybe he's living on investments."

"I met him," I said. "But he's over there, so I know nothing."

"You'd have to go outside, all the way outside," she said. "How is it with Diane? Is she right there in the room?"

"Yes. Of course. It's fine, I understand. I need to call Morgan and tell her we're all OK so she doesn't see something on the local news."

"All right," Chantal said. "I'll call when I'm leaving."

"Talk to you then."

I waved the phone at Diane, who was, by now, sitting on the sofa with Leo, combing his ears. "I gotta call Morgan," I said. "Be with you in a minute. You're getting this whole story, yes?"

"Somebody died across the way," she said, waving in the wrong direction.

"Up here," I said, pointing in the right direction. "Up at this end. Not very close to here, but two houses from Chantal. That was her."

"Got that," she said. She held Leo's ears at their base so when the comb hit tangles she wasn't yanking the ear. She looked like she was doing a great job and he looked like he appreciated it.

I called Morgan, got her voice mail, left a message saying

there was another death but not to worry. After I said it I realized I hadn't talked to Jilly and I really didn't have a clue where she was. I'd expected her back right after lunch.

So I called Jilly and got her voice mail and left the message again.

Then I put the phone down on the kitchen counter and went out on the deck to see if I could see anything down toward Chantal's house, but I couldn't see much through the trees and whatnot. Police cars, lights flicking around the place from police cars, but that was it.

Diane followed me out to the deck with Leo in tow. She sat down. He jumped into her lap. "I always thought this was a nice place," she said. "But I think I maybe won't look at those condos she was talking about."

"Whatever," I said. "Stuff happens."

She changed ears but kept on combing.

"We had a guy up the other way who was supposed to be a dealer," I said. "He had lots of friends who used to come visit him for very short periods of time, like minutes. He would always meet them outside, in their cars. His aunt owned the place and he lived with her. At least that's what Parker told me. Then some neighbors complained, and then there were cops around, and then the kid wasn't there for a while, I mean, like a couple years."

"I remember the drug dealer," she said.

"That's right," I said. "You were in residence."

"Yup," she said. "I waved at that guy all the time when he was hanging around outside. A friendly wave. Neighborly."

“That’s the don’t-shoot-me wave, yes?” I said. “I can’t believe I forgot you were here then.”

“I didn’t want to interrupt you.” She finished the second ear and hugged Leo, rocked him in her arms. “We don’t like to interrupt, do we, Leo?”

“You want to take him out for a walk or something?” I asked.

“Maybe in a minute,” she said. “Who’s coming now? Jilly, the woman Chantal, is that it? Morgan will probably stay up in Houston? Your Bernadette, who could show up at any minute. That woman cop you were talking to? Who was that?”

“Her name is Jean Darling,” I said. “Detective Jean Darling.”

Diane pursed her lips too dramatically. “You got a lot of women around here, don’t you? You got practically a bevy of women.”

She was right. It wasn’t lost on me that I had mostly women friends. On the other hand, I didn’t really want a lot of men friends. Too much trouble. Always huffing and puffing, this way and that, control issues, roosters strutting around, including me, of course. I was content, maybe more than content, to stay out of the barnyard.

“It’s true,” I said to Diane. “A large group of people or things of a particular kind. Exactly what I like.”

## 27

# A BAD NIGHT

Ella Maria Parker fooled everyone and returned shortly after we got the letter declaring her innocence in the matter of her husband's death. She arrived in Kemah at Forgetful Bay with two guests, whom she introduced as members of her family. One was a woman confined to a wheelchair with a broken ankle, which she reported had been recently repaired through several surgeries during the last of which a plate had been inserted into her ankle, screwed directly into the bone. She invited all comers to "feel the plate" in her ankle at every opportunity. This was Ella's sister Sig, short for Signe, which was said to be a French name that the sister had gotten by virtue of her father's fascination with French New Wave cinema. The other traveler was Peter Rohe, a former television commentator for Velocity TV, who was only to be with us for a very short time given his demanding overseas schedule.

"I met Peter in New York," Mrs. Parker said to us as we gathered at Bernadette's condo to commemorate her homecoming. This was a command performance arranged by Bernadette in an effort to prevent any appearance of HOA complicity in the sub rosa sentiment said to exist against Mrs. Parker's return. Present were myself, Chantal, Detective Jean Darling, Jilly, Bruce and Roberta Spores, assorted others.

Diane had, by this time and after more than a few days at my place, removed herself to a local residence hotel called the Candlewood Suites, which she found quite comfortable, having a suite of two rooms on the first floor, allowing easy egress and ingress to attend Leo's needs, such as they were. She had looked at two condominiums in Forgetful Bay and found both "possible," though she was not ready to commit to either and was still looking at real estate with her broker.

"And how was the Alaskan portion of your trip?" Roberta Spores inquired. "Was it as beautiful as it is on television? We love Discovery and Nat Geo, don't we, Bruce?"

"We do," he said. "We are closet Alaskans."

"It was very pretty and very sad," Mrs. Parker said. "I could not forget the loss of my beautiful husband, Duncan. I wept in my cabin."

"This is true," stated her sister Sig. "I was with her much of the time and she wept constantly. Never have I seen Ella Maria weep so much."

"We're so sorry," Bernadette said. "It is wretched what happened to Duncan. Everyone thought he was looking forward to retaking his post as president of the HOA."

"I know he was," Mrs. Parker said.

I started to ask why he'd given up the post, but then realized I had misplaced a data point, the suggestion of misconduct with the dancer Olive Mars, and I realized this line of conversation would lead nowhere anyone wanted to go, so I coughed instead of speaking, covering my mouth with a napkin I had picked up off the table where Bernadette had laid out the chocolate chip cookies. The cookies were very tasty, and when I recovered I commented in that regard. "The cookies are excellent, Bernadette. Are these from the Toll House recipe?"

"McDonald's," she said. "Surprising good, yes? McDonald's sells three for a dollar, two for a dollar if you're in a bigger city. Or maybe it's a franchise option. Anyway, here it's three." She picked up the plate of cookies and passed it around to the guests. I took another, but I was not the only one.

"We had another death in your absence," Jean Darling said, earning herself a wicked look from Bernadette.

"Another?" Sig said, rolling closer to the table to see what treats remained.

"Mr. Peterson, Oscar Peterson, was, uh"—and here Jean seemed to realize the difficulty; she stopped right there in the middle of her sentence, paused, and then continued—"well, it doesn't matter here today. We're so glad you are back, and please, if I can help you in any way, you can count on me. I live here and I'm available at the station or here at any time."

"What happened to Mr. Peterson?" Sig said.

Bernadette shook her head. "I don't think the police have refined their investigation yet."

"So it was not natural causes?" Sig said.

"Was it a shooting?" Mrs. Parker said. I was surprised by

the way she asked, it was casual, she was eating a cookie at the time, chewing, and she asked the question as if it had no particular emotional connotation for her, no connection.

"No," Bernadette said. "No evidence of shooting."

As I remembered Duncan Parker's description I spent a good deal of my nontalking time eyeing the widow. She was, indeed, overlarge. She was tall like he said, but she must have slimmed down on her trip, because she didn't look particularly overweight. She wasn't model thin, but she fit in her clothes, wore heels in spite of her height, and was altogether striking. Perhaps he had exaggerated the girth of her. I had a hard time imagining her and Duncan Parker as a couple because she seemed very much a nonmarine wife, a striking woman who would have, perhaps owing to her size, an easy go of it in the matter of a companion. Parker was a smallish man, five foot seven, maybe eight, and kind of ordinary, whereas Ella Maria was anything but, what might be called, in the lexicon, an exotic.

"I think we need to meet Diane, don't we?" Chantal said to me.

We weren't meeting Diane, but it was our prearranged exit line, so we shook hands, nodded, wished all the best, and said good-bye, taking Jilly with us for the imaginary meeting. On the walk back to the condo, Jilly said, "Man, that thing is huge."

"I wouldn't kick her out of bed," Chantal said.

"You people," I said. "She seems pleasant and attractive."

"I liked her, too," Jilly said. "And her sister was something, wasn't she?"

"Like what?" Chantal said.

"Abnormal, I guess. She sure was interested in the eats."

"Those cookies," I said.

"The Peterson deal was awkward," Jilly said.

"She handled it well," Chantal said. "I think she killed her husband, though. That's all I could think about. Her shooting him in the face. In the head. Where was he shot, anyway?"

"Forehead, I think," I said. "Or temple. One of the obvious suicide spots."

"Mouth would be one," Jilly said. She was kicking a half-size black-and-white soccer ball we happened upon in the green space we were crossing.

"It was twenty-two caliber, wasn't it?" Chantal said. "I don't think you use those in your mouth for suicide. Have to shoot the brain."

"That would be a brain shot, wouldn't it?" Jilly said. "Shooting upward through the mouth?" She put her finger in her mouth to illustrate. "Did you look this up or something?"

"No," Chantal said. "I'm probably wrong."

At the house Jilly said she was taking a shower and disappeared into her room. Chantal and I took up spots in the living room and clicked on the big flat-screen television. She changed some channels and I watched the screen and read the closed captions I always had on. After a few minutes of this, Chantal gave up the remote.

"I had a thing with Peterson," she said, her voice chalky. "Long time ago now. Well, a year and a half, nearly."

"Really," I said. I looked at her and she was staring at the screen, or in the direction of the screen. A vacant stare. Like she was hypnotized.

"We started up one day. He was walking, I was outside. We talked, hit it off, went in for a water, had a drink instead. Was easy after that. We went with it. Kept going, weeks, months. I met the wife, their kids. I thought she'd snap to it, but that didn't matter, somehow. He was a lovely guy. Gentle, kind, thoughtful. It was sexual but more than that, a privacy that we shared, a hidden world, it was like we both let it all go at the same time. I felt like we might eventually be together, so it was storybook—you never expect it and then it drops in your lap. Hadn't happened before, not husbands, lovers, nobody. And we didn't talk about it. We sailed along, secret meetings, he'd come to the restaurant, we'd meet at the house, wherever."

She stopped there. The room was cold, as if someone had turned the air-conditioning down an extra ten degrees. Chantal reached in her purse and brought out a pack of cigarettes.

"Do you mind?" she said. "Just this once?"

I waved OK.

She lit the cigarette and took a hefty drag, let it roll slowly out between her lips. "Don't be afraid of women, Wallace. Women are not poison."

"So how did it end?" I said.

"Did I say it ended?" Chantal said.

"Oh," I said. "Sorry. I assumed."

She laughed. "I'm kidding you. It did end, and badly. But

that's another story." She scooted to the edge of her chair, sat there, and slipped her feet into her heels. "What are we doing for dinner? Let's take everybody. Is Morgan coming down?"

"Not today," I said.

"Let's drive somewhere," she said. "Galveston. Let's go see if John's Oyster Resort is still there. See if that mouse is still running around. What do you say?"

I knew better, but I said yes.

I squared it with Jilly, who didn't seem to think it was a big deal, at least until I invited her to come along. Then she made a face and shook her head. "Another time," she said.

So Chantal and I headed for Galveston. The night was balmy, a sweet breeze signaling a shift in the weather, the scent of the salt water carried in the air, the small lights along the coast highway and others reflected in the water, behind us the moon, up in the southeast and moving fast. I asked Chantal to tell me about Peterson. At first she shrugged, waggled her free hand—she was driving—then she said, "It's always complicated, isn't it? Two random people shuffled together. What chance have you got? Everything is so unlikely, and yet you get enmeshed. Options disappear. You're in a UFO beam that renders you helpless."

I made an otherworldly noise.

"Sorry," she said. "Anyway, that was me. He was perhaps less taken by the romance. And lost interest from there."

"I hear that," I said.

"Yeah," Chantal said. "Sometimes you live with it, sometimes you find alternatives. You could make a list—departure, withdrawal, punishment, violence, cruelty, replacement."

"You do, don't you?" I said. "Every time."

"Yeah," she said. "It's best to simply detach the head of the offending element, a clean, brutal cut. Then it's over and repair begins. The wound is cauterized."

"Perfect," I said, but I wasn't thrilled with the conversation and I started to say that, then figured she was already feeling bad so I'd let it go. Her reaction to Peterson's passing surprised me. Where she'd remained apart from things at Forgetful Bay, this time she was hooked. That said everything. I decided to change the subject.

"Anything else going on? Restaurant OK?" It was a poor effort, but I had hope.

"Nothing," she said, staring straight out the windshield. "Nothing much."

"You know John's Oyster Resort isn't there anymore, don't you?"

"Sure," she said. "I wanted to drive awhile. You eager to get back?"

"Not immediately," I said. "We could stop at your place if you want."

"Tinker's there," she said. "Came back yesterday."

"How did the exhibit go?"

"She seemed disappointed," Chantal said. "She added a bunch of stuff to her piece, both in the video and in the physical presentation. She told me she picked up things she found in the neighborhood and dumped them in her space. Things like tree limbs, garbage, cardboard boxes—for some reason she's in love with cardboard boxes."

"Cardboard has a great smell," I said. "I like the crisp new boxes, ones that have never been used."

"You and Tinker ought to get together," Chantal said. "So she dragged all this crap into the gallery and I asked her how do you re-create that, like if somebody wanted it? And she said, you don't, you make something similar. So I asked her what happens when she dies? What happens then? She said there would be photographs of the different states of the work, plus videos, texts describing the process, and so on and so on. It's an idea, but as soon as somebody offers to buy something it changes completely."

"Becomes commerce," I said. "I've seen that before."

"She wants it to be changing all the time, out of control."

"I know the feeling," I said. "But some of the extremes don't work. Who was that guy a hundred years ago who cut his penis off? That wasn't a good move."

"That's an urban legend," she said.

"No, I think it was real," I said. "We can Google it, if you want. I could do it now."

"Forget it," she said. "What's one penis more or less?"

"Right you are," I said. "So, you want to stop by and see her?"

"Not really," she said. "Speaking of the severed penis, did you hear about the ref?"

"What ref?" I said.

"This referee got in a fight with a soccer player he was

throwing out of a game and the fight escalated and the referee eventually stabbed the guy, so the player was taken to the hospital and died en route, and meanwhile the game was still going on and the crowd found out the player died and they rushed the field and killed the referee and that's not enough, apparently, so they quartered him, cut him limb from limb, and decapitated him, and stuck his head on a stake in the middle of the field."

"Hail Mary," I said. "Where'd you get that?"

"Tinker. She collects stories like that. She's done it for years. Any story that's grotesque or full of gore she saves for her artworks. She used to know this other girl, named Jen something, who did it, and she picked it up. I guess she wants to have the work reflect the extremes of the world we're stuck with these days. Sometimes I wonder about her."

"Extreme gawker," I said.

"Who isn't?" Chantal said. "Watch TV news much?"

"I suppose," I said.

We rode in silence for a while, the sound of the air whizzing by the car, the motor, the tires buzzing on the highway, the cars passing us going the other direction, trucks, echoes off bridges and overpasses, a small plane, big horns from the water. I got the feeling that I wasn't so comfortable anymore. I was aware of it not as the discomfort but as the awareness of the discomfort, and that it was happening with Chantal, whom I'd been fond of so quickly, and then afraid of. I still liked her, but now things were sputtering, like we were being ejected on different paths from target material due to bombardment of the target by energetic particles—going off the rails—and there was no stopping it. It wasn't a onetime thing, either, not a bad night, but something larger, something about our whole act. The best thing to do, I figured, was to get away from it, see if this particular minute, this evening, this drift, would blow over, and see if we could get back to normal at another time, a day later, a week.

"I think we ought to head home," I said. "I'm getting winded here." I waved out the car window so she'd know I was making a phony joke about being buffeted by the wind.

She delivered the slightest of smiles, a twitch, really, that barely creased her face. She slowed the car.

# 28

# HOA

"I'M NOT sure what I can say to you tonight," Bernadette Loo said, opening the emergency meeting of the Forgetful Bay Homeowners' Association. "We've all been unnerved and saddened by recent events, and surprised, too. And confused, and even frightened, I dare say. We've had an appalling parade of unlikely events here in the last few months, and everyone is on edge. I don't have to rehearse these events today as I suspect they are uppermost in all of our minds. I have asked Detective Jean Darling, a member of our community and of the Kemah police force, to bring us up-to-date on the situation in which we find ourselves. Then I hope we will take questions and try to lay all the cards on the table. With that, let me turn the meeting over to Jean."

Jean Darling rose from her seat in the first row of folding chairs and turned to address the group. As she did, there was some commotion in the back of the room. When I turned to look I saw Hilton Bagbee on the floor with two people on their knees alongside him. There was shouting. "Call 911," somebody said. The guys down on the floor were yanking at his shirt, waving at other people gathering around. "It's his heart," someone shouted. "Spread out, spread out."

Everyone in the room was by then paying attention to Hilton in the back of the place. Jean and Bernadette Loo were both heading back there, as was Bruce, and some people were dragging chairs out of the way, scraping them on the floor, making a racket the way metal folding chairs will when banged into one another.

"Is he OK?" Bernadette shouted as she pushed through the crowd.

"He's not breathing," someone replied.

A guy who looked like a jock leaped into the melee and pushed a woman aside and started mouth to mouth. It was as if there were an explosion at the back of the place, and every sound in there echoed like crazy, ricocheting around the room.

Jean Darling pushed open the front doors of the clubhouse and shouted, "Everybody out. Let's get out of the way, please. Outside! Please!" She started pulling on people, ushering them toward the door. In the rush several others in the room fell to the floor and in the effort to get out were scuttling along like crabs. Bernadette Loo had been pushed out of the way and she was try to funnel bodies toward the front. People were grabbing their stuff and screaming for one another to move. The thing was pandemonium. Jilly and I both tripped on a folding chair and landed on the floor.

"You OK?" she said.

"Go," I said.

Bruce and Roberta had been sitting next to us, but now I couldn't find them in the crowd as we went for the doors. A few people were back with Hilton, and the rest were rushing out. Jean got rocked by a heavyset woman I didn't recognize, and went down for a second in the doorway, but was up quickly and was torqued around, pushing people past her.

"I'm OK," Jean said. "Get out, get out." She was reaching for her radio, which had fallen a little ways into the room. I scooted the radio toward her and returned to Bernadette, who was behind me by now.

"Is he all right?" I said.

"Don't know. Can't tell anything."

A chubby kid with lots of hair was on the floor between two rows of chairs that were still more or less upright. "Who's this?" I said to Bernadette, tugging her arm and pointing to the guy.

"Nasser," she said. "Lionel Nasser. He's a teacher."

The place was clearing. I went through the two rows shoving the chairs out of the way and didn't have to get too close to Nasser to see that he was OK but had a nasty cut on the side of the head, lots of blood.

"You all right?" I said, grabbing at his shoulders.

"I hit the chair," he said. I was glad that was it and I didn't have to check for a pulse because I probably couldn't have felt a pulse if he'd had one. Helping him up I got blood for my trouble and wiped it on the back of his shirt.

"They're coming," somebody yelled, and I heard a siren in the distance.

"Is Bernadette OK?" Jean said, her voice raspy.

"She's fine," I said. I looked around the room and almost everyone was gone. "Everybody's out, looks like, except the guys working him." I waved toward the back of the room. "You ready to go?"

"Yeah," she said. "I think so." She started to go out and tripped over something, and I tried to help but seemed to be in the way. She shook me off and got to her feet. She was wobbly.

"Bernadette," she said.

She was right alongside us, heading out. "We're OK," Bernadette said. People outside the doorway were bunched in little groups.

Cops and EMTs arrived. People were gathered in the circular drive, talking, smoking, lots of gestures and exclamations.

There was a deep rut across the lawn where a motorcycle had torn up the grass between the pool gate and the drive. The emergency people were inside pretty quick.

Jean Darling was limping around talking to other cops. Bernadette was sitting on the bench in front of the clubhouse talking to Jim and Elizabeth Sims, two other longtime homeowners I'd met recently. Jilly was there with Bruce and Roberta.

"So, is he all right?" I said.

"I think he wasn't breathing," Roberta said. "He fell like a shot."

"That's what I thought, too," Bruce said.

"I couldn't tell. That big guy was doing cardio," I said.

"That was a less than orderly exit," Roberta said.

"Was Chantal inside?" Bruce said. "I didn't see her."

"No, I don't think so," I said.

Bruce said, "People are dropping like flies."

"Bruce," his wife said.

"What about Parker's wife?" Bruce said. "Where is she, anyway? What happened to her?"

"Didn't see her," I said. "She's back, but I didn't see her tonight."

"Bernadette should put it in the newsletter," Roberta said. "If she wants to update us, do it there. Or online. I'm not coming to another meeting."

"Me neither," Bruce said.

The medical people came trotting out of the clubhouse with Hilton on a stretcher and slammed him into the back of the ambulance and sped off.

I circled the drive toward where Jean Darling was talking to Bernadette and a woman I didn't know.

"Rosa Lima," Bernadette said, pointing to the woman.

I nodded hello. "How's Hilton? What did they say? Anything?"

"I was inside a minute. It's not good," she said. "I guess that's obvious."

"Not good at all," Rosa said. She had an accent. It wasn't as overdone as an overripe TV actress's, but it was there. And she had the look, too. A certain looseness about her shirt. She looked like she could use some bananas on her head.

"You guys OK?" I asked, speaking to Jean and Bernadette at the same time.

They said "Yes" simultaneously.

Rosa said she'd heard about me.

"Oh?" I said.

*"The Real Housewives of Forgetful Bay,"* she said, dropping her shoulders.

Bernadette made a face, then said, "I didn't see this coming. Hilton, I mean. He's older, but I thought he was healthy."

"We're all older," Jean said. "A run of bad luck."

"Some run," I said.

"People die," Rosa said. "I mean, they do. I've lived in places where people died. When I was a kid people died in the neighborhood. One year three or four people died on our street and the next one over. People my parents knew." She fluffed up her hair, sort of shaking it behind her head. "Really you've only had a couple of people die here, and one was probably suicide, so that doesn't count."

"Does too," Jean said. "Just as dead."

"What about Peterson," Bernadette said. "That's the scary one."

"A lot of times when people die you don't know them," Rosa said. "They live down the street and they die, and it all gets taken care of and you really don't take much notice of it. Somebody will tell you and you might send a card."

"Miss Buzzkill," Bernadette said.

"I've seen lots of this sort of thing," Rosa said. "Some places there are many more troubles."

It was kind of quiet out there in front of the clubhouse. The cop cars were running, but you couldn't really hear the engines, and the lights were silent as they flickered around, strafing the clubhouse and the other buildings nearby and some of the residents. I heard police radios, but they were like background. The whole scene sounded like a small party with people talking, excited voices rising and falling. It was peculiar, even a little festive, as if we were gathered in the garden of someone's nice home in the glow of an early summer evening. A lawn party.

# 29

# LOCKUP

Cal looked silly in the orange jumpsuit. His slip-on sneakers were three sizes too big, a thing that looked to be typical of all the sneakers on all the inmates we saw in the cells that lined the waiting area of the Pilgrim County Correctional Center where Cal was being held in preparation for transfer to one of the state farm units. Diane had insisted that I join her for a visit with Cal, scheduled to last at least fifteen minutes and maybe more if the guards were feeling generous. The fact was I'd never set foot inside a county jail before, though I'd seen my share of police stations from the inside, and the PCCC was not a bright spot in my ideal tour of administrative wonders. It was surrounded by a pair of fifteen-foot chain-link fences thirty feet apart, both of which were topped with comically unappealing razor wire. Both fences were electrified, we were told. There were parking lots outside the fences and inside the fences, but we didn't get to go inside in the car, so we had a healthy walk to a ramp that led up to the entrance to the facility. Inside, there were exhibits, as if it were a state welcome center. There were maps of outlaw territories and historical photographs of famous outlaws and good-for-nothing low-down scoundrels—some hanging from makeshift gallows in these pictures, some standing on similar gallows with thick ropes around their necks and expressions of dissatisfaction on their dirty faces, some leaning in proud nonchalance against the doorways of old taverns and what may have been whorehouses. There were airport-style racks of chairs around, high windows that showed only sky and the cutthroat wire, and a large glassed-in section at the back behind which were dozens of uniformed individuals dealing with six lines of raggedy people at six little barred windows such as you might have found in a busy train station years ago.

We took our turn in one of the lines, and after handing over identification and getting in return photo passes, we were escorted down a stairway behind an unmarked door to a level belowground, where there was another, smaller waiting area lined with holding cells that were fitted with electric doors with keypads and big sheets of double-pane chicken-wire glass, in which cells were what I took to be criminals awaiting disposition.

In this smaller waiting area we got in a new, shorter line, presented our materials again, and waited for an officer to fetch us and take us down a long, slightly sloping hall to a tiny room in which sat Cal, looking forlorn. We were well and truly underground by now, and we were ushered into the adjacent room, equally tiny, and settled at a narrow table pushed up against an opening into Cal's room. This being an old and temporary facility, there was an actual grille between the rooms, and we could talk to each other without the telephones you always see in prison-visit scenes on TV. There were guards in both rooms.

"You look great," Diane said. "Prison suits you."

"Gee, thanks, doll," he said. "I've got that sun-don't-shine look." He raised a hand and pointed at me. "Hello, Wallace."

"Hey," I said. "How is it so far?"

"It's been worse," he said. "They're transferring me out west is what I hear, I got no idea why. I can tell you this is no place for an innocent man."

"I expect not," I said, figuring whatever he said I was going to go along with.

"So what's doing out in the big wide world?" Cal said.

"Seems like people are dying willy-nilly at Wallace's fancy-pants resort community," Diane said. "Mr. Oscar Peterson, no relation, died last week of unknown causes. In his car in his garage. Coroner has not provided a cause of death."

"Fewer than a half-dozen fatalities," I said. "Counting car crashes."

"Not including Dan," she said. Then, to Cal, "Someone collapsed there last week, causing more yammering."

"She could be held on suspicion of yammering," I said to Cal.

"Ha," he said. "He's a funny guy, ain't?"

"Not," Diane said.

"You guys should take it easy," Cal said. "I'm the one in jail here."

He had a point. Our nerves weren't helping him. I wasn't bent on helping, but I didn't want to pile on. He was having a hard-enough time, even if he had messed up more often than anyone ought to be allowed. I signaled the guard asking him to let me out of the room. "I want to give them some time," I said, drawing a thumb over my shoulder at Diane and Cal. "That OK?"

The guard got the door for me. "Stay right out here, will you?" Then, as he closed the door with me in the hall, he said something I couldn't hear into the radio attached to his shoulder, to his epaulet. In a minute another guard appeared and stationed himself across the hall from me.

"How you doing?" I said.

"Fine," he said. "You related to this one?" He leaned his head toward Cal's room.

"Not hardly," I said. "She's my ex. For some reason she's seeing him, or was. I don't know what the deal is. I'm along for the ride."

"Huh," he said. "Your ex. That's something."

"I guess it is. We were married ten years, now divorced. The guy was married to this other woman I know, who I used to work with."

"Threesome, huh?" He grinned. Joke.

"If you believe in time travel," I said. "You been here long?"

"Twenty years, give or take."

"So you've seen it all."

"Pretty much. It's all reruns after the first couple years."

"I'd go out of my skull," I said.

"You got an iPhone?" he said.

"Yes," I said, reaching for it, then remembering I'd put it in the basket with my other things upstairs. "Why?"

"Thinking of getting one," he said.

"They're good," I said. "I've had one since the fours."

"Trouble innovating," he said. "Apple. That's what I hear."

"You never can tell what they've got up their sleeve," I said.

"Maybe. No flies on Samsung, though."

The conversation went on like this, barely keeping its head above water. I was watching Diane and Cal chatting in the two glass rooms. They seemed to be having a good time. I had let Diane hook me into coming. It was like she wanted me to see this scene, her and Cal in the prison, me out of earshot. I was hoping she'd hurry up, but she was taking her sweet time, and the head guard, the one who had let me out of the room, didn't press her.

"Is there a time limit on this visit?" I asked my guy in the hall.

"Up to Jerry," he said. "I've seen 'em go hours."

"No shit?"

"Days," he said. "Jerry's very empathetic."

The guy smirked and then I got it. I settled down on the floor and shut my trap.

* * *

When Diane was done we drove to the Chinese place in Kemah that was about to go out of business because it refused to do a buffet, which, as everybody knows, is the only way to make money on a Chinese restaurant in Kemah. The owners were a couple who had come from China, he from the north, she the south, and they'd been running this restaurant outside town for a half-dozen years. At first they'd done a lunch buffet and a dinner buffet, but they dropped the dinner buffet because the woman, who had taken the name Betty, said that the buffet was wasteful and that they ended every night throwing away too much food. It was profitable, but wasteful. That was her line in the sand. Thereafter they did a lunch buffet for a time, but eventually gave that up, too, and for the same reason. We were friendly because Jilly and Morgan and I were constant customers at Mandarin House. Betty and George—that was the husband's American name—invited us to all their Chinese New Year celebrations, where the food wasn't American Chinese but something a lot more Chinese. Maybe too authentic for crackers like us. Still, we went each year, picked around the edges of some strange and occasionally offensive food, encouraged everyone there, being mostly their Chinese friends, to make fun of us, and in that way navigated the event and kept up our part in the friendship. We did try, but Anthony Bourdain we weren't.

So after the trip to the prison Diane wanted to meet

Morgan and Jilly at Mandarin House, and we did that, took our usual round table in the back corner of the place and tried to stare down the menus, which at least three of us knew by heart. Finally Diane said, "Cal's doing OK in there."

She turned to me for confirmation, and I nodded and said, "Yeah, he seemed good. I mean, within the prospects available to him. I got kicked out of the room so the two of them could, you know, talk."

"There wasn't a need," Diane said. "I thought you wanted out."

"I was uncomfortable," I said. "It felt crowded in there. Besides, I had a nice talk with a monosyllabic guard."

"No hill for a stepper," Jilly said.

"I wanted to get cozy with him," I said

"Cal seems to have made his peace with the plea deal, the sentence, the whole thing," Diane said. "He's one hundred percent with the program. He even wrote a letter to the girl apologizing and all that."

"Oh, ick!" Jilly said. "Double ick!"

"And that's just for starters," Morgan said. "I knew that girl, that girl was a friend of mine."

"Girl was a dirty leg, pardon my French," Diane said. "That's what she was."

"Whoa!" Morgan said. "It's the Wayback Machine. Nineteen and fifty-eight."

"I'm rehabbing it," Diane said.

"How long you figure he'll do?" I asked. In the car she'd

said two years, tops. But she wanted to talk about Cal at dinner, so I was helping out.

"He got three years. Some things the lawyer said sounded like that was too much, other things like it was a bargain. I think they make half this stuff up as they go along."

"That sounds right," Jilly said. "No news there."

"She's a little bit cynical in her old age," I said, smoothing the stained red tablecloth on my part of the table. It was cotton and frayed, but friendly. "Anyway, I thought he was going to do less than two?"

"That's the hope," Diane said. "But we don't know for sure. They have to do lots of meetings and petitions and reviews and all kinds of crap. It'll help if the victim writes something undiscouraging. Sometimes they come to all the meetings and cause a ruckus."

"Those damn victims," Morgan said. She had a light touch with the line, shaking her head with a confused expression on her face. She was good at that.

"I'd rather have him out than not," Diane said.

I looked at Jilly and she was silent on the point. She looked back but wasn't giving anything away.

"You really don't want anybody to spend time in jail if they don't absolutely have to," I said. Then I stopped and said, "Sorry. Possessed by Anderson Cooper. Please disregard this message."

"Cal's all settled in there," Diane said. "It sounds crazy, but he's looking forward to it. Like going on a retreat, a religious thing. Go to the mountains, sit by a stream, reflect."

"That would be better," Morgan said. "By a stream."

"I agree," Jilly said, finally. "I married him once."

Betty brought out a plate of steamed dumplings and a set of plastic appetizer plates, small and oval, and we passed the dumplings around and ordered while we were doing it. Betty was pleasant and funny, repeating our orders in her broken English, swatting Morgan on the shoulder and laughing when Morgan answered some question Betty asked in the same broken English.

"You make fun," Betty said. "You come China, try speak. You leave Betty alone. I do fine. You want pancake?"

Morgan had ordered *moo shu* pork and did want pancake and said as much, then turned to me. "So what is latest in Land of Walking Dead?"

"You already know everything," I said.

"Give us a rundown," she said.

"Oscar Peterson died. They think it was natural. Parker is ongoing. Hilton Bagbee, heart attack. Parker's wife returned. Someone said she was living at Candlewood."

"What about Miss Chantal?"

"Nothing," I said. "The detective, Jean Darling, thinks it was a spoof."

"Art violence," Jilly said.

"Not sure Jean gets that particular aspect," I said.

"What aspect?" Diane said.

"The art aspect. The special blue and all that."

"Oh, yawn," Morgan said. "Double yawn."

"Now, children," Diane said.

The food arrived and we began to eat. There was less talk during the meal. It was as if everyone at the table was suddenly pouting, or maybe we all got tired at the same moment. I was worried about Diane and what she was going to do with Cal in prison. I was hoping she'd go back east. With Cal tied up in Texas that did not seem likely.

# 30

# CAR WASH

I TOLD Jilly and Morgan I'd meet them later at the condo, dropped Diane at her hotel, and drove down the coast to see Chantal. It was still light out, after seven, and the light was speeding up, taking its bows, and traffic was thin as usual. All the seabirds were flying back where they'd come from earlier in the day. What I thought was that things were a little out of whack. The people I wanted to see were heading to the house and I was going south to see Chantal, drawn there by—what? Something I'd started and was caught in—expectations, mine and hers, hopes, the same pair—and I knew way too little about her, and what I did know, or thought I knew, wasn't choice. Chantal was something the cat dragged in, as my mother used to say. A cipher, not a zero but a mystery. A woman I might have been interested in if we'd met thirty years ago, with a whole life out in front of me and the time to do anything, the time to work on it, the time to invest in a prospect, to play a thing out, to see what might come. But now all that seemed a little silly, something from a fairy tale, a fantasy that we grow up with, that we have something enough and time, whatever that line is. World. And here I was losing another night on this woman I had been charmed by some weeks before, but for whom the interest had faded. I suddenly felt real distaste for her. She scared me, depressed me. Or maybe the depression was just mine, a wave of it swept over me. That used to happen all the time, about anything, coming out of nowhere. Overtaking me, heavy on my shoulders, at the neck, a weight. I let the car slow down, then pulled off to the side of the road shy of an elaborate combination gas station, truck stop, and restaurant, and sat there for some time with the engine idling. I watched the sunset off in the west, which was in all ways extraordinary, exquisite, a remarkable panoramic canvas rendered with utmost delicacy, and yet it seemed ordinary to me, another pretty sky, a showy repetition of yesterday, a duplicate due tomorrow. I went into the glove compartment and got my pills. Took a couple, shook the bottle to gauge how many were left. Plenty. I didn't seem to have the strength to steer the car, to turn it around and head back home, and now I didn't want to see Jilly and Morgan, either, not feeling the way I was feeling. I didn't want to see anyone I could think of, anyone I knew. I felt a little sick to my stomach, felt pressed into the car, my shoulder aching, my hands resting on the edges of the seat. Anywhere but where I was, I thought, I would prefer to be. Anybody that I wasn't, I would prefer. To be. The hissing in my ears grew louder the more I listened to it. A whistling, a wire, a sizzle. I knew I wasn't going to see Chantal after all. Maybe another day. And not Jilly and not Morgan, and surely not Diane, and not Jean Darling or Bernadette, or Bruce and Roberta, and not Oscar Peterson, not Duncan Parker, or Mrs. Parker. Not the gay neighbors or the new neighbors. Not my first wife, God rest her soul. Not my mother or father or my brother Raleigh, whom I kept alive in my heart but who was, in fact, long, long gone. I wanted to weep about all this, I thought that would be fitting, but my eyes wouldn't cooperate, they were desert dry, arid. I wanted a cat, a monkey, a pet of some sort, a companion dog, a bakery. Comfort. Relief. Rest. I put the car in gear and rolled forward on the side of the highway, slowly, then turned into the parking lot of Tommy King's Highway Oasis. I rolled through the parking lot to the car wash, which was a drive-through unit at one end with five additional wash-it-yourself bays. I stuck my credit card in the meter for the drive-through, punched up my desired wash, and pulled forward as instructed, shut my eyes while the water and the soap streamed over the car, sprayed and misted and sprayed again, and the soap curled on the windshield, and the great U-shaped arm of the wash swept back and forth alongside, around, over the car. And when the thing stopped, when the buzzer buzzed and the light came on and said DRIVE AHEAD, I did that, I drove ahead, circled around through an empty wash bay, and inserted my credit card in the meter again. I pulled forward. I waited for the rain.

# 31

# FLIGHT

DIANE CALLED. "She's in love with you," she said.

"What are you talking about?"

"Jilly," she said. "You really ought to do something about that, one way or the other."

"Where are you calling from?" I said. My phone said it was midnight and I was still in the car, in the car wash, where I'd been for the last three hours or more. I'd taken a good nap. It took me a minute, like it always does, to get my bearings. "You at the hotel?"

"Airport," she said. "Houston. I was going to leave without a word, but decided I needed to help you out with this problem. Did you see Chantal? I called the house and Morgan said you had not returned from Chantal-land."

"That's what she called it?"

"Word for word," Diane said. "I get the impression she's not too thrilled with your late-stage dalliance."

"What are you doing at the airport?"

"Returning to my snug harbor in the Northeast," she said. "I decided it was easier than coming back. We don't know where Cal's going to be anyway. One of his guys said he thought they'd send him out to Marfa, some special penitentiary out there for sex offenders. Apparently Cal is dead lucky he didn't get huge time."

"I wondered about that, the girl being, you know, a ten-year-old."

"Not funny," Diane said. "Anyway I grabbed a plane up east and I'll be gone before sunrise. Are you going to miss me?"

"I think so," I said.

"I'm serious about Jilly," she said.

"Don't be messing in my stuff," I said. "You are entitled to many things, but that isn't one of them."

"You are so sweet, Wallace. And I'm telling you what you already know. Jilly has hung on with you, kept you upright, washed, dried, and folded for these many years, way before you and I went south. You owe her, and more than that, you love her."

"You think?" I said. "Not your call anyway. And Jilly needs lots of room, lots of time. I don't see her pushing for consummation."

"Oh yeah, right. It's only what? Fifteen years you've been hanging out with her?"

"I'm not discussing this, Diane."

"So what? Are you with that dangerous chanteuse of yours?"

I looked around at Tommy King's Highway Oasis from my spot in the car wash and said, "Not hardly. I'm taking a rest at Tommy King's Highway Oasis and Car Wash. Been here since nine or nine-ish. Car is real clean and I've been sleeping."

"That a joke?"

"Nope. I had one of my spells. You may remember my spells."

"I do? Oh, you got sad. Sudden-onset melancholy."

"Whatever. Yes. I didn't want to see anybody, so I pulled into Tommy's place and then I washed the car maybe forty-nine dollars' worth, which would be seven times at seven dollars a pop—the Semi-Deluxe Detail Wash—and on the last go-round I must have fallen asleep. I would still be asleep save for your call."

"So here's what I think," Diane said. "I think you ought to ask Jilly to marry you, and you guys ought to move someplace new, away from Forgetful Bay. Didn't you go look at property in Florida?"

"How long before your plane takes off?" I asked.

"Hour and forty minutes. Why?"

"Are we going to talk the whole time? My job is to help you wait for the boarding call?"

"That's one way to look at it. Or you could say that we're old friends and former lovers, ex-husband and ex-wife, still close after all we've been through together, and I'm taking this opportunity to clue you in on your love life, about which you have not an inkling, as per usual."

"You are kind," I said. "I'll give you that. Especially in these later years."

"I try," she said. "We both do. Plus, I'm the only remaining wife in your stable at the present, may Lucy rest in peace, so I am assuming the duties."

"OK, got it. Will think about taking action per your prescription. Can you hang on about twenty minutes? I've got to pee."

"No fun for Wallace and Diane. Call me back, will you? If you get done before I take off."

"Love you, dear," I said.

"You, too," she said.

I went into Tommy King's Highway Oasis store and sought the key to the lavatory, which was freely given. Having concluded my business there in a timely fashion, I returned the key and purchased a three-dollar bag of peanut M&M's and mounted up, slipped the car back onto the highway headed north this time, and considered punching up Diane's number on the iPhone, which was, naturally, linked to the hands-free Harman Kardon twelve-speaker stereo system in the car, including four satellite tweeters. Then, instead of calling Diane, I turned on the radio and scanned the spectrum of stations available until I found something suitable for my mood and cranked that up to earsplitting and rocked all the way home. Van Morrison.

Jilly was on the couch when I arrived. She wore shorts and a little shirt. She was watching one of the Lisbeth Salander pictures, the one where she throws the gasoline on her father in the car and lights him up. "I think we need to watch these all over again," she said when I sat down next to her. She sighed, as if she felt a heavy responsibility that she did not particularly want to discharge.

"Why?" I said.

"They're all tied together and if you read the *Wikipedia* page the whole thing makes sense, but I never quite got the whole story before."

"I'm guessing that's not so important," I said.

"No? Why not?"

"It's more the fabric of the thing, the atmosphere, the climate, the mood, the character, the feel of it, this girl, against all, this wonderful girl, her extraordinary power, David and Goliath, the feel overall, the way everything feels is what's important."

"That's a pretty negative attitude toward narrative in film," she said.

"It's like *The Killing,*" I said. "It's all about the tiny stuff that goes on between the characters, the shadows, eyebrows, looks in the eyes. All that endless rain. Her face through a smeared car window. His voice coiling up an octave then fading when teasing her."

"Got it," she said.

I stared at the flat-screen TV. "This is great," I said. "I'd like to watch them again. They remind me of forties movies somehow."

"Forties?"

"Never mind," I said. "A previous time period. Is Morgan sleeping?"

"Think so."

"Is there anything to eat?"

"Peanut butter and ice cream," she said. "So how did things go with Chantal?"

I got up and headed for the kitchen. "Didn't see her," I said. "I stopped at a roadside place and took a nap."

"A nap? Since eight-thirty?"

"Don't ask," I said. "Then Diane called from the airport. She's headed back to Rhode Island."

"I thought she was coming back to join the force," Jilly said.

"Nope. She's waiting on Cal. Seems to have a thing for Cal. Strange as it may seem."

"More power to her," Jilly said. "I wish her well. He may have changed by now, anyway. When he was up here talking to me that time, that night? When you were out? He didn't scare me that much."

"Good to know," I said. I got the raisin bread out of the freezer and dropped two slices into the toaster, then fetched the chunky peanut butter, the Breyers chocolate ice cream, a knife, and a spoon and a bowl. All these I arranged on three sheets of Bounty paper towels on the countertop where the toaster was doing its job. I tapped the knife on the countertop, drumming unconvincingly. I was a drummer once but so bad at it I didn't deserve the name. Now I couldn't keep time with one hand, let alone two. And the feet.

"Quit that, will you?" Jilly said.

I stopped, the toasted bread popped up, I made my sandwich and put a half cup of ice cream into the bowl. I put away the ice cream and the peanut butter, wiped the knife and placed it carefully in the sink, slipped the spoon into the bowl of ice cream, and took my snack to the dining table, which was small, seated four, and Scandinavian. "Want to join me?" I said to Jilly.

"Sure," she said, and punched PAUSE on the remote, stopping the TV in its tracks.

"I wonder if you might want to go back to Florida?" I said. "Look for a place there."

"What? A vacation place? It's already a vacation right here, isn't it? You got water, boats, oysters, scenery, guys in Bermuda shorts everywhere you look."

"Just wondering," I said. "Don't get overwrought."

"I wouldn't mind," she said. "I don't know. Sure. If you want to. I'm the baggage here, you know?"

"Come on," I said. "You're more like the jewels of the Madonna."

"Oh yeah? Good to know. When did that happen?"

"Dunno," I said. "Long time ago."

"I don't remember an announcement on this point," Jilly said.

"It was truncated," I said.

"And then some," she said.

She was having a good time. I was wondering why I'd let years go by since the divorce without saying something. It wasn't only Diane's instruction, it was time, it was time going by faster than it could be counted. Diane was right. Something had to be said.

"I'm kind of attached to you, Jilly. Terminally. If that's OK with you. I mean, if you want to be, you know, terminally attached to. I don't know why you'd want to, but I'm not all that bad, I guess. You could do worse. There's Cal. He's an outlier. But maybe you'd rather hunt up a couple dozen guys your age."

"Sounds great," she said. "Clubbing, scouring date sites, posting on Craigslist, putting butt-naked pictures on all the better meet-a-man sites. Good idea. Did that all last week. Turns out I'm the runt and ugly duckling rolled into one and all those great guys won't touch me with a striped stick."

"I must have phrased that wrong."

"A little bit," she said.

"And I think you mean buck naked," I said.

We sat there for a minute regarding each other. It was a long minute. One of the longest. It kept on unraveling. After a while she picked up my sandwich and helped herself to a sizable bite. Then she put the sandwich back where she found it. "You think I would actually say *butt naked* in the real world?"

"Ah," I said. "I'm slipping."

"Do tell," she said, and she covered my hand with hers. Covered might overstate it.

"How about some ice cream?" I said, inching the bowl her way with my free hand.

"Why not?" she said. "You're going to discover the truth of

me sometime." And she gave up my hand and took the bowl and spoon and wolfed down what ice cream remained.

"Maybe we can talk more tomorrow," I said.

"Yes," she said, licking the spoon as she got up and headed for the kitchen, the bowl in tow. "Let's revisit this issue then. Meanwhile, I am going to retire secure in the knowledge that tomorrow will bring satisfactions beyond measure."

She came back to kiss me on the cheek. The lips were wet, soft and parted.

32

# TATTOOS

I TRIED Chantal but she didn't answer. I called again and got voice mail after two rings. That meant something. I'd seen it on a TV show. TV shows are always alerting us to things we don't want to know. Or maybe that's city life, and down in Kemah we make no distinction between voice mail after two rings or four rings.

In any case it was three A.M. and Chantal did not pick up so I left a message, invited her to call back when ready, and took myself to bed early for once.

Bernadette called the next morning and said she had to see me at once. I asked if we could meet later and she said no, that she wanted to meet right then. So I said fine and dressed and headed down the road to her place, which was one of the two-bedroom cottages on Smoky Lake.

Bernadette was not alone. Jean Darling was with her, and two men I didn't recognize who were introduced as police officers. All four of them were sitting in Bernadette's living room, somewhat uneasily it seemed to me. I said, "Is there some new crisis?"

"Peterson," Bernadette said. "It appears that he died naturally."

"The best way," I said

"Coroner says heart attack," Jean Darling said. "Not induced."

"You can induce a heart attack?" I said.

"Sure," Bernadette said. "It's all over the Internet. Full of ways. Potassium chloride, sodium gluconate—"

"Calcium gluconate," Jean said.

"And there are others," Bernadette said. "Air—like air bubbles in the bloodstream, that kind of thing. I saw that on TV."

"And many more," Jean said.

"What about Hilton?" I said.

"Do we have any reason to think it wasn't natural?" Bernadette asked. "He had a bad heart and it went."

"That's likely," one of the two cops said. The other one nodded agreement. This appeared to be their routine.

"The coroner is suspicious," Jean said. "But he's a flake."

"We were wondering about Chantal," Bernadette said, ignoring Jean. "The rumor we've heard is that she had a, well, a relationship with Peterson. Would you know anything about that?"

This seemed odd to me, but I didn't see any way to avoid reporting my conversation with Chantal. "I talked to her after he died," I said. "She seemed very upset. She indicated that they were close at one time. I wasn't clear on when. At least I'm not clear now."

"Why is that?" Jean Darling said.

"I don't remember the details. I was there as a sympathetic listener."

"Who didn't listen carefully?" she said.

"Right," I said. "She was feeling lousy, I was trying to comfort her, so that's what I was concentrating on, not what she was saying. I didn't take notes."

"He didn't take notes," Bernadette said to the two hulking policemen, who, I suddenly noticed, looked pretty much like the Blues Brothers—identical shoes, suits, shirts, ties, etc.

"What we've heard is they had a relationship and he broke it off recently," Jean said. "And that she was not happy about the breakup."

"She didn't seem angry. She seemed saddened, upset by his death," I said. "But you can ask her."

"Can't find her," Jean said. "She's not answering her phone, she's not at her condo, and they haven't seen her at the restaurant for a couple days."

"No kidding?" I said.

"You haven't seen her, either?" she said.

"No. I've called her, but no answer. Haven't talked to her or seen her."

"You went with your ex-wife to see someone in the prison last week?"

"Yes," I said. "Jilly's ex-husband Cal. He's in for—"

"We know," Jean said. "Do you know if Chantal had any

dealings with Duncan Parker? Didn't I ask you this once before?"

"Someone asked me," I said. "You or Bernadette. And no, I don't know about any connection to Parker."

"Or his wife?"

"She told me she'd seen the wife walking in the neighborhood, but not to talk to, I think."

They asked more questions, pointed questions about Chantal, also about Chantal's daughter, Tinker, who had been seen around the development recently, and I said I'd met the daughter and she seemed a little strange but not strange enough to cause alarm. In fact, I was defensive about Chantal and didn't want to add fuel to the fire, so I may have edited my answers to their questions more than I might have otherwise.

"She has a lot of tattoos, the daughter?"

"I wouldn't say a lot," I said. "But then I didn't see a lot of her. She has some tattoos in places that are ordinarily visible. Ankles, feet, hands, wrists, arms, shoulders, neck, even her face, I think she has one on her face. I don't mean she has tattoos on each of those, but those are the places I might have seen tattoos on her."

"Any others?"

"Not that I've seen, though I suspect there are others, yes."

"Would you say a lot?" Jean asked. "More than most people?"

"More than most," I said. "But people with tattoos tend to, you know, get more than other people."

"So she's a tattooed person," Jean said. "Not like a student who got one little tattoo one night after a party or something."

"That's correct," I said. "My memory is she has several tattoos. Maybe many tattoos. Maybe even large and elaborate ones. So what?"

"Well," Bernadette said. "Apparently one of the neighbors saw a tattooed girl."

"Tinker was staying at Chantal's house, right?"

"We know," Jean said.

"So that could be it," I said.

"It could be, yes," she said. "We have people looking into it."

"A lot of people down here have tattoos, a lot of women," I said. "I see them everywhere."

"I have a couple myself," Jean Darling said.

"Well, there you go," I said. "Maybe the neighbor saw you?"

"Mine are hidden," she said. "Not apparent to passersby."

They let me go back home and go to sleep and I did, with a vengeance, making it all the way to three-thirty in the afternoon. There's nothing like the pleasure of waking up in mid-afternoon and knowing that the day is almost gone, and that evening is that much closer. Morgan and Jilly were both there when I made my appearance in the kitchen. Morgan was chopping up fruit and Jilly was playing a game on her iPad, and they were talking about Destin.

"She wants to go to Destin," Morgan said. "She won't tell you that but I wheedled it out of her."

"Thanks," I said, going into the refrigerator to see what was there to eat.

"I didn't say that, exactly," Jilly said. "I said it was pretty. But I like it here, too. It's more stinky-coasty, you know?"

"That's a benefit?" I'd found some chocolate pudding in the refrigerator and got a spoon and was cleansing my palate with the pudding. "I'm cleansing my palate," I said, when Jilly gave me a look about the pudding.

"Stinky is less oppressive, more natural, whatever that is. Smells more like the water here, the bay, even the Gulf. There's that scent of seaside living here, shrimpy, but it's sort of missing over there."

"Smells too good," Morgan said. "And fewer people die all the time."

"That's the ticket," Jilly said.

"You know what I thought the other night when I was driving back?" I said. "I thought about my mother and father in heaven with my brother Raleigh, sitting up there, all three of them grinning like fools watching us down here. Like we were in the sack race and they'd already done their stint and were up there watching us tumble home."

"More like a game of Whac-A-Mole," Morgan said.

"You got that from me, darling," I said.

"I'll footnote it," she said.

"Peterson's death was all natural," I said. "The heart attack was unassisted."

"Who did they think did it?" Jilly said.

"They were thinking Chantal."

"Your recent and poorly thought out six-night stand," Morgan said.

"Who's counting?" Jilly said.

"His insta-paramour," Morgan said. "Congratulations, Dad. Did they have you as an accessory?"

"No, and they didn't have anything on her, other than she had a thing with Peterson in a recently past life."

"What about the other guy?" Morgan said. "The one they thought the Amazon wife killed."

"Parker," I said. "They asked about him and Chantal. I think they were working on a scheme deal. Multiple murder."

"I guess you're the one who got away," Jilly said.

"Could be," I said.

"Well," Morgan said, "at least he's on top of this news-gathering thing."

I finished my pudding and placed the bowl and spoon in the sink, ran the hot water into it, and rinsed the sink. Then I got interested in cleaning the other dishes and getting them into the dishwasher, so I pumped some soap on the sponge and rinsed the dishes that had been left in the sink earlier in the day. I liked washing dishes, I'd always liked it, since I was a kid—the hot water, the visible progress, the pristine way the sink looked once the dishes were done. The way my hands felt when I dried them on a dishrag or some paper towels. "I'm still nervous," I said. "I think you guys ought to be nervous, too."

Jilly and Morgan looked at each other for a minute, then said, almost in unison, "Nah."

"We're fine," Morgan said. "These are normal things. And I never cared so much for Parker anyway. It's too bad, but, you know, stuff happens."

"Three guys from our office died last year, remember?" Jilly said. "Thompson, McCarthy, and that other guy, what was his name?"

"Harper," I said. "Or Piper. Was it Piper?"

"Yep," she said. "Harper's still munching his way through the coffee-room rations."

"And it's not *my* office anymore," I said.

"Oh," Morgan said. "I forgot that we are scarred forever by our mistreatment at the hands of the vicious commercial art industry."

"We're not thrilled," I said. "And I think it is time for me to take a shower."

"He said, leaving the two women alone in the kitchen with their thoughts," Morgan said.

"Let the record reflect I am leaving the kitchen as well," Jilly said. "Candy Crush Saga summons."

"Are we doing anything today?" Morgan said.

"Yes," I said. "Bernadette wants to go into Chantal's condo. She may have already done it, but I told her I'd go with if she could wait for me to sleep."

"Has she been deputized or something?"

"No, she's president of the HOA. Apparently there's a clause in the covenants that allows such."

"Is Chantal actually missing, or just sort of, like, unaccounted for?" Morgan said.

"Nobody knows," I said. "Now I wish I'd gone down there the other night."

"I don't," Jilly said. "Wish you'd gone down there."

"What's that on your sleeve there, girl?" Morgan said.

"Thanks, Jilly," I said. "I don't, either, come to think of it. Was a figure of speech."

"Take your shower, Dad," Morgan said. "Hurry up. We women want to go check out the late paramour's digs."

Bernadette had waited, as it turned out. I called her after my shower and she said she'd been waiting for my call since one. I said I'd slept a little more than I'd intended. We went to Chantal's condo with Morgan in tow. Jilly bowed out at the last minute. Bernadette had a passkey and we went in the main door under the building. The place was immaculate, as it had always been when I had seen it before. The kitchen was spic and span, the floors looked a little dusty but otherwise clean, the windows were clean, the beds were made, the closets perfectly orderly, the baths pristine. One of the faucets in the master bath was dripping, but I remembered that it had dripped previously. The last bedroom, where we'd previewed Tinker's show, was a bit of a wreck, hastily tidied. Her cleanup was no match for the rest of the house. But there was no sign of Chantal.

"Let's don't touch anything," Bernadette said when we returned to the living room having passed through the rest of the place. "Just in case."

"Doesn't look like she's been here for a while," Morgan said.

"Probably been staying at the Velodrome," I said. "We should go down there. Or someone should."

"Looks like the girl cleared out, too," Bernadette said. "I guess we can leave now. Truth is I was a little afraid we might find her in here, Chantal, I mean."

"What, you mean, like, dead?" Morgan said.

I raised my hand. "Occurred to me, too."

"Man, you guys are some ghouls," Morgan said.

"It would fit," Bernadette said. "Just saying."

We filed down the stairs and Bernadette locked up and we walked back toward my condo. About halfway back Bernadette split off, said she was going to walk a bit. Morgan wrapped her arm around my waist and pulled me close to her.

"So, I guess things are finally on the move with Jilly?" she said. "I think that's great, you know. She's fun and smart and I like her."

"I guess. I mean, we've talked a little. Diane pushed it, when she left. I always thought I was too old, you know. I got twenty years, nearly. But I guess that doesn't matter as much as it used to."

"I don't think it matters at all," she said.

"Well, you're a brazen young hottie," I said, kissing her forehead. "Why would you think anything mattered?"

"I think all the correct thoughts, Dad. Among others. You taught me well."

"You are a blessing," I said.

# 33

# POOF

Chantal was gone. That was the message Bernadette left on my phone a few days later. Chantal was gone and Tinker was gone and the manager at the Velodrome had no idea what to do and the police were interested in the disappearance, and would I please call her "as soon as humanly possible." I could and did, within hours of receipt of her message.

"There's an APB out," Bernadette said. "And a BOLO."

"Ten-four," I said.

She ignored me. "Did you know that Chantal was once, you know, sort of in trouble with the authorities? Not here, but before?"

"In Mississippi and other states nearby," I said. "Yeah, I heard that."

"What, were you keeping that for your memory book?"

"I didn't think it was anyone's business, really."

"How about the police?"

"Especially the police," I said. "Besides, they knew she was here."

"They did?"

"Yeah, I was with her once at the Velodrome when they came to see her."

"Local police?"

"I don't know who they were. There were a couple in uniform and a couple plainclothes guys, and they had marked cars, Texas cars. They may have been state police. I didn't really get into it that much."

"And so how did you get the story?" Bernadette said.

"She told me. There was a trial and somehow before it really got going the DA over there dropped charges. Sounded like it was a big deal over in Biloxi or someplace."

"That's the story," she said.

"Who told you? The cops?"

"Jean did," she said.

"So they're still looking for Chantal?"

"Parker was shot with a twenty-two in the temple, like her husband."

"That's silly," I said. "Lots of people get shot in the temple."

She laughed at that. "You a detective suddenly?"

"OK," I said. "So I don't know that, actually. Parker shot himself, like, with the gun in his mouth, didn't he?"

"Somebody said that, but that's not where he was shot."

"Not lucky for Chantal."

"Any other reason you know of she would have up and left?"

"Nope. Got no clue."

"You guys were a thing?"

"Little thing," I said. "Not a big thing."

"How you feeling right about now?"

"Funny," I said. "Is the idea she had a relationship with Parker, too? I mean, both Peterson and Parker?"

"Maybe," she said. "What Jean told me was that they were 'interested' in her about Parker. They're reviewing Peterson, too."

"What about the daughter?" I said. "She's a piece of work."

"I know nothing about her and Jean didn't mention her. You know something about her?"

"She said some stuff when I met her. She was doing an art piece for a gallery up in Houston, a video performance thing. She read some stuff off the Net. And told some gruesome stories. Hard to tell what was real."

"Stories?"

"Some guy beat her up, the usual stuff. Said she shot him. Runs in the family, apparently."

"So the mother killed her husband, and now you're telling me the daughter did, too?"

"Didn't kill him, just shot him. The daughter."

"We have to tell Jean, you know that," she said.

"That's fine. I'll tell her if you want. That's all I know about it. It was supposed to be some time ago. She had the guy's car, a convertible, I think it was."

"We better sit down with Jean," Bernadette said. "You available now, if she is?"

"Sure. Whenever. Call me back."

* * *

She called back within minutes and we arranged to meet at her place and I went over there and repeated the story as best I could remember it to Jean Darling, who recorded the conversation on a small digital recorder, starting with various formalities about the time of day, the location, who I was and how I was speaking willingly and without a lawyer present and so forth. I figured she knew what she was doing. I went through my meeting Chantal and our dalliance—that's what I called it, though I was embarrassed when I said that—and then about Tinker, and Tinker's story, as much of it as I remembered. As I talked about Chantal and Tinker the story seemed stranger than I thought. Fraught—that was the word I used, the only time in my life I ever used it. When we were done, Jean said she was shutting down the recorder and stated the time, date, location, my name, her name, Bernadette's name. Then she hit the STOP button and thanked me for agreeing to the recording and said that it probably wouldn't be the last time I had to tell the story. "They're going to want to bring you down to the station and get you to tell them like you told me today. Don't worry about it. If you remember other things, try to remember, when you're retelling the story, to tell the officers that you remembered something after we had this talk."

"I can do that," I said.

Later I was reading a story about the lionfish in an online magazine where it was reported that, prepared correctly, lionfish were said to make a tasty meal, but one prick from the fish's venomous spine could cause an excruciating death. Lionfish had become a problem, apparently, and the scientists that study this sort of thing were trying to figure out ways of preventing the oceans from being overrun with them. Apparently the largest lionfish were the worst offenders, as they routinely delivered many more baby lionfish than smaller siblings.

"Are you reading that article?" Jilly said, looking over my shoulder at the iPad.

"I am," I said.

"I read it this morning," she said. "It says we should be eating lionfish but that they are so pretty nobody wants to eat them."

"They look grotesque to me," I said.

"Well, so pretty or so grotesque," she said. "Sometimes it's the same thing."

"It says here that according to *National Geographic,* lionfish have moist, buttery meat that is often compared to hogfish."

"Hmm," she said. *"Darling, could you pass the hogfish?"* She came around the end of the sofa and sat next to me. "Meanwhile, about Florida. I've made up my mind. I can take it or leave it. Either way I'd like to maybe hang together and muddle through. Ditch Point Blank. I loathe and despise et cetera."

"Great news! You'll move? You going to live in?"

"Can we get a boat?"

"Sure," I said. "You know how to run a boat?"

"I can learn," she said. "I'll look it up online. I'm sure there are sites that explain boat ownership. We can download some books from Amazon. How hard can it be?"

"My brother Raleigh had boats all his life and he said it was a living hell. He was always repairing this and replacing that, redoing the keel or whatever."

"Puking over the starboard bow," she said.

"I'm serious," I said. "He said it was awful. Powerful people always want to go out in your boat if you have one, and they always get drunk, and then you have to be careful they don't fall out, and it's a mess."

"Forget the boat," she said. "I've lost interest in the boat."

"I gather the police may suspect Chantal."

"Of?" Jilly said.

"Parker, I was told. I guess she decided to skip. She told me she'd shot her first and second husbands. Only one died. Second one. Could have been making it up, you know, the allure of the femme fatale. She was charged, had a trial, all that."

"She had a trial?"

"So she said. But charges were dropped. Didn't I tell you this? I can't remember who I've told what anymore," I said. "Maybe I told Morgan."

"She would have told me," Jilly said.

"Anyway, I figure she decided there was too much attention and took off. Maybe she took Tinker with her."

"Her work here was done," Jilly said. She stretched across me and grabbed the remote and clicked the TV on, scrolled through the listings on cable. "Want to watch *Professional Hair Removal, Part Two*?" she asked.

It was a rhetorical question, I think.

* * *

The *Kemah Sentinel* reported that a former Triple-A baseball pitcher Hilton "Bones" Bagbee, seventy-four, died recently in the clubhouse at Forgetful Bay Condominiums. Bagbee played baseball professionally for nine years, most recently forty-odd years ago pitching for the Commerce Keystones. He also logged time in the Texas minor leagues with the Whips, Redheads, Quail, and Cookies, appearing in ninety-six games, mostly as a reliever, though he did make seventeen starts. The highlight of his career came early when opposing batters complained that the full-facial mask Bagbee wore to protect himself from line drives was designed to distract batters and thus make his pitches harder to hit. The Triple-A commissioner thereafter ruled that Bagbee had to stop wearing the mask on the mound, as it made him look like Jason, of hockey-mask fame, though the reporter may have had the time line screwed up there. He was often confused with another pitcher, Justin Miller, for whom the "Justin Miller Rule" in MLB was later named.

The county coroner's office confirmed Bagbee's death, and a spokesperson stated that the cause of death had been determined to be completely natural.

# 34
# STATUARY

Two weeks had passed since the commotion about Chantal, and nothing had changed, but, like always, the interest came in waves, and the last week had been low tide, which was fine by me. I left a couple more calls for Chantal, called the restaurant, too, but got nothing. Morgan was back up in Houston for her classes; Jilly was back and forth. The neighborhood seemed to have absorbed Peterson's death and Parker's death, not to mention the assorted additional deaths and discomforts in the neighborhood, so there was a lull going on for which we were all grateful, though I suspect everyone was still giving some thought to all and sundry. But we were, for the moment, the living, and the living only pay lip service to death, unless it's very close. In the family, a parent or a lover, maybe a pet or a dear old friend. So it was a quiet midsummer week at Forgetful Bay. The weather had gone cool for Texas summers, lots of storms and fronts pushing through, which kept things bearable in the afternoons and did that magic with the light that makes everything look a whole lot better than it does in the pounding sun. People were in a good mood. I saw Bernadette and the neighbors chatting in the road at sunset, other folks passed by walking dogs of various descriptions, usually one large dog and one small dog was how they rolled, and people waved, nodded, said hello as they passed or if I saw them on my occasional walks. The neighbors had been watering a lot earlier in June but now, with the rain coming and going, there was no need.

One night about one I decided to get out and get something to eat, a hamburger or chicken sandwich, something drive-through, which was the only thing open at that hour anyway, and I didn't turn my nose up at a McDonald's burger or whatever in any case. I didn't want another homemade sandwich, and getting a little fresh night air was a bonus. We'd had a shower earlier in the evening, so the streets were still wet, glistening with that slow-drying shine, and there was a lot of that on the car windows, too, as I left the house. I took a tour down by Chantal's condo to see if there were any lights, and there weren't, so I turned around and came back past Bruce and Roberta's place. He was in the garage, it looked like, no doubt working on his perpetual machine. He'd sent me a link to the website of the guy in Utah he was working with, a site that was called Never Ending Power, LLC, and it looked to me like it was phony as a two-dollar bill, but I hadn't said that to Bruce. I rolled past my condo and noticed, a couple places later, that the gay couple with the Virgin Mary statue that I'd taken a picture of on the ice chest, and which had since been placed in a very prominent position in the front flower bed, complete with tiny sun-driven lights illuminating it, was no longer alone there in the yard in front of their condo. Now they'd added a much larger, maybe four-foot-tall statue of Saint Joseph or Saint Francis or some other saint unknown to me, standing smack in the middle of their driveway, back up against the siding between the two parking spaces under the left and right halves of the building. My first reaction was like, crap, more junky stuff in the neighborhood, but an instant later I started smiling about it, thinking how really crazy it was to put religious statues around your property, it was so cracked it seemed almost magical. And so I decided to make another circle of the Forgetful development, to come by that house again, but also to see what other people had in their yards. Normally I paid not too much attention to neighbors' houses, so I was suddenly aware that I really didn't know what people were doing in the neighborhood, yardwise. I decided to take a tour all the way around the crooked little street that circled our properties. By this time I was nearing the north entrance and it was half past one and the car tires were making that sticky sound they do on wet pavement, and the air smelled like rain and seawater, all mixed up, so I drove past the entrance and on around for the hell of it, just to enjoy the smell and the sound and the air out there near the bay. The lights on the highway outside the property, and all the commercial crap that lined the highway, were lit up as always, making the Forgetful Bay Condos look like a lonely little roadside settlement. There were more lights along the edge of the bay, and a few out in the darkness of the bay, and all of them were blistered by the water on the windshield, though I could see them clearly out the side windows that were rolled down. I drove by the Parkers' place and noticed that they had a statue, small and hard to see, at the edge of the driveway, and then at the late Oscar Peterson's condo there was a large concrete angel in the side yard, I mean a serious-sized angel, maybe five feet tall, with great wings and everything, and then Chantal's where there was nothing much except a garbage can that had been kicked around in the driveway, and then at Bernadette's there was a set of yard gnomes and a black fountain with running water in front of the entrance to her place. At Jean Darling's there was a dog statue I'd never noticed before, looked like an almost life-size Labrador retriever standing guard in her yard, and as I kept going around the cottages, I saw more statues—behind one of the cottages two women in flowing concrete robes at the edge of a little pier on Smoky Lake, one with a bird on her outstretched arm, the other holding a snake. I also saw various pieces of pottery, jars and jugs of different kinds and sizes, planters, one elf, a giant peppermint candy cane that I figured to have been left over from some Christmas, and, as I got back around by Bruce and Roberta's I passed their house and mine, and the one next to me where Ng had lived, which was still packed with Mercedes automobiles, though not his, of course, and then I slowed to a crawl as I passed the Virgin Mary condo again and took a hard look at the new statue, which was in shadow and looked like it was dark to begin with, and it was the size of a seven- or eight-year-old kid, and

I guessed, this time around, that it was Saint Francis, given the way the guy was standing, with his arms out, like welcoming the birds, and I started grinning again and thought maybe I ought to get me a statue or two to lively up the place. I mean, I liked the idea of people who went ahead and put statues of saints in their yards or driveways or behind their houses. I mean, why not? Where's the harm in a little blind faith, a little hope in the face of the grotesque spectacle of ordinary life in this century? I loved the impulse. It was enchanting. I drove all the way to McDonald's grinning about it, the bay air blowing herky-jerky through the car, the sky really dark with those white shadowy clouds roaming around. I was really happy about these people and this place; I was giddy as I splashed into the McDonald's lot and pulled up to the order screen.

35

# MOONLIGHT

At about four that morning I was out on the back deck watching the night, reading things on the iPad, using Flipboard and the other aggregator, I forget the name—oh, Zite. They were carrying news from all the usual organs—the *Times, Washington Post, Slate,* the *Guardian,* BuzzFeed, BBC, NPR, Mashable, *Chicago Tribune,* Politico, AP, Al Jazeera English, *Forbes,* the Verge, *Pinball, LA Times, Globe and Mail, Zip & Fiddle,* and so on and on in the new world. I read the junk that showed up. Stock stuff, world news, Palestine, Syria, politics, celebrity crap, movies, Mac news, a *Times* piece on Mandy Patinkin, puff, but everybody loves Mandy Patinkin. Whatever. Apple didn't look like the evergreen anymore. What's her face, Miley, had startled everybody again with some performance; a guy somewhere, a kidnapper, had been found dead in his cell; should we or shouldn't we bomb somewhere; were the Republicans being horsey in the House; what was the deal with Michael Douglas and what's her face—the stuff that drains out of the gaping Internet wound endlessly. I sent an e-mail to the real estate guy in Destin saying I wanted to come back and look at condos again, thinking maybe it wasn't such a bad idea to get out of Texas for a while, maybe permanently. Jilly was up for it, so I figured we'd go over there and we'd set up house, though I wasn't sure what the rules and regulations would be. I could imagine it being a pretty good setup, whatever the rules were. I was in the back of the house, on the small deck off the master bedroom, and the moon had moved over the top of the house and was slanting down into the western sky, a full moon on the Forgetful Bay grounds, and on me, sitting there on the deck. There were some lizards out there, crawling on the walls, geckos, which I looked up on *Wikipedia* because of their transparency and found this footnote, quoted here in its entirety.

> ^ Santos, Daniel; Matthew Spenko, Aaron Parness, Kim Sangbae, Mark Cutkosky (2007). Directional adhesion for climbing: Theoretical and practical considerations. Journal of Adhesion Science and Technology 21 (12–13): 1317–1341 http://www.brill.nl/journal-adhesion-science-and-technology|url=missing title (help). Gecko "feet and toes are a hierarchical system of complex structures consisting of lamellae, setae, and spatulae. The distinguishing characteristics of the gecko adhesion system have been described [as] (1) anisotropic attachment, (2) high pulloff force to preload ratio, (3) low detachment force, (4) material independence, (5) self-cleaning, (6) anti-self sticking and (7) non-sticky default state.... The gecko's adhesive

> structures are made from ß-keratin (modulus of elasticity [approx.] 2 GPa). Such a stiff material is not inherently sticky; however, because of the gecko adhesive's hierarchical nature and extremely small distal features (spatulae are [approx.] 200 nm in size), the gecko's foot is able to intimately conform to the surface and generate significant attraction using van der Waals forces."

Which was a poem to me, and interesting, too, because we had a fair number of geckos crawling around, most of them the clear pinky kind, sort of, and the way they moved was a constant amazement. More than that, I was sure Monsanto had at least four dozen people tucked away in some Area 51 equivalent working on geckos, trying to figure how they could improve all of us with that gecko adhesion system and its high pulloff-force-to-preload ratio.

Meanwhile both Jilly and Morgan were sound asleep inside, comfortably sawing wood and looking forward to tomorrow, when we were going on a field trip to Texas City to tour the Great Fertilizer Disaster Museum on the site of the worst US industrial accident and largest nonnuclear explosion in history, which took place in April 1947, killing between six hundred and nine hundred people and wounding thousands. The numbers are disputed because many of the victims simply vanished in the blast that blew the four-thousand-pound anchor off one of the ships in the harbor there a full two miles away, where it remains to this day.

I was pretty happy about the change in the arrangement

with Jilly, or the prospect of it, and touched by the approvals of Diane and Morgan. I had been comfortable with the way things were, all things considered, but this new acknowledged thing was, well, it was something I guess I'd hoped for but kept quiet about, figuring it would probably not happen. You hang out with people and you get really attached to them, and you sometimes get too attached, and things go haywire, and unless the people are, or become, family, more often than not you lose the connection—that richness, that warmth and closeness, that feeling that you're with them in a keenly personal way that will outlast the normal friendships and connections. That sounds more schematic than I mean it to be, but I had lost some people I'd rather not have lost that way, so I was pleased that both of these women, my daughter and my—what?—my friend, partner, maybe, *inamorata,* were resting comfortably in my house, maybe our house. I knew Morgan would leave eventually, live her own life, and I was glad for her but regretted the distance it would likely put between us. She would always be with me in one way or another, however literally separated we became. Jilly, on the other hand, seemed to be signing up for the duration, which was a remarkable lifesaver, so much so that it made me want to say a prayer of thanks to whatever omnipotent intergalactic energy resource put this whole shazam together in the first place.

I was lounging on the deck there thinking my own thoughts, reflecting on events, thinking of Chantal and Tinker roaming the countryside again, maybe together in

Tinker's copped Cadillac, flying across the desert of Arizona maybe, top down, headed for Flagstaff, the Grand Canyon, or parts west, Vegas, LA, who knew. Somewhere to disappear, take up new identities, new friends, new lovers, always testing them carefully before admitting them into the inner circle, and even then keeping them at arm's length in case things turned nasty or inquisitive or threatening in any of the ways they were both accustomed to things going bad. It was ironic that Chantal would ask me if I'd ever known anyone who had killed someone after telling me she had. Maybe that was a test, too. To see if and how I could handle it, and I guess I did all right, at least for a time. I also knew I'd failed longer term, that Chantal, or both she and her daughter, had read me correctly as being a little less brave than was essential to play in their game, to travel their roads. Some people are too dangerous. And they knew I was out of my league as soon as I knew it, or maybe before. And they never said a word about it, never pushed it in my face, or made me feel bad about it, but instead just vanished. I loved the idea of people vanishing. Some of those who vanished were no doubt ripped from lives they loved, and I felt for them and wished a speedy return to what was lost. But for the others, the ones who left by choice, who wanted to disappear, I had only envy at their good fortune of having taken the step into the new world. Every time I walked out of Walmart and looked at the big board of missing persons I got this chill of excitement for those who had voluntarily left, who had fled whatever arrangement they found themselves in, preferring the prospect of a fresh start, a new identity, a new life, a new place in the world, with all new people and all new things, a pristine and unknown landscape, a daily life the fabric of which would be immaculate and unknown.

So as the moon slid across the sky, inched across and down, I heard an engine off in the distance, a drone-like sound, a small plane, and not one of the new ones, either, an old prop plane, and I scanned the western sky for it and at first found nothing, though the sound kept coming, becoming clearer, and also louder. I got up and went out to the railing so that I could scan a larger slice of the sky to the west, as well as north and south. Finally I located blinking lights on an airplane to the south and some distance west of us, as if following the Gulf Freeway north from Galveston up to Houston. It was still some good distance away and appeared against the black sky only as twinkling lights. I sat down again and resumed watching the moon, which was gold by now, maybe sixty degrees off the horizon, occasionally obscured by streamers of clouds slipping across its face. I went inside to get a fresh bottle of beer and when I returned the airplane engine was louder, a steady drone that warbled a bit, like it was hitting my ears at two different times or something, like a car or maybe motorcycle engine struggling a little going up a steep hill. Then, suddenly, the engine cut out entirely. The silence was shocking, the absence of the sound louder than the presence of it had been. I got up and looked south again trying to locate the plane and saw the lights bobbing up and down, as if the plane were rocking. Then the engine kicked over, started roaring, and it seemed that the lights brightened, but that could have been a trick of vision. It was close and low by now, still to the south but much closer to the coast, well off where the freeway was. I started to get my chair and pull it to the rail, thinking I would prop my feet on the rail and watch the moon and the passing airplane, but as I turned to fetch the chair the droning engine cut out again, and when I turned back around I could not find the aircraft in the night sky. I kept scanning the southwestern sky but still couldn't see anything, only the endless black of the night, the tiny stars way off in the distance, and the moon, which looked almost as if it were drifting, and the clouds standing still as it slid behind them. There was a guy down in one of the outlying marinas to the north who seemed to be loading up a boat for some early morning fishing. I suddenly got the plane's engine drone again and, barely behind that, the thumps of the heavy coolers this guy dropped onto the boat's deck. Maybe I saw those more than heard them. The plane's engine was cutting in and out, and the noise was aggravated and booming as it started and quit. When I turned back to the southwestern sky there was nothing but engine noise, growing louder, and then, suddenly, deafening, and then I caught the glint of moonlight hitting the fuselage, for a second, and it was strangely close then, the engine noise was like a hot rod, somebody in a dragster in the neighbor's drive blipping the throttle, and the plane looked like it had crossed over toward us from the Gulf Freeway, and it was almost sailing in wind, not flying like any plane would fly but wobbling back and forth, and dipping up and down like a kite, wings racking back and forth. I was up and turning to go inside to get Jilly and Morgan, but the plane was way too close and out of control, the wind shrieking, the motor hammering, and then it was right in front of me, full size, blocks away coming out of the night sky, shooting toward me at astonishing speed. I knew I'd never make the door. I stayed perfectly still, stared as the thing roared toward me and the house and the neighborhood. I was almost certain that it would recover at the last minute and miss us all.

# ABOUT THE AUTHOR

FREDERICK BARTHELME is the author of fourteen previous books of fiction. Until 2010, he directed the writing program at the University of Southern Mississippi and edited *Mississippi Review.* He now edits *New World Writing,* an online magazine started in 1995.